Wearing My
Halo Tilted

Also by Stephanie Perry Moore

Chasing Faith

Perry Skky Jr. Series for teens

Beta Gamma Pi Series for teens

Published by Dafina Books

Wearing My
Halo Tilted

STEPHANIE
PERRY
MOORE

KENSINGTON PUBLISHING CORP.
http://www.kensingtonbooks.com

DAFINA BOOKS are published by

Kensington Publishing Corp.
119 West 40th Street
New York, NY 10018

All Kensington Titles, Imprints and Distributed Lines are available at special quantity discounts for bulk purchases for sales promotions, premiums, fund-raising, and educational or institutional use. Special book excerpts or customized printings can also be created to fit specific needs. For details, write or phone the office of the Kensington special sales manager: Kensington Publishing Corp., 119 West 40th Street, New York, NY 10018, attn: Special Sales Department, Phone: 1-800-221-2647.

Dafina and the Dafina logo Reg. U.S. Pat. & TM Off.

ISBN-13: 978-0-7582-5165-7
ISBN-10: 0-7582-5165-3

First trade paperback printing: February 2008
First mass market printing: January 2010

10 9 8 7 6 5 4 3 2

Printed in the United States of America

For Leon, Syndi, and Sheldyn
(my three babies)

I know you feel your parents are tough
and sometimes wear their halos tilted.
Though we aren't perfect, we are believers.
And always know we have perfect love for you.
Even now we're praying that your
future-marriage unions
will be blessed and built on God's rock.
As your dad and I daily work to straighten out our
own crowns,
may you and every reader do the same.

Acknowledgments

A tilted halo . . . doesn't even the strongest Christian wear one at times? None of us will be perfect 'til we're with God. But let's admit that we can straighten ourselves up a bit. I loved telling this story of a struggling marriage needing grace to be whole. Maybe if we showed a little more compassion to one another, this world would be a better place. Let's face it, it is hard to make it out here; and it's hard to get along with people that act like they have no morals. But when it all seems hard to bear, bring your woes to God, and have faith that He can fix your drama.

I've learned in my research why we fall short, and that most times the difficult moments draw us closer to the Lord. In other words, in our weakness, He is strong. So when we fall prey to temptation, we must allow Him to renew in us the right spirit of holiness, righteousness, and goodness. Though it is in man's nature to sin, we can conquer the enemy and walk upright. Here is a heartfelt thank you to all those who helped me get to His business and finish this inspiring tale.

Thanks, Dad, Dr. Franklin Perry Sr.; Mom, Shirley Roundtree Perry; brother, Franklin Dennis Perry Jr.; special author friends: Robin Jones Gunn, Beverly Jenkins, Vanessa Davis Griggs, Marjorie Kimbrough, Victoria Christopher Murray, Matthew Parker, Michele Andrea Bowen, Lysa Terkurst, Daaimah

Poole, and Paula Chase Hyman; agent Janet Kobobel Grant; assistants Ciara Roundtree, Torian Colon, Cynthia Peace, Andrea Johnson, Nakia Austin, and Jessica Phillips; publisher Kensington/Dafina (especially Selena James and Adeola Saul); extended family, *sorors,* and friends; my children: Leon, Sydni and Sheldyn; husband, Derrick Moore; and my readers. I could have written something cooler, but I'm having a tilted halo moment. Seriously, you know I could not have done this without you.

And thanks, Heavenly Father, for another opportunity to tell a story that will bring people closer to You. Keep helping us all because we're so fragile. Personally, I do pray to become more like You daily. I can't wait to be with You and finally receive the perfect crown in heaven that will always stay straight. 'Til then I know you'll help me to push my tilted halo up.

Chapter 1

Wish

As I balled up on the cold, hardwood floor in our master bedroom, I prayed that my irate husband wouldn't come back upstairs and haul another lamp across the room, actually hitting me the next time. I was too afraid to budge from the corner, scared that my watery eyes would cloud my vision and I'd accidentally step on the shattered glass. Never in our contented four years of marriage had Dillon become so over-the-top angry that I felt threatened. But one time was one time too many for me to live with a man that handled conflict by screaming at me and punching the wall. I wasn't going to go through mental drama with him. I had to gather my courage, compose myself, and figure out what was next for me and my girls.

I was so sick of the downward spiral our marriage had been on. For the last six months, Dillon had managed to sleep in numerous places in our three-story contemporary house. Everywhere that was other than beside me. The truth was, he was tired of me asking him to perform his husbandly duties. Was it so wrong that I wanted him?

Maybe I was overreacting, trippin', or something. Maybe I was blowing this whole thing out of proportion. I was sure there were plenty of women who would love to have a faithful husband like mine. At least Dillon paid all the bills so that I could stay home, raise our two daughters, and write Christian novels. Even though he wasn't in my bed and his insecurities took from me the best of him, at least he was home.

Four hours earlier when his black Escalade had rolled into our circular driveway, I had no idea asking him to satisfy his wife would cause such trouble.

"Alright, Lord," I said, realizing I needed to find Dillon and address things rationally. "This isn't what I signed up for. I'm just twenty-nine and Dillon's thirty-one. Why are we fighting like this so early in our marriage?"

After I'd finished moping, I quietly opened the door to the closest bedroom to ours, which happened to be occupied by our youngest daughter, Starr. She had just had her first birthday at the beginning of the month. I certainly didn't want to wake her. I cracked the door just enough to see she was sleeping soundly and that her daddy wasn't once again sleeping on the floor. I could've gone through the bathroom that linked one daughter's room to our other daughter's, but mad and upset, I wasn't thinking. I took the long way around to the other door, which was Stori's, my three-year-old daughter's room. Her eyes sparkled as she called out my name.

"Mommy, is it time to get up?" she asked in her most precious voice, which almost made me forget I was furious with her trifling dad.

I walked around her hot pink room and saw she was the only one in her bedroom. I pulled up her covers, kissed her on the forehead, and said, "No, sweetie, it's not time to get up. Get some rest."

"Okay, Mommy. Love you." Stori rolled over and hugged her snow white teddy bear.

My anger seeped back in. Even my daughter had someone to cuddle with.

I continued the search, growing madder with each step. The door to the guest room across from Stori's was open. However, I could clearly see my husband wasn't in there. I headed down the winding staircase into the great room and then went to the keeping room. The TV was on, but Dillon wasn't on our sectional leather couch. There was one other place he could be—his favorite spot—the basement.

With every step I took, I became more and more ill. I thought, *Why do I have to be the one that always tries to not go to bed with anger seething? Maybe I wasn't the only one ready to call it quits. If I have to be alone in our bed, we might as well be separated.*

"Shake the thought," I told myself as I passed the six framed NFL-team jerseys proudly displayed on the stairs. Those shirts quickly reminded me that maybe that was part of his problem.

Dillon was still frustrated about not becoming successful in the league. Though he was there long enough to get vested, he never was a starter. And ever since he'd been cut, because of salary cap reasons, he'd been a little crazy. If it wasn't mood swings, he was downing other players in the league. For a year, he had no job. Thankfully, we had savings, but mentally he was scarred. Sometimes he went off on me for no reason, or I'd find him in a corner crying alone. Seeing him go through that was unbearable. After finding our way to each other for comfort, we prayed and God came through. His old college coach from the North Carolina Tar Heels who was now head coach at the University of South Carolina, offered him a chance to be a position coach. If that hadn't happened, who knows where my husband would be.

He'd been out of the league for three years and the coaching world was difficult at best. The Gamecocks last two seasons had been subpar. I knew if they didn't have a winning season this year, Dillon could be out of a job.

If he did still have issues about not playing pro ball, he didn't have to take it out on me. Plus, he didn't need to be stressing anyway. This was June. Football season was coming up in two months. God had blessed him to still be a part of the game. He was known as the best linebacker coach in the Southeastern Conference. Though he wanted to be a coordinator and head coach, this job was a stepping-stone. The chump needed to be grateful. He might not be playing in the league anymore, but at least he had a job. God had blessed him and he needed to get over it.

Flipping on the light switch, I saw his fat, funky self comfortably sitting in his La-Z-Boy with drool sliding down the left side of his face. I pushed his head lightly with one hand, while my other one rested on my hip. The jerk didn't move.

"What are you doin'?" I screamed, trying to startle him.

He bounced up and became inches taller than me. "Shari, didn't you get enough of messin' with me?" he asked, as if he had no intention of apologizing.

He looked meaner than an upset pit bull. But I'd been bummed out too long. I was as ticked off as a struggling single mother who hadn't gotten paid child support in over a year. My jaw was tight and my eyes were squinted. If I was white instead of the caramel brown sister I was, I would have been red hot.

"I really don't think we should talk right now. Let me just go to bed. You really need to head upstairs and leave me alone," he said, clutching my hand and turning me toward the stairway.

I jerked away from him. "Don't pretend like everything is okay."

"Don't bring that up again." His voice stiffened, like I was the one with the problem because I was mentioning it. "You're beginning to be a little intolerable. Don't make a big deal out of it." He turned away and went to lay back down on the couch.

With frustration, I pouted and headed up to the main floor. I heard Dillon behind me, but I wasn't waiting on him. When I stepped foot into the kitchen, I decided to let him know that he was no longer welcome in our bed.

Huffing, I sighed. "I hate you. You know what? Don't even come upstairs. I just need to bring your stuff down here."

"This is my house. I can go anywhere in it I want to go," my husband argued back.

"You're right. It is your house, and it's mine too.

But since we need time apart, let's be apart for real."

With eyes more malicious looking than I'd ever seen, he said, "Shari, don't tell me what to do. I'm grown."

I was beginning to hate him. I never used those strong words before, but that's how I felt now. Boy did I wish my current experience was just a nightmare, but this was my reality. I hadn't really pushed him to please me for months now. He thought everything was cool, but it wasn't.

"What? Why you standin' there like that?" he said, looking at the smug glare I'd pasted on my face. "What's your problem?"

That was all I needed him to ask me. "You're my problem! You call yourself a good Christian man, but every time I question you on stuff I feel you're not doing right, you go off on me, screaming and yelling."

"You're screaming now," he cut in.

"I have to scream so that you can hear me! When we do have sex every other month, it's not that good. I'm not even thirty yet, Dillon. Why are you treating me like you're gay or something? Are you into me? I don't understand."

"You're pissing me off again, Shari! You better watch your mouth," he said.

He came closer to me and I backed up. I wanted to be tough, but the sane side of me instantly recalled I wasn't sure what he was capable of if provoked. The last thing I wanted was to be dead. Who'd take care of my girls with his butt in jail for murder?

"You know why I don't want to be with you? Because you nag me too much!" he yelled as he punched a picture in the wall. "Go on upstairs and get out of my face!"

As the tears ran down my cheeks once more, we heard a little voice cry out, "Daddy, Daddy, please don't yell at Mommy."

Right around the corner was our three-year-old, Stori, trembling uncontrollably. Dillon went over to pick her up, but she ran to me. "No, I want Mommy!"

I knelt down, looked at her, and said, "It's okay, sweetie."

Stori cried out, "Mommy, why are you crying?"

I realized I couldn't even console her. No way could I tell her it would all be better, because frankly I didn't know. I stood up and looked at him viciously.

I wiped my face. "Don't be scared. Mommy's okay."

I jogged up to my room with Stori in my arms. We laid in my bed, and I didn't move until she drifted off to sleep. However, I couldn't rest. I got out of bed and my knees just buckled to the floor, as if my body wanted to cry out to God. I used to pray every night growing up as a child, but when I got married, I stopped. Maybe that was a major reason why I had so much marital turmoil.

My husband was a strong believer. He was an awesome speaker. He'd been discipling some of his players, leading them to the Lord. Why then did it seem he was leading his family more to hell than heaven? We didn't tithe. He always found some reason or another why our money needed to go somewhere other than God. I'd catch him on the phone lying to people about why he couldn't make an event he promised to speak at. We didn't have family meals together anymore, so the girls and I blessed the Lord for our food alone. We didn't have quiet times like we used to in our dating relationship. We never even prayed together. So in a way, I had strayed away from praying alone.

With a breaking heart, I prayed out, *"Lord, you gotta help me. You gotta help us. My heart is turning so hard toward him. Only you can soften it. Or am I supposed to leave him? I know you don't want this for me."*

I got up off my knees and wiped my cheeks clean. I joined my oldest in bed. Snuggling with my child, I inwardly felt more messed and alone.

"Shari, baby, why you got that mad face on? Smile, girl! You in church!" my eighty-two-year-old grandma said to me, as I sat beside her the next day, in the front pew, reluctantly watching my husband preach at my granddaddy's small Baptist church.

I'm not saying Dillon was a hypocrite or that all men and women in the pulpit should be perfect. But in my opinion that morning, Dillon McCray should've been sitting beside me listening to somebody telling him how to get himself right versus telling other people how to walk with God.

My husband wanted to be a preacher just as much as he wanted to be a head coach. So when my granddad came to him with an opening on youth Sunday, just once a month, Dillon jumped at the chance to see if his passion for the pulpit was legit.

His sermon was taken from Acts chapter one, where Jesus told the disciples to go and be witnesses for Him, but my husband wasn't a witness at home. He couldn't even talk to his wife with compassion. He had no business giving advice. If I could've gone up into that pulpit and knocked him upside his head so that he would start confessing to everybody he needed to practice what he preached, I would have.

But my grandma had me on lock down. She had her hand on my hand, making sure I didn't move. Though my grandma was up in age, she had fire. She had spunk. She had wisdom. She had instinct. By the way I squeezed her hand so hard, she knew I was mad at that man I wished wasn't mine.

"You don't want the whole congregation to know your business, baby," she leaned over and whispered to me. "It's all in your eyes, girl. You hear me?"

I nodded. Even my husband must've noticed I was frustrated, because he said what I wanted to hear. He confessed to the congregation that he was frail and weak and needed God just as much as the next man.

But he said, "At least we're trying. At least our halos are on even if they're tilted."

What a crock, I thought. I strongly believed that if the halo wasn't on straight what was the purpose of wearing it. Some of us needed to quit hiding behind the fact that God gave grace.

Obviously, I was in the minority, because afterward he got huge applause from the members and a bunch of "amens." When he sat down, he looked at me and smiled. I wish I could say that gesture melted my heart, but it didn't. I was in God's house and I had no forgiveness inside my heart. I was only there to keep up appearances. I also came to see my folks. With my grandparents on their last leg, any day could be their last and I didn't want to ever let them down. But I wasn't gonna be a hypocrite in the Lord's place.

A part of me wished I felt differently. I wished I could feel like he did a marvelous job. I wished I felt full that he acknowledged me as his wife at the beginning of his sermon, but that was too small. I was tired of the little crumbs he threw at me every now and then.

Maybe I was selfish and immature for feeling that way. However, I saw no other way to feel. I'd change in a heartbeat if it'd make a difference.

Later we went over to my parents' house for a big Sunday dinner. My mother loved cooking for her children. Though my dad's coarse joking usually got on everyone's nerves, the large spread of two meats, five vegetables, and three desserts would be enough reason for any adult to ignore him.

Stori and Starr loved going over there to see Mama and Papa and play in the playroom designed especially for them. My granddad loved having his family around him for Sunday dinners so that he could tell many stories of days gone by. During dinner, I couldn't even play the role of Dillon and I being such a happy couple. When Dillon asked me to pass the hot sauce for his collard greens, I did so without looking at him. When he thanked me, "You're welcome" never parted from my lips.

After dinner, I helped my mother clear the table. For a while she and I cleaned the spacious kitchen in silence. But I knew that would change. She always piped unwanted advice into my life.

"Shari, you know I can see you're mad at Dillon. Whatever he did, you can't pout like this."

I wanted to break the glass she just handed me

to dry. My mom had a way of loving me that was unnerving. She always thought that she was giving me medicine I needed, but she always gave me advice that pushed me farther away from her.

Drying the black-iron skillet, I looked at her and said, "You don't even understand what's going on in my family. You always think I don't have a reason to feel anything other than happiness."

"Shari, you can't expect marriage to be great everyday. And I know you. If things aren't perfect you want to bail," she said, as she stared out the window over the sink to the open field.

I was fuming. Why was she treating me like a child? Those days had passed. If she didn't notice my curves, I was grown. And I wasn't going to live my life ignoring any problems that came my way like I'd seen her do over the years with my dad.

She turned to me and said, "I don't know what's really going on with you and Dillon, but as hard as you think I am on you, I'm on your side. I know marriage can sometimes be crazy. But you have two little girls."

"And what does that mean, Mom?" I replied in despair as I went and took a seat at her table.

"Those precious girls don't need to be walking around here with one parent. You two need to watch what you say around them. Because little Stori told me she heard her dad yelling. I'm not going to ask what it's about."

"Well, at least ask me if it's true. You can't just believe what my three-year-old daughter tells you," I said rather sharply.

"Girl, please. She's too young to have made that up. She simply said what she heard," my mother said, placing her hand on my shoulder. "Shari, you've got to make it work. It's more than just you two."

I heard her but I wasn't really letting her advice seep in. I nodded politely. As soon as Dillon was ready to go, so was I.

As the next few days passed, it was more of the same at my house—me sleeping in one bedroom and Dillon in another. It seemed like it was just me in the marriage. My feelings were all that mattered. Maybe that wasn't the Christian way to think, but I had to be real with myself. I was in a marriage that I didn't really want to be in anymore.

Every now and then, I caught myself thinking we could work stuff out. Sometimes he could be tolerable when he cut the grass, ran through the house chasing our girls, or cleaned the house from top to bottom.

The *work it out* mentality didn't last long though. He still wasn't taking care of me. Did he ask me if I wanted a back massage? No. Did he bring me any flowers or offer to cook dinner? Please! And when he did come home from the campus, he was more into his children than wrapping his arms around me. It didn't appear that he cared to save our marriage, which was more of a reason why I shouldn't care either.

I was so thankful for my college roommate, Josie Dennis. She had more sass than anyone I knew. I loved her silky milk-chocolate skin. And how come everything she put on looked like it was tailor-made for her size-four frame. Her relationship with God was not that strong. But she was a believer. Plus, Josie was a better person than most preachers around our town. My husband included.

I was so happy she phoned me midweek to have lunch. She worked in corporate America and was holding down six figures. She was my only friend in Columbia, but one true girlfriend was way better than numerous fake associates. When we met to gobble up steaks, I was relieved I had a real forum to vent.

"So your mama said stay with him though she knows he's crazy, huh?" my girlfriend asked after I filled her in on all that went down.

I nodded my head, chewing on my rare meat. Honestly, I was somewhat embarrassed. I was really considering heeding my mom's advice. He could get mean again at any time. Why didn't I have backbone?

"See, that's why I hate that old school mentality. Telling me because I have two kids I have to stay. Uh-uh. Girl, if it ain't workin', we are way too young to be tied down forever in a loveless marriage. Sometimes you just gotta show him. You just gotta walk out and let him know you can live without him. That'll make him straighten up," she said, cringing at the sight of my red meat.

"Well, it also sounds like you don't advise me to stay. But I'm not like you. I don't make even close to one hundred thousand dollars. How could I support myself?" I said, throwing down my fork and knife.

She placed her hand on my head and said, "You're working. You're writing books. You're doing well enough to survive."

"Josie, I got one book out. I won't get another

advance until I turn in the next book and if it gets accepted by my editor. And the first book only made me twenty-five thousand dollars. My agent's shopping deals for me. And even if I do get paid more on my next advance, I'll have to pay taxes, my agent, my transcriber, and marketing and travel expenses. Really, I won't see much more than I'm seeing now."

"Shari, I hear you, but the only thing I'm saying is you need to find a way. You've got to make Dillon understand that you're not going to live like that, 'cause you see men dog out women, leave women, and cheat on women because they feel that we are just weak. And you are not weak, Shari. You have a degree. And if you gotta do something other than write them books, girl, you need to figure it out. Don't let that man hold you hostage. Particularly when he ain't treatin' you right. You'll be in that house and continuing to be unhappy, and the next thing you know your girls will be bitter kids. You'll pass that stuff on directly down. You might as well leave. If y'all are supposed to be together, then shoot, it'll work out. However, if you want the same results," she leaned in and sternly said, "keep on doing the same thing. Be a fool and stay."

I dropped my head. I was a wimp.

"Maybe I need to back off and not tell you what to do. I won't push. I just love you, girl. You've got to do something different to make him stop that. Live in an empty house for a while. He'll get the picture. He just can't treat you any kind of way. I don't know, girl, you might get out there and not want him back." She was smiling. "There are plenty of other men that will treat you right. Can't you just imagine a hunk treating you special and making you feel really satisfied."

She was a mess. But maybe she was right. Some changes in my marriage needed to occur.

Josie went on to tell me that her insecure husband was trippin' as well. She made more money and he was resentful. It seemed to say, united in matrimony may not be in the cards for either of us. As we headed to our cars, we gave each other a warm embrace of encouragement. That let me know that if I did make a bold move, Josie would be there.

After talking to my mother on Sunday and then my girlfriend on Wednesday, by Friday I was really confused. Do I stay or do I leave? Do I stay for the kids or do I think of what's best for me? I needed some counseling.

Thankfully, my scheduled lunch with my pastor's wife, Mrs. Kindle, who also happened to be an author as well, was perfect. I never had to hold my tongue with her either. I was just amazed that over the years she and I had spent so much time together. I'd grown to love her and depend on her so much. Her answers were never as rigid and one-sided as my mom's. Nor were they as out there as my girlfriend's. They were sort of well thought out and actually in the middle. As we talked in-depth about my marriage, her counseling gave me a clearer perspective.

"It sounds to me like you're saying you still do love your husband. You admire all he does for your family. There might be a few things you need to work on with his physical appearance, because that's making you less attracted to him. But all in all it seems like he's the one you love," she said.

"I do, but lately it feels like I don't."

"Don't confuse frustration for not being in love with him. There are certain things that you want him to do that he's not doing. Before you decide you need to leave, Shari, I'd say make a list of the things he's doing right. Then write a list of the things that irritate you. Also, make a third list of what you think would be idyllic between the two of you."

"And then what am I supposed to do with these lists?"

"Sit down and go over them with him."

"Believe me he's not gonna do that. Anytime I voice my opinion or say how I feel—I don't know. He's just not gonna do that."

"Don't think negative about it. You've gotta really get at the root of what's bothering you. Maybe after you two talk, if things still aren't resolved before you look at him leaving or you leaving, maybe you guys should have professional counseling with my husband."

"Please. Dillon wouldn't sit with Reverend Kindle. It's a great idea and I know that's what we need to do. We do need counseling, but he's just—I don't know. He says one thing, and then he does another," I said, gritting my teeth, wishing this wasn't so. "He'll communicate with everybody else maybe, but he won't even talk to me. Why can't our life be perfect?"

Our server came and gave us our pasta. I ordered a shrimp Alfredo dish, and she had a marinated chicken over a bed of fettuccini. As we ate, we made the conversation a little lighter. She said life is far from perfect for most of us. She talked about her son who had recently gone to jail on drug-related charges. She told me about her younger son who had just gotten married, but was already having problems getting along with his wife.

"These young people are rushing into marriage," she told me. "He didn't need to marry that girl in the first place. He's trying to be the president of a college and she dropped out of college years ago."

I always thought her world was perfect. You know being the pastor's wife usually meant always having things together. But then she confided that women in the church want private prayer with her husband for anything but prayer. Then I started to realize that I would be all alone. Maybe it was too soon for me to make a decision about whether I was to leave or stay. Dillon and I had issues that needed to be dealt with. But hey that was okay.

As if her discerning spirit felt my confusion, she held my hands and said, "Lord, please guide this lady. She's got a good heart. She needs Your help with her marriage and with her writing career. Lord, You are precious and we honor You. In Jesus' name we pray, amen."

I didn't expect things to automatically be changed with my marriage. But for some reason I did have hope that I never felt before. Maybe I wouldn't have to leave. Maybe things were going to be better soon. God could work miracles.

It was June 18th, my thirtieth birthday. It seemed like it should be such a happy time, but I had no plans. There was no real reason for me to celebrate. I didn't make much money as an author but

I was thankful for the few pennies I did bring in. Dillon and I agreed that I could put that money into myself. Therefore, from 8 AM to 2 PM everyday, Stori and Starr were in day care, and I needed to be productive. But as I sat behind my big mahogany desk in my leather swivel chair, fit for a president or CEO of a big corporation, I couldn't come up with one word.

I knew I had to write something down on paper. I was only halfway through my novel that was due to my editor a month ago. My untraditional way of writing books was dictating it all on tape. It was an effective one when I actually had something to say. But on those days when nothing came to mind, nothing was put on tape. I was getting further and further behind. The book had to get done. My little assistant, seventeen-year-old Malika Avery, a rising senior in a nearby high school, lived not too far away in an apartment complex.

Lord, I silently prayed, *if I could just have one birthday wish it would be . . . Okay, let me at least be honest with you. I want more than one birthday wish. I need to finish this book. I need the desire to spend more time with my girls. I'm sick of being depressed. And Lord, I'm so unhappy. I need a miracle in my marriage. I woke up this morning and Dillon was gone. No "happy birthday," no kisses, and not even a small good-bye. I don't know what to do. I keep on panting after him. But not again. This morning I am thirsty for You. Fill me up, because I feel so drained and so empty. Though today I'm only thirty, it feels like I'm eighty. Help me, Lord. Give me some good—*

The loud ring of my office phone interrupted my prayer abruptly. I twirled my chair around toward where the computer and fax machine were located and took my left hand and placed it over my heart. My chest skipped a few beats when I noticed it was my agent. She was well-known, and I'm still amazed that she had taken me on as a client. But then again it didn't surprise me that much. She worked with my pastor's wife and I believe Mrs. Kindle pulled a few strings and got her to take me on.

My first novel, *Luv Right or Git Left*, hit the *Essence* bestseller's list. Word of mouth was making it fly off store shelves. Even though I was with a small Christian publisher, my distribution placed the book in mainstream bookstores like Barnes & Noble and Borders, mass-market stores like Target or Wal-Mart, and most Christian bookstores like LifeWay or Family. Released last year, it had sold almost fifty thousand copies. For a new author that was very good. So my publisher was eagerly awaiting the release of the next one.

"Don't answer the phone," I said out loud to myself, although I knew I had to.

My book was a month late and I was nowhere near finishing the first draft. It wasn't like I'd been on extensive tours or anything, but I did have a new boss. Starr was a year old now and I knew when I signed the deal that I'd be having a baby. I felt more depressed than I thought. Whoever said that creative writing was a way to cope with life was lying.

Truth be told, a part of my depression was because I had wanted a boy both pregnancies. I never considered myself one of those ladies who were into girly stuff. After all, I married an NFL player. I liked sports and I think deep down I was closer to my dad than I was with my mom. I just didn't think female bonding was possible and I guess in some ways I shied away from totally giving my all to my girls.

But as so many people have told me, every time I looked into the eyes of my precious daughters, I realized God knew what He was doing. I was handling the barrettes, bows, dolls, hula hoops, ballet, and tap. I knew even my husband had wanted Stori and Starr to be Dustin and Dawson.

"Shari, are you there?" she said when I pressed the speaker button.

"Hey, Tina."

"Dear, it rang eight times. I can never get a hold of you when I want to. I called yesterday and you hadn't responded. We can't operate like this, honey. You need to respond more promptly and be more accessible."

"I didn't get your messages, sorry."

She spouted off sassily, "Well, you need to check them. Do something."

"I've been really, really working on the book," I said, looking up in the air as I knew to myself that that wasn't the truth. "Okay, I've been really trying to work on the book, but nothing is flowing. I have true writers block."

"Well, you need to get to working. But, honey, that's not why I'm calling."

All of a sudden I sat up in the chair, took the phone off the hook, and listened intensively. "What's going on? You're not calling about the new book?"

"No, baby," she said.

I could imagine her making things happen very

comfortably from her big New York office. She was probably sitting back with her feet up on her desk, laid back in her, even bigger than mine, chair. I really admired Tina for all she had accomplished. I just wished she wasn't so hard on me. A lot of people said that was for my best interest.

Even Mrs. Kindle felt that though Tina got results, her harsh tactics could be toned down. Yes, she was the agent, but she wasn't my mom. Every time we talked she was ordering me around. I was intimidated. However, I knew she was able to make me the impactful author that I wanted to be. Her message was always blunt. I guess if I was going to continue to deal with her, I was going to have to get a little more backbone.

Breaking my thoughts, she said, "You remember what I was telling you about before?"

"Yeah, the play guy?"

"Yes," Tina said. "I told you he was interested in buying the rights to *Luv Right or Git Left*."

"Uh-huh."

"Probably like in January."

"Yeah, what about that?"

"Well, because I didn't want to come to you until I had something really firm to bring to you, it seems we've struck a nice deal. Not only will you get a nice payment for the acquisition, but the play *Luv Right or Git Left* will go on the road in a month."

"What?" I said. "That's so soon."

"I know, girl, but it seems they've been rehearsing since March. The presales were strong enough for them to stop trippin' over money and close the deal. They'll have a packed house.

"So the script still reads the same?"

"They changed a few things here and there, but the premise of it is your story. Bottom line, they are paying twenty thousand dollars."

"Are you serious?" I screamed, very excited as I stood up from my chair.

"Yes, I'm such a good agent that you solely own your play rights. The publishing company won't be getting fifty percent."

I still had to pay my agent fifteen percent. But what I'd be left with was a nice amount. This was such good news.

"But that's not all," Tina said, as if I could see her patting herself on the back. "You will also get five percent of the play's profits. Listen, they are about to hit the road soon. The publishing company has agreed to pay for you to go on tour and sell your books. The producer, Trey Colon, will get ten percent of the book sales. So we have enough room for everybody."

"Well, how long is the play going on?"

"Through September."

"I can't do that Tina! What am I gonna do with my girls?"

"I don't know sweetie, but you have to figure it out. It's the summer. It would be a really nice opportunity for you. Getting away for a while might help you finish that book on the road. You won't have no husband, no babies. All you have to do is sign during the day and sell books at night. And then while you're traveling, you can be writing and when you come back to the hotel you can be writing."

"But I talk on a tape recorder. I wouldn't have anybody to transcribe for me."

"Girl, send them tapes home to that little girl you have over there, the little fast high school girl.

"Or you just gotta be like all them other writers, take that laptop with you and do it yourself. Just think about it. But I do need an answer tomorrow because I've got to put all your accommodations in to get you ready to go out. The first tour goes to Atlanta. Either way, you'll get something. That's cool with you, right?"

"Yeah, yeah that's fine. Thank you, Tina." How could I ever even think of getting rid of her? This was definitely good news.

"Call me tomorrow now. I've got to go into another meeting and figure out a way to tell them their book is horrible. I thought I had a deal for it but now I gotta go over here to this publishing company and try to sell them to somebody else."

"Alright well, take care."

"Shari, call me tomorrow, please, with an answer. Oh yeah, yeah, yeah, and happy birthday."

"Tina you remembered!"

"Of course I remembered! Consider this bonus as your present."

"Sounds good." I hung up.

All of a sudden, I got down on my knees and just praised God. I ran upstairs and found a CD from my favorite gospel artist, John P. Kee. Playing the song "Show Up" really spoke to my situation. God let me know He was there. He had showed up and shown out in my life. My blessing was on time. I played Kee's song four times repeatedly.

I ran a hot bath, sat down to soak in it, and closed my eyes. In heaven was I, as I imagined Dillon and me making love in our king-sized bed. I thought that if I told him the news he'd be real proud of me. And he'd express his gratitude by pleasing me. I could almost feel his kisses all over my neck. Taking my index finger and sucking it passionately with his tongue. Yes, my dream was good. But my whole body longed for it to be reality. Getting my groove on was going to be my birthday present to myself. The real thing was going to be much better than the dream. I was sure of it. Well, at least I hoped so, because it was my birthday wish.

Chapter 2

Big Dipper

Actually, maybe I was getting excited about nothing. Dillon hadn't said anything about my birthday. We hadn't even been speaking in the house.

Going over to my closet to find something to make his head turn, I assumed he had planned something to celebrate the date of my birth. He had always done something special for that day. Five years ago, he took me to Charleston, South Carolina. We stayed in a villa overlooking the water. Not only was the room romantic and cozy, but the mud bath was gritty and sexy. He'd been trying to outdo himself every year since then. So I just knew, even in the midst of all our trials, this was going to be another magical night.

Knowing Dillon, I would need to secure a baby-sitter. We'd had stupid arguments before, because he'd told me I should have known what part of the date was my responsibility—the sitter. Honestly, I was last minute in getting to that because the anger

I'd felt for him over the last week made me not even want to see him in public, much less be together on some romantic outing.

Remembering, I dashed over to the phone and called my assistant Malika. She was on point and only lived a few houses up the road. Because I talked into a digital voice recorder, I needed someone to transcribe my words. I felt bad that I hadn't had any chapters to give her this last month. I knew she needed extra money for the car she was saving up to buy. Hopefully, getting her to keep the girls would be something she was up for.

"Malika," I said in a mischievous tone like I wanted something.

With a teary voice, she said, "Ms. Shari, I can't talk right now."

"What's wrong?" I asked with serious concern.

"If I tell you you'll hate me," she uttered.

That statement really scared me. I'd known Malika and her mom for the last three years. We both moved into the exclusive neighborhood around the same time. My heart ached for her because she'd just lost her father in a horrific train accident. He had been the conductor of a freight train and there had been a faulty part that had gone bad causing the engine to explode. Thankfully, her mom's settlement would help ease the financial burden of not having him around.

From the moment she batted her sad eyelids at me, we clicked. I was like her older sister or mentor. And since her mom was gone most of the time working on community service projects, Malika spent a lot of time helping me. What could be the problem? She was a straight A student with complete focus.

"My mom has me on lock down," she said, slowly revealing details. "I'm pregnant."

My heart plummeted, like an elevator shaft falls. Why did a girl with so much promise veer from the path the Lord had intended for her. She'd already had it tough. How was she going to endure more?

"Shari, are you there?"

"When did this happen? I didn't even know you had a boyfriend."

We hadn't talked in a few weeks. I know she wasn't that gullible to fall for some weak line from a deadbeat. I was ticked at myself for not checking in on her. What was a seventeen-year-old going to do with a screaming infant? She was still wet behind the ears herself.

"My mom is yelling for me again. I gotta go. Please don't hate me," Malika asked strongly.

"My love for you is unconditional. Go see what your mom wants and we'll pick this up soon."

Malika said, "Thank you, Shari, for being so understanding. Everyone else is freaking out. You get me."

"Wait now, I am disappointed. But God loves us in spite of ourselves. Hold your head up and seek the Lord. He'll help work this for the good."

"You believe that?" she asked, as timidly as that of a new preschooler who is unsure if his parents will pick him up.

"Yes, I wholeheartedly know God can turn a mess into something exquisite. Believe in Him, girl."

She said, "Thanks. I really needed this. Bye."

When we hung up I prayed for her. I had peace that though this isn't what I wanted for her, the

Lord would not forsake her. I vowed to be more involved in her life.

The evening was drawing near and I was faced with having no babysitter. My mom, dad, younger brother, and his fiancée were off visiting her parents somewhere in Baltimore, Maryland, so they couldn't help me out.

The only person I knew I could trust with my babies was Grandma. I hoped she was home and not at one of her many church concerts. She was the organist for about twenty local churches. It wasn't that many, but every time I turned around she was playing for somebody different. She said she didn't even need to practice. Whatever she struck up playing, the choir would chime in singing. She was a strong black lady.

One day I got into her business, and I said, "Please tell me you ain't doin' all this for free." I'm not saying the Lord isn't good, but they were using her and wearing her out! She told me that she was getting a little something on the side so I was very excited that Grandma had business savvy. She was racking up with all them churches.

Glad for a fashion breakthrough, I pulled out a sexy, black cosmopolitan dress. I needed something to excite Dillon. I wanted badly to energize him more fully than a charged battery.

"Oh, yeah, this is it," I said, trying on the piece that had been in my closet for far too long.

It was strapless and it was form fitting at the top. At the bottom it flowed out like a fishtail. He wouldn't be able to resist me. I was sure about it. I was actually quite happy about being happy about us. Grandma just had to be available!

"Shar-*ri*," she said with a country twang, "I just don't feel well. I'm quite tired, not tonight."

"Yes, Mame," I said, sounding polite, but saddened.

"You understand don't you, sweetie?" she said, sounding even more pitiful that she couldn't do it for me.

I couldn't get mad at my grandma. Of course, this was last minute and she was getting old. She needed to rest, but I just was counting on her. I wanted to yell, "It's my birthday, Grandma, please! It'll be alright, the babies will sleep. Come on, it's my birthday." I could hear that she did sound quite weak. I didn't push it.

"Mommy!" my oldest yelled as she ran into my room and tugged at my housecoat.

She didn't care that she didn't give me any respect while I was on the phone. Dillon had her so spoiled that she wanted what she wanted when she wanted it. Breaking her out of that would be my mission.

Cutting my conversation short with Grandma as I told her to get some rest, I said, "Okay, Stori, what's so important, sweetie?"

"The baby fell, the baby fell!" she squealed.

At first, I couldn't hear screams coming from my child, but when I listened more intensely and walked to her room the horrifying sound became all too clear. I jetted into my baby's bedroom at that point and found her blaring at the top of her little lungs.

At that same insane moment, the garage door went up. I knew I needed to calm that child down before Dillon came in the house. He goes incessantly crazy whenever he thinks something is wrong with the girls. Our night would be ruined before it began.

Trying to figure out what happened, I thought back that she had been asleep when I put her down. I guess Stori went in there and woke her up. Starr had a few more minutes before she normally got up and she must have decided to climb out. It was okay because I handled it. No brain damage was done. We broke the crying for that matter. She was fine.

I was so proud of myself as I held Starr and walked her around in circles. Saying sweet little lullabies in her ear made the noise dissipate. The problem was last month I told Dillon to let down her crib two notches 'cause she was now able to stand up. He kept putting it off. So if there was anybody he'd need to get on, it was himself.

It didn't matter. My oldest had gotten to my husband anyway. I heard him swiftly stomping up the stairs.

Dillon barreled into Starr's room and asked, "Why weren't you watching the baby? Stori said she fell out of the crib while you were on the phone?"

I couldn't respond to that at first because I was still stuck on how in the world was I going to break the news to him that we wouldn't be able to go out? That was until I looked in his empty hands and was a little dumbfounded that he held no flowers. Giving him the benefit of the doubt, I thought that they were downstairs or still in his car. So I walked over to him and tried to give him a kiss but he walked around me.

"No, no. I'm serious. Did she fall out of the crib, Shari?"

I couldn't believe that he had a little attitude with me. He was the Negro that didn't let down the mattress. He could see she was fine. Let it go and tell me, happy birthday.

"She's okay, baby," I said, still trying to diffuse the situation.

Dillon wasn't having that though. "Answer my danggone question. Did she fall out of the crib or not?"

"Yes, she fell out," I said quite rudely. "Because you didn't let down the stupid mattress like I told you to. You said you'd get to it this weekend. Well, this weekend wasn't soon enough."

His tail couldn't say nothing then. He went ahead and grabbed the screwdriver that I'd had on her white-washed dresser since May. Knowing that I was right, he tried to let down the crib mattress. He had screwed the thing on so tight when she was born that he was struggling to undo the screws.

Actually, I was happy he was straining himself. Shoot, I got no happy birthday words from him. He didn't say I've got some place special to take you. He didn't even tell me I looked really beautiful. Even though I hadn't put on my spiffy outfit yet, he was still supposed to notice me. I was crushed when he didn't do that.

After he finished adjusting the crib, I handed him his daughter that he was so concerned about. He could see up close that his baby was okay. I walked down to the kitchen; Stori quickly followed behind me. When I got there, I was quite upset that I saw no flowers, presents, or anything. It appeared he hadn't even made plans. No wonder he hadn't mentioned them.

I picked up my three-year-old in my arms and headed over to the TV in the family room. I found her favorite *Barney* tape, popped it in, and she danced around. I sat on the couch and let a few droplets fall from my face. A few moments later when Dillon appeared, I didn't even see him staring at me. No part of me cared.

Sensing my agitation, he calmly said, "I was a little rough on you, I'm sorry. You know how I am about those girls though. I didn't mean to make you cry."

I stared like a zombie at the television. The little stuff he was talking about was a poor excuse. I was hurt, I couldn't help but show it.

"Evidently," he said, "since you're going to be mad at me, you're probably not planning on cooking. Am I supposed to go and pick up dinner? I thought you'd have something ready, and I'm hungry."

"Why? I thought you knew," I finally said, peering over at him with very evil eyes. "It's my birthday! I've just turned thirty. I guess it's no big deal. 'Cause I thought you would've had plans for us."

His eyes went wide. The jerk had actually forgotten. Football was intensive, but darn I was supposed to be foremost on his brain.

The words, "I hate you," just came out of my mouth as I got up and went upstairs and locked myself in our bathroom.

"God, this just isn't fair! Tell me why we are so unhappy? I mean, help us. Why did this happen on my birthday? Oh, Lord," I cried in desperation to the Heavenly Father, as I physically felt like just keeling over.

I heard Dillon on the outside of the door.

"Open up, honey, please."

"Please don't give me any lame excuses, Dillon. I just want to pray, okay? There is nothing to be said." I had my knee up on the toilet looking out of our small window at a tree and a little bird. I really wished the bird was me so that I could fly away too.

"I'll be right back," he said. "Relax, baby. I'll take the girls with me."

I didn't need for him to try to piece everything back together. My high hopes for the night had already taken a big dive. When I made it to our bed, I quickly fell into a deep sleep.

About an hour later, Dillon tapped on my shoulder and one of my favorite dishes was before my eyes. He had brought dinner to me. Sautéed mussels, scallops, and shrimp was embedded in pasta with marinara sauce. I hadn't had that in a while. Also, we rarely drank. For him to buy wine along with all of this, he was trying to make up for his mistake. Sipping on the chilled glass of white Zinfandel relaxed me.

"The girls are asleep," he said, as he fed me a piece of the garlic bread.

After I finished my first glass of wine, he kissed me intensely. His firm hands slid all over my upper body. A masseur could not have made me feel better.

"Oh, you smell good," he said, as he undid my robe and took in the apricot-grapefruit body spray on my body. "I did forget your birthday and I'm sorry."

His nose traveled me like a dog in heat. Deep

breaths kept me from losing it. I couldn't give into the arousal he was making me feel. I was angry.

"I know I usually have plans or something, but with what we've been going through lately, I guess . . . Know that I do love you. I know I give you a hard time. I know I'm a jerk," he said, as he placed my left toe in his mouth and made my butt twitch from one side to the other.

Gosh, Dillon did all the right things and all the moves. He wasn't as wild and adventurous as the dream I had the day before, but my husband definitely softened the blow of my disappointment with how I wanted my birthday to actually be. Dillon McCray had something special and he was really making me want it. And since it wasn't often enough, he had me. Being with him felt so pleasurable.

Problem was his release came too quickly for me. Within ten minutes the passion was over and I hadn't even gotten the most enjoyment yet. However, too bad for me. He was no longer into me. He reached for the remote and started flipping the channels. No more intimate talk. No more body rubbing. He was just there, but in another world. Yeah, he was in our bed this time. But I still felt alone.

"Good night," I said, disappointedly, as I pulled the covers over my bare, unsatisfied body.

I silently prayed, *I'm just not content. I'm telling you, Lord. You need to speak to him or he's gonna lose me.*

I tapped Dillon one last time after my honest prayer with God. He didn't even tell me good night, happy birthday again, or baby I'm sorry. As

I watched his actions, I thought, *Yup, he's already lost me.*

During the night, I went to check on Starr. I ended up holding her in the rocking chair until she and I fell asleep. I was asleep until Dillon lifted her out of my arms and placed her in the crib that was finally the right level. He then lifted me up out of the cushioned chair and took me back to our bed.

"I need to get up," I said, still quite disappointed in the way my birthday turned out.

"I'm gonna feed you this morning," he said, trying to be sweet. "But before I do all that, let's talk. The girls are still down."

I couldn't believe what I was hearing. He wanted to talk to me? We hadn't had a heart-to-heart in months.

"What's going on with us, Shari?" He was propped up on his elbow, and with his left hand he stroked my eyebrows.

On my back, I peered over at him. Maybe God does answer prayers. Was he really ready to listen? There was only one way for me to find out.

The concerned stare in his eye made me believe my husband was truly ready to dig deep down into the root of our problems and try to solve them. Life was beginning to be a lot like the hair I was growing under my chin. I'd shave it the first couple of times, but that wasn't enough to stop the irritating problem from resurfacing. Before the morning came, little stubbles were coming out again. It wasn't until I pulled the unwanted hair

from the root that I really removed it. Such was
the case with my marriage. I needed to get the trouble out of our marriage or at least pull it with the
tweezers from the core. Dillon and I needed to dig
deep and straighten some of this stuff out so it
wouldn't just keep popping up.

"I had a talk with Mrs. Kindle the other day," I
said softly.

"Yeah, your regular lunch," he cut in, as he
smiled.

Putting my back to him, I said, "I know you
don't like it when I share so much about us."

"I understand you need counseling," he replied,
as he turned me back to him. "She's around you
for a reason."

"I told her that I was real unhappy."

"You told her that?" he said in an upset tone,
telling me that he truly did not understand, like I
knew he wouldn't.

I nodded my head.

"What did she say?" he asked, a little calmer.

Reaching for his hand, I said, "That maybe we
need to do what you're willing to do now. Really
talk things out. Talk about the stuff that I love, talk
about the stuff that I hate, and talk about what I
think is ideal for us. Really try to see if we can work
through our issues."

"Things aren't that bad, Shari, seriously now.
You exaggerate stuff," he responded, as he ignored my hand and sat up in bed.

I sat up beside him and spoke with conviction.
"Maybe not for you, Dillon, but for me. I don't
know. I just don't feel loved."

As soon as I said that he moved to the edge of
the bed and retorted, "I don't feel loved either.

When I come home, what's supposed to be my castle, it's a mess. It's not like you have to keep the girls. They're in school most of the morning and part of the afternoon. I don't get here until what—four or five hours after that. And the place is still like a pig's pen. I have to step over my own clothes. Clean the heck up, girl, if you want me excited to be here."

"Do you want to know what I'm thinking or am I just supposed to listen to you?" I asked, trying to hold back my own frustration. "You can tell me what's wrong and right. But you don't want it to be a two-way conversation. You bully me with your overpowering demeanor. I'm sick of it."

Dillon stood up and peered out the window. He knew I was telling the truth and the brotha' wouldn't look at me. He could dish it out, but it was high time he took the criticism as well.

Sliding nearer to him, I said, "I'm not saying that I'm trying to cast a stone. I'm just trying to tell you that you forgetting my birthday and trying to make it up the way you did is just not enough. You don't really talk to me to find out what's going on with me. I don't feel appreciated either."

Dillon turned toward me. He gave me a look like I was lying. It took me no time to give him specifics.

"Okay, example, you never come in and ask me how my day is. You just run to the girls and see what's going on with them. Over the last six months, *I* have planned date nights for us—*you* don't even plan one. To me it's like you're not trying to put anything into our marriage. You just take it for granted that I'm here. I'm supposed to love you. I just turned thirty and it seems like I'm sixty or something, because we make love, what, maybe once a month? And even when we do it's not that good."

"You trying to humiliate me now, huh?" he said, turning back to the window. "We're together more than that. And you never complain."

I shook my head with disgust, and said, "Alright, sometimes maybe it might be twice in one month, and I might not say anything bad about it, but that still proves my point. It's not even enough and I don't complain, because I don't want to hurt your feelings. But don't you think I'm disappointed when it's over as quickly as it began. You're a selfish lover."

He stormed to our bathroom. I wasn't out to tear him down. And I surely knew I wasn't without fault. But I could admit when I was wrong. He needed to hear me out. I wasn't yelling. He had to know how I felt about him, darn it.

Sitting beside him on the edge of our Jacuzzi tub, I said, "I think you look like a big slob sometimes. And I'm not trying to be mean, but you can't even wear any of those clothes in your closet. You've gone from a size thirty-six to a forty-two. I'm a tiny girl. I want a good lookin' brotha', not Fat Albert."

Walking over to the shower and looking into one of our many mirrors, he said, "I'm running every morning. I'm working on my weight. I even watch what I eat so it's not like I'm not trying to do anything about that. But what about you? You've got three rolls in your back."

"I didn't even know you noticed. And I only have one left, thank you kindly. Plus, I had a baby. What is your excuse?" I asked to be vindictive.

He was right though, so I couldn't be too mad

at him for telling the truth. I had gained some weight in my tummy and my back. I had a double chin, almost, and in addition, I had hair under it. If my current changing body was an indication of what I had to look forward to as I grew older, I was going to hate myself.

"You're completely unattractive," he told me bluntly, as he grabbed the side of my waist. "And your nagging doesn't make me feel attracted to you either."

"You're saying my body and my mouth is the reason why you're not trying to jump my bones every single week, or better still, every other night like I would hope?" I asked. "I'll take your constructive criticism. Maybe I'll try to do something about it."

"I'm just saying, Shari. Don't think that I'm the only one that's changed, because you are dramatically different too. You write this book, but we don't see any income from it. I gotta work overtime in football. Coach is always giving me something to do. Most of the time I think you're mad at me because I come home late or whatever. I'm trying to do what I can to help coach win so next season we'll have a chance at the national championship. Do you even remember what the athletic director said at the end of last season?" Dillon uttered in frustration, as he bent down over his dirty sink that I hadn't cleaned yet.

I remembered for sure. After the team went 7-6 the last two years, the athletic director told the head coach that they'd better win at least eight games this year or he'd fire the whole staff. For that reason alone I hated his profession. There was no loyalty or stability in coaching.

He looked at me through the mirror, and said, "If I'm fired what will we do then? NCAA coaching jobs are hard to come by, especially for black coaches."

I hated to admit it, but he was dead on. Shoot. Approximately eighty-five football scholarships are given out per school, with about sixty-five of those going to black players. Yet, Division I schools averaged two black coaches out of a staff of twelve or sometimes fourteen. Pitiful. In my opinion, black boys needed to protest or go to historically black colleges. They'd make the necessary changes then.

After waiting for me to give an answer, he said, "You can't support us. You can't even support yourself."

He said that last comment sort of under his breath, but I heard him. Any other day that little crack might have hurt my feelings, but not this time. My career was doing better and so were my emotions.

Jumping on his back, I playfully taunted, "I'm glad you mentioned that because I'm about to get seventy-five-hundred dollars from this production company that is turning *Luv Right or Git Left* into a play! And in addition to that, my agent wants me to go on tour with the book for the summer. How do you feel about that?"

Sliding me off him, he said hastily, "Go on tour with the book where? For how long? And who's gonna keep the kids? No, you can't do that. I know you told her no!"

Overall, Dillon was a good husband where the finances were concerned. He never badgered me about how much money I spent. He just asked that

I keep the checkbook balanced. It definitely felt like his money was mine.

But I was sick and tired of him saying that I couldn't take care of myself. Though he was right; I couldn't. I wanted more for me. I had two girls for goodness sake. How in the world was I going to dig deep and tell them that they could be all that they wanted to be? I was settling for less in my own life. I wanted to spiff up my career a notch. I had to take opportunities when they came, and Dillon surely wasn't holding me here. Actually, the conversation confirmed that I needed a break from him. He was too controlling.

"I didn't give her an answer earlier. But now I've decided I'm going on the tour," I said boldly, as I turned on the shower for it to steam up so I could get in it.

I could tell by his stern body language that he wasn't in agreement with me. I didn't care though. Nothing was holding me back now.

He quickly turned the water off. "Girl, we got two young babies. I'm working a full-time job. You're trying to take them on tour with you to some play? I've been to them plays with you. There's too much going on night after night. No, you're not going to be on the road like that. Not my wife, not my kids. That's that. You need to call whoever you need to call back and tell them the answer is . . ."

He rolled his eyes and looked at me so that I could finish his statement, but I couldn't finish it because the answer he wanted me to give to Tina was not the one she was going to receive. I had made up my mind. I was sick of him.

Yeah, he was the head in this relationship, but he wasn't acting like someone worth following. Therefore, in my mind he had defaulted his right to tell me what the heck to do. If I was wrong, I was just going to have to deal with it, but I kind of felt like I was right. Though I couldn't tell Tina yes. I didn't know what in the world I was gonna do with my girls, because I agreed with Dillon on one thing. Out on the road, living out of a suitcase, and jumping from hotel-to-hotel was not good for the girls. We were probably traveling on a bus and that was no place for toddlers. I needed to come up with a solid plan.

Dillon went over to the closet and started throwing dirty clothes out into the hallway. "See this is what I'm talkin' about. You talkin' about going out on the road and you can't even do your job here. There is nothing for me to put on. I'm really sick of this, Shari."

He went into our bedroom and pulled out three drawers and started throwing shirts on the floor. He was ticking me off because now he was messing all that up, as if I needed more work. He was showing me more and more that we couldn't be in the same space right now.

He was right. I wasn't a tidy maid or anything. It wasn't nasty, but it was cluttered and unorganized. Yeah, I needed to dust and clean, but with two young ones pulling on my arms and then trying to finish a book, I just couldn't get any housework done.

He needed to be me for a week, for a day, shoot for a couple of minutes! Then he could see I had it hard. All he had to do was sit around a board-room most of the off season, drinking loads of coffee with boring white men, and strategizing about how they'd win a darn football game or two.

"Can you buy me some more briefs? All my underwear got holes in them. I know we ain't that piss-poor broke," Dillon ranted with three badly torn pair in his hands.

I knew he was madder about the fact that I was willing to go on the book tour than he was about not being able to find clothes, because as soon as I walked over to his underwear drawer I found three pairs that were wearable. They had little stains here and there that didn't come out with the Clorox, but they certainly weren't as bad as the other three he found that I needed to completely discard. Plus, the stains were his problem. He was just as bad as the girls. The joker needed to wipe better. Really, it was probably dirt from his work-outs. And since I let the dirt sit for a while before I actually washed loads, when I got to it, most times, it was hard for the dirt to be lifted. Dang. I had to do better. Maybe a break would refresh us both.

"I'm serious," he said, as he took the three pairs from my hand. "You don't need to do that play. I know I give you a hard time about not working and all. I'm sorry, because you do have a job. You got those girls and this is summertime, you know. Write another book from home. No matter what happens to my job, we'll be alright."

Unwavering, I looked over at him, and said, "I don't know if we're gonna be alright and I'm really kind of tired of just settling. I'm gonna go on the tour."

"No, you're not!" he said in the harsh tone I hated, just knowing that I was gonna take his fussing.

Whatever, I thought, as I looked at him with empathy. I was so fed up with the Negro before me that I could have cut him. Maybe I just had to show him with my actions. He wasn't hearing my words. Yup. Someway, somehow, I was going to have to show him.

"Hey, Shari," Tina said to me through the receiver, after I dialed her number early-Saturday morning. "Tell me the good news, lady. You're going on tour, right?"

I actually had no idea what I was going to do. I just told her that I would call since she told me I had to. I certainly couldn't let her down, but now she was putting the pressure on. She needed me to go on this trip and it wasn't just for her benefit. I had benefits too. But my husband said no and in no uncertain terms meant no. What in the heck was I going to do?

When I delayed in responding, she said, "I've been praying for you. And I can't really say God has told me to tell you this or that, but I just feel led to say you need to finally make a commitment to you. If going on tour for the whole summer is too much to commit to, then we can try two weeks at a time. Neither party should care. I mean, the publishing company will still benefit from the books that you sell and they won't have to pay expenses if you're not traveling. And Trey, the play guy, he's gonna benefit from whatever books are sold, whenever they are. So that's money you didn't have. So why not take a few baby steps before you walk totally? Try it. Say yes. I've seen you in action. You can't be scared of the public."

"No, no, no," I said, cutting in and defending myself. "The public is my best mode of selling."

"Then what's the hold up? I know you've got your man in check just like I've got mine," Tina responded, sternly. Everyone knew she wore the pants in her nine year marriage. She had helped her husband build up his bookstore empire. I think at last count they had nine stores in the midwestern and eastern region. Their goal was to add one every year. Their bookstores were doing exceptionally well, because with other black-owned chains struggling, and in some cases shutting down, they were expanding. She was a marketing genius. If she said I needed to be on this tour, I needed to take heed and be there.

The words, "Yeah, I'm going," just sort of slipped out. "Two weeks is good for me to commit to in the beginning. Thanks, Tina."

"Okay, girl. Well, I gotta go. Stanley and I are headed over to his store. I'll talk to you Monday morning and give you the details. But you need to plan to fly out on Wednesday."

The next thing I knew, I was sitting there in my office going ballistic. Everything was pushed up. I thought I'd have more time. I was trying to figure out what in the heck I was gonna do with my kids. Not to mention, I needed a way to get Dillon to believe this was his idea, so that he wouldn't be pissed I went against his wishes in the first place.

"Hey, there!" my dad said in a zany voice from my garage door as it opened.

"Y'all better start locking these doors," my mom said in a thwarted motherly tone.

"Where's Dillon? I don't see his car," my dad

said, talking normal as I heard him walk toward the front of the house, where my office was located.

"I don't know," I said in a smug tone, not wanting to go there with my nosy folks.

"Uh-oh. He might be under the doghouse." My dad laughed as he entered my office.

I couldn't believe my dad was a superintendent. Let my grandparents tell it, he barely got out of school himself. He was such a big jokester. I didn't need him being sarcastic. However, I couldn't push the wrong buttons with my folks and I needed them to buy into what I was about to do.

So I hugged my daddy, and said, "What's going on?"

"Hey there, cuz. What's up with you two?" my dad asked, as he planted a kiss on my cheek.

I released him from the secure embrace and lied. "Things are cool, Dad."

The glare he gave me told me he didn't buy what I was saying. My mom knew Dillon and I had issues. She always shared all my business with my dad. So I knew she'd tell him whatever she thought she knew. And that always irked me.

He wasn't in any position to give me advice. He cheated on my mom when I was in high school and college. Though they got things back on track, he knew I was like him. If my daddy could fall into temptation, it was probably in my blood to do the same.

I could never cheat on Dillon. It would be over. And as much drama as I had to go through with one husband. Another man probably wouldn't make it any better.

I had to make my mom buy into keeping my babies. She really was my only option. I'd never leave my girls with anyone else. I had to appeal to her feminist side. She was the biggest advocate I had for me pursuing my writing career. I would say I felt like I didn't have to work a couple of years ago, but my mom told me I needed to do more with my life. And she was my biggest cheerleader since my book came out. Even though it should be easy for her to say she'd keep the girls while I was gone, my mom was still a young grandma. She was just over fifty. Her life was planned out.

Smiling at her, I thought, *Lord, please soften her heart. I really need my mom's help on this one.*

"I see you, Shari. What's going on? What do you want?" she called me out, as I headed over to her smiling pitifully.

I really needed her help a lot of the time. In fact, now was no different. But never had I asked her to keep my kids for two weeks straight. She'd only agree for one week for the summer. But never had I had an opportunity like the one before me that could soar my career through the roof.

"I know something is up. You might as well go on and ask, what is it. What's going on?"

"She didn't get you a birthday present yet. You better tell her what you need," my dad said, as my mom cut a sharp eye over at him. "You know you gotta help your only daughter out, cuz!"

I had no extra time to figure this out, so I told them all about what was going on. After a long pause, my mom surprised me and said, "I can shuffle some days around and keep the girls. You need to go on this tour. It sounds like the play is going to be impressive. Go. The girls will be fine."

Full of excitement, I squeezed her so tight, and

then thinking of a possible problem, I said, "I leave in a couple of days though."

"Well, how long have you known about this? I know you're not telling us at the last minute," she responded brashly, sounding like the mom I knew.

"Just got the word," I assured her.

"And big head?" my dad said, talking about my husband. "Is he okay with this? Or does he want you to stay cooped up in the house?"

I just kind of giggled. Why was my dad right on? Maybe he could help me convince Dillon I needed to do this.

"Yeah, I know him," he said without me even affirming his thoughts. "He wants you to get a job, but he don't want you to do nothing. You need me to talk to him?"

"I was just thinking that, but no, Dad. I don't want to rock the boat more, it's already tilting."

"Seriously. Everything alright, Shari?" my dad asked in a way that made me love him more.

He was so concerned about his little girl, and I appreciated that. It kinda gave me confirmation that this was the right thing. My parents weren't all freaked about me leaving my kids behind. I needed to do some things for me, so that I could be a better mom to them and possibly be a better wife to Dillon. I had something happening in my own life. I honestly wasn't close enough to God to see what He was telling me, but somehow going felt right.

"He can come over and see the girls. He'll be fine," my mom said to comfort me when she saw I looked like a girl afraid this may cause me to lose my marriage.

"You go ahead and do what you gotta do. Tell

'em. He'll be okay," my dad assured. "But if there is a problem you call me."

I just smiled and then hugged my dad tighter than my three-year-old hugs her baby doll. My parents were really precious to me. I sometimes really hated that my husband's parents' situation wasn't the same as mine. That's maybe why he didn't understand how a husband and wife were supposed to function together. His dad was never around. He left when he was three, and his mom, I wouldn't even get into thinking about her right now. It was a whole separate issue all together. If she wasn't calling our house asking for money, she wasn't calling the house at all.

"You got that paint ready?" my dad said, as he headed upstairs to my oldest daughter's room.

Stori wasn't a baby anymore so we were painting her palace a bold Disney princess pink color. When I pointed to the paint in the corner of her room, it was off to the races. Like Stori's room getting a makeover, I hoped the play would revive me as well.

Finally finding a place for my girls to stay, now all I had to think about was how in the world I was going to tell my husband what I was going to do. He would be okay with it. He had to be. If not, our marriage was going to be stretched, strained, and pulled apart as far as the stars go, from one end of the sky to the other, making the Big Dipper.

Chapter 3

Far

How in the world am I gonna tell him? I thought to myself the morning I was supposed to take a five o'clock flight to Atlanta for the start of the play. Dillon had just gotten back from a last minute two day speaking engagement in Raleigh, North Carolina. With him gone for a bit, I had time to pack up my things, as well as get all the girls stuff over to my mom's place without interference.

My husband and I had talked a number of times while he was out of town, but nothing about my plans came up. Actually, nothing about me came up. He only asked about Stori and Starr when he called. Occasionally, I felt guilty about not telling him, but I dismissed that thought. I didn't want to stir up trouble with him away. I had to clean up so that I could figure out what I needed to pack.

Before he left to go to Raleigh, I was going to

address the issue. But it just didn't seem like the time. He was rushing to leave because his head coach asked him to fill in as the evening speaker at a Fellowship of Christian Athletes boy's camp he could not do. It actually was good he was gone. Now I'd only have a quick minute to hear his displeasure. If there was major drama, the needed distance would already be in place. However, I just wasn't feeling the vibe to get into it.

Finally, I came up with a plan to soften the blow. The girls were already at my mom's and I knew the first place he'd go, when he came in, was to their room. When he didn't find them there at eight in the morning, an hour before they were to be at day care, I knew he'd come charging into our room asking tons of questions.

"Where are the girls?" Dillon said in the testy voice I expected, before stumping his toe on one of my black Coach luggage pieces that I adored and had rarely used. "Ow, why is your luggage in the middle of the floor packed and ready to go?"

I was in our little sitting room connected to our bedroom, sipping on a cup of hot green tea, as if I was waiting on him at that exact moment. The look on his face told me that he wasn't happy and I didn't know which question I should answer first. So I kept still for a minute, staying calm. He was losing patience with my not responding as his eyebrows arched. He clutched his foot then gave me a look, like nothing in the world you can say could explain all this. So I got a little nervous. However, I had already been putting this moment off, but there were no more stall tactics that could be used.

I put down the cup, leaned forward, and gently said, "The girls are fine." I smiled trying to ease his mind. "They're at my mom's."

"They're in Greenville, why? You didn't tell me they were going. You're going up there too? Is that why your stuff is right here?"

I shook my head and looked away. All of a sudden the pain had gone out of Dillon's foot as he stood strong and tall and came over to me. He knelt down and we were now eye level. He reached his hand out for mine. As I held his, it actually started to scare me that his gesture showed sweet concern.

He said, "Shari, you got a whole bunch of bags out there. It's like you packed up everything you own. You're not leaving me, are you?"

Never in the world did I ever think he'd believe that was a possibility. But I was actually happy that something in his dominant brain had allowed him to see that he wasn't the only thing in this world for me. Yes, he was the sole breadwinner and I probably would be struggling like crazy if I left him, but that didn't mean that I couldn't and wouldn't make it on my own.

Taking my hand out of his and cupping his face, I said, "Nothing could be further from the truth. I'm not leaving you, Dillon. I'm just doing a little something for me, that's all." His face squirmed, not at all getting what I was talking about. "I'm going to Atlanta today."

"For what?" he said, bitterly letting some of the niceness subside a bit.

This was where the rubber was about to meet the road. I decided to choose another path other than the one he told me I'd had to take. Surely that wasn't going to sit well with him. I knew it, and now it was time for me to take whatever the consequences were going to be. But I wished, hoped, and prayed that it wasn't going to be that bad. In my mind I believed, when I explained to him my rationale, that he'd really be proud of me. After all, my plan didn't involve him altering his schedule in any way. It was time for me to follow my dreams.

Standing to my feet and smiling down at him, I said, "I'm going on the road with the play."

As he stood to his feet, he towered over me like the giant did over Jack in the story *Jack and the Beanstalk*. And like that mean character, his eyes were fiery and his hands were on his hips. He was *not* digging the answer I gave him. So he quickly let me know that was that.

"I already told you you're not going on that play tour. You've got responsibilities here. What about the gi—"

Before he could even say the word "girls," I said, "That's why they're gone. They're at my mom's. She's gonna keep them."

"You're moms goin' to keep them for two weeks? She barely wants to keep them for the weekend. How'd you pull that off?"

"You know she's supportive of my career, Dillon. You know she's behind me. She thinks I need to do more things for myself."

"You probably pushed those girls on her. It's not goin' to work."

"No, I didn't, and if you wanna call her yourself, you can. My dad's in support of this too. I'm going." I walked out of the sitting room and headed over to pick up my first bag to take it downstairs and put it by the front door.

I already knew Dillon would be acting silly, so my little brother was prepared to come and pick me up and take me to the airport. He wasn't going to stop me. This was my moment.

"What is this?" Dillon said in a disappointed tone.

I turned around and faced him. "Nothing."

"Why are you doing this, Shari? I told you I didn't want you to go. I don't even know where you're going anyway. I don't know who you're going to be with. Uh-uh. You're a married woman, not some groupie who can follow a tour."

"Groupie! What are you talking about?" I said, completely offended.

"Yeah, that gospel singer, Bryce Maddox, you always joked is the one you'd leave me for if you could. He's starring in the play. I'm supposed to be okay with letting you be on the road with him?"

I actually hadn't even thought of who was going to be in the thing. But Bryce Maddox, yeah! His smooth sounds and fine self would certainly pull in the crowd. Dillon had to have gotten that off the radio. *Bryce Maddox. Very cool,* I thought.

Knowing his thoughts were ridiculous, I said, "First of all, you also said you'd leave me for Vanessa Williams. We just mess with each other on that stuff. Plus, he's married anyway. What are you talking about? You sound so stupid. Don't you trust me?"

"Don't you trust me to lead our family in the best way I think we should? I told you you're not going and yet you made all these plans to go. You're defying me."

"Well, I was trying to do something for us."

"I'm going to get my kids. You are going to be

here and take care of them. And your parents have no right interfering in our lives."

"Fine then, Dillon. Go get them," I said, feeling the tears start to well up in my body. "We can keep them here and be all dysfunctional when you gotta go to work. Or you can let them stay with my mom for two weeks while I try this thing out and see how it goes. And I might stay longer, Dillon. But either way I'm going. I'm at least going to try this, because I have an opportunity to advance my career. I love you," I told him. "And I'll provide the complete itinerary of everywhere I'll be. I gotta do this, Dillon. I got to."

"Do it and it shows me that you don't love me and you don't love this family. Shari, if you leave you might not have a place to come back to. You better think about that." Dillon picked up his keys, rushed down the stairs, and the next thing I knew I heard the garage door go down, quickly letting me know he had left.

I dropped to the floor beside my many bags. Balling my knees up to my chest, I rocked myself back and forth as the tears finally dropped.

Okay, I thought. *He's made himself clear. If I leave we're over.* I hoped that Dillon was just talking noise and his anger was allowing him to say tons of stuff he didn't really mean. But if he was being serious I had to be ready to deal with his ultimatum. Did going on this tour mean that much to me? Was it more important than keeping harmony in my marriage? I wiped my eyes with the back of my hand. I realized that we were out of sync long before I decided that I needed to do this. If I wanted the vibrant Shari to come back to life, I had to take action.

Already I was needing the Lord to mend this before I had even left. Though I wasn't completely sure the Lord wanted me to go, I didn't feel that torn up about my decision. So I wasn't gonna change my mind now. My mom had said yes, my ticket was waiting for me at the airport, and my stuff was ready. I was going on that tour, and if I didn't have a marriage when I got back, I'd deal with that then, because I had to do this now.

Hours later I was flying off to tourland. My eyes focused hard on the Bloody Mary that was beside me. Watching the passenger seated next to me, that I didn't know, enjoy his drink made me question if I too needed to unwind. I practically walked out on my marriage. I made a decision that I knew my husband didn't approve of. Only the Lord knew what would happen next, and though my life was in His hands, I might've just made a huge mistake.

"You're a pretty lady. Why are you looking so sad?" the blond, handsome gentleman, appearing to be in his forties said in a flirty way.

I knew he was slightly intoxicated. I could smell his breath. This was his second drink, but it made me chuckle nonetheless. I just wished my husband had some of that flirtatious sense in him. Not saying I wanted him to go and say something sweet to another woman, but just to appreciate the beauty in his own lady. I wished that it somehow would trickle down to him to be interested in me instead of always wanting to hold me back in my place. What place was that? One I surely didn't feel comfortable with. I looked down at my three-karat marque stone snugly fit on my finger and stared back at the man.

"Oh. Wedding problems," he guessed. Puckering my lips and then letting the corners of it roll up into a soft smile affirmed his statement. Looking back down on my hand and playing with the gorgeous ring, which was one of the last few gifts I got from my husband being a four-year linebacker in the big leagues of football, I wondered why in the world I forgot to bring my band.

When my book was first released last year, I was mugged. Someone stole my ring. While I was signing a book for a man, he attempted to take my ring and I screamed. When the crowd gathered, the guy ran away.

The next day when I got home Dillon bought me a platinum band. He and I agreed I'd only wear my ring when I was in a safe environment. More and more I found myself wearing the band because it was less flashy. It didn't draw too much attention to the fact that I was hitched.

As the plane accelerated off the ground I leaned back thinking about the nosedive my marriage had taken. Happiness was not just automatic. Somewhere deep down my feelings for my husband had started to fade away. I'd never gone against his wishes before. But this was a new day and I only hoped tomorrow would be brighter.

I knew I had thoughts of not claiming him, but I should've brought the band, I told myself.

"Well, I've been married for nine years," the gentleman said in a fun-filled voice, giving unsolicited advice. "It's never been easy, but just like anything else in this world, that you want really bad and if it's worth having, you gotta work for it. You both must work at it to get it. Work to keep it. Just believe and somehow it'll work out."

I laughed. I don't know if it was the spirits or if it was just the truth that I needed to hear. But how was I going to work on my marriage when I was miles apart? When we touched down in Georgia, I thought maybe that was the start of it. I mentally needed to work through our problems. Maybe time apart from Dillon and the girls and my somewhat boring life would give me time to do just that.

I was picked up in grand fashion. There was a limo waiting for me as soon as I went to the curb. Tina told me to get ready for first-class treatment.

However, I guess I wasn't ready and neither was the limo driver. He looked at me with tenseness, like he didn't know the person he was carrying was black. Not that it should matter to him, because my money was just as cucumber colored as anyone else's, but when he didn't open my door or offer me anything to drink—water, soda, something—I realized he had a problem. I sat back taking up only a fraction of the big cushy space. Then I thought, was this a sign of the way my life was gonna be from now on? Full of luxury, but unable to really enjoy it. My cell phone startled me. I quickly picked it up, not noticing the number was that of my husband.

"Shari," he shouted testily in the phone. "I got your little note saying you were gone. There's nothing you can say, Shari. You made your choice and though I don't understand it, don't expect to come back here."

Before I could respond the receiver went dead.

I didn't have to wonder if that was a sign or not. That was an answer. My marriage was over. I was glad that the limo driver wasn't paying any attention to me. Now, I was a complete basket case. I took both of my hands and placed them over my eyes, as I stroked back my medium-length hair. Pulling it as if I wanted to hurt myself physically so it would get rid of the pain in my heart I felt inside.

Yeah, it was my choice to leave, but just to hear Dillon say we were through made me question once more if that's the outcome I wanted. And I could probably fight for him and get on a plane and go back home. But something inside of me couldn't do that. I was all messed up. I was not fit to be a mother to my girls and certainly not wife material right now. My husband couldn't reach out to me and understand what I needed. How in the world could he expect me to reach out to him? He wanted to be the leader. He said God placed him as the head of the family, but yet he acted more like the tail. I was tired of him showing his behind.

I needed to talk to somebody, but it couldn't be my mom. Though she supported me coming, if she knew Dillon was really against it she would probably tell me I better come home. I knew as mad as he was at me he wasn't gonna go over to my parents house and act a fool. He was foolish but he wasn't stupid.

He couldn't take care of the girls all by himself. I knew Dillon. I knew he respected my mom. He always wished that his mom had some of that class. That get up and go. The bottom line, he was scared of my mom. Not really knowing that all the while, she was on his side more than mine anyway.

I wanted to talk to my girl, Josie. She'd be screaming in my ear shouting for joy that I had stepped out and did something for me. But that surely wasn't what I needed either for myself. I did need counseling, but I could not call my mentor. She was still my pastor's wife, and I didn't want it known that I'd taken off. I might not have gotten judged, but I couldn't take any chances, so I was in a pickle.

Who could I talk to? I wondered. And that's when my dear old daddy popped into my brain. I couldn't dial his number fast enough. However, the call went straight to voicemail. I knew if I dialed my parents' home, my mom would probably answer and I'd be stuck explaining. She always played the role of my dad's gatekeeper. Not only did she make sure his other faculty and staff teachers didn't get too close to him, I believed she liked keeping him at arms distance from me. I called her out several times and she said she wasn't doing that, but she did. I called and I got the third degree; I just wanted to speak to my own dad. So sometimes I just didn't call.

My mom couldn't know everything. She was way over the top. Still wanting to run my life when I was grown. She didn't know how to handle things I didn't agree with. What was I to do with no one to call on? It was like God just reached down from heaven and thumped me on the head and said, "Listen, why don't you talk to Me?"

Placing down the phone and getting on my knees in the limo, I bowed my head and said, "Lord, I really don't know what to say. My life is kinda good, but it's extremely crazy. I don't know if I did the wrong thing. Surely you want my marriage to last, right? I mean, Dillon and I love our kids with all our hearts. But if he's not loving me like You love the Church, then maybe this is my way out. What are You saying? Can You give me some direction? Right now I just think I did what was right. Show me how to walk Your way please. I feel so separated from You right now, that if You told me to turn left I'd probably go right. Speak to my heart, Lord."

I was so deep into my prayer that I didn't realize the car had stopped. All of a sudden the limousine door was opened. The mean driver looked at me like I was some project kid that had no business being in the ride.

Rudely he said, "Ah, it's time to get out."

Gathering my stuff, I saw the Ritz-Carlton hotel and realized again that this was really going to be first class all the way. Reaching into my pocket, I saw the three hundred dollars of cash I had on me and gave the gentleman a five. I didn't want to give him that. He looked extremely disappointed like, "Yeah, I know why I hated that you were black."

I said to him with a smile, "Treat me better and you'll get more. Be glad I don't have the energy to report you."

I walked away beaming inside, thinking, *Yeah, the same thing goes for my husband. That goes to show him dagonnit. That's what he gets. If it's over then let me move on.* As quickly as I thought it, I sighed. *Is moving on going to be easy though?* In the depths of my soul I doubted it. What choice did I have? I was alone now. Then again I wasn't. I had hope because God was with me. And I had already turned all this mess over to Him. So somehow, someway, it was going to work out for the best. I just had to learn how to follow Him.

I was so excited, and I had only an hour to get ready for the big night: the premiere of the play. Everything I had in my suitcases I hated. I needed a completely new wardrobe but lack of money wouldn't allow that to happen. Though I was getting a small mint, it took weeks for it to be sent from the production company, to my agent, then on to me.

My hair couldn't wait for my bank account to rise. Looking in the mirror in my completely clean bathroom, I wondered what in the world I could do to make my hair look better than it was. Thankfully, I had gotten a perm six days before, but my regular hair day was on Thursday. I hadn't noticed it before flying, but I had big flakes all up in the front of my bob haircut. I was thankful that I hadn't gotten it all cut off because I was able to wash it quickly and pull it all back with some gel. It was a chic look, not the nicest, but definitely not shabby either. Just a touch of class.

I found my black dress, which was fitted at the top but flared out at the waist with a cute little sash. It was black on one side, brown on the other, and the sleeves—oh, the sleeves—were completely stylish as they flared out on both sides, almost as long as my skirt. Right at my chest there was a nice little circle cut out. Nothing was revealed, but it would definitely tempt any man that looked my way. They'd say, "She looks hot." When I turned around in the mirror and saw three rolls in my back, I realized maybe my yucky body was the reason why Dillon didn't care too much to keep himself in shape for me.

I gotta stop thinking about him, I told myself, as I hit my head with a quick thump. Five minutes before six, my telephone rang. It couldn't have been my husband; he didn't have a clue as to where I was. It must be someone with the play who was going to be my ride, wanting to know if I was ready. This was cool. Black folks running a little early. I was diggin' this. To my satisfaction I was right.

"Hey, Ms. Writer, this is Melvin Jenkins, but you can call me Mel. We're so glad to have you," the deep, husky, baritone-sounding voice said.

Off that I could tell this guy was friendly. That made my chest, that was beating way too fast, as if I had just come from running a marathon, slow down a pace or two. I had to relax and not be nervous.

"I'm running a little early because I know y'all black women. I needed to call you and let you know that the bus was going to be pulling out in five."

"The whole cast is here at the Ritz?" I said, quite surprised that the producers of the play were spending those kind of bucks. I had been affiliated with some black plays before. When I was in college, I toured for six months with one. We stayed at so many Motel 6s and Days Inns that the light was left on for us.

"Yeah, but I mean, you got your own place. Most of the folks are four to a room! You ready?"

"Yeah," I said with a little confidence.

"Cool. It'll be good to meet you. Come on down. Let's rap."

After hanging up the phone, I went back into the bathroom. Quickly, I put on a girdle to hide some of my rolls and made sure I had on the cutest jewelry I owned. I splashed a little peppermint oil over my body and knelt by the tub to talk to the Lord.

"Father," I cried, "this is a gospel play, but I don't know if I'm really out here doing Your work. I kinda feel distant from You now. Please calm me down. Stay with me, Lord. And Lord, I just pray also for my husband and my girls. You be to them what I can't right now. In Jesus' name, amen."

"Could you hold the elevator please?" I yelled before it closed, bringing my untamed side to this upscale place.

My five minutes had turned into six, after I pampered myself a little more and prayed. I could only see part of the gentleman that held the elevator door open for me. But the part of the caramel man I saw was masculine, but tailored. When I stepped on I was speechless. It was him! Bryce Maddox was standing before me, even sexier than he ever was on TV. I stared with my mouth hung open.

"Okay, it seems you know me, but I don't think I've had the pleasure of ever meeting you, lovely lady," he said, extending out his hand.

He looked at me so intensely it felt like his eyes were cutting through my flesh. Instinctively my eyes batted. I couldn't have disguised my blushing. Oh my, gosh. *What in the world is happening to me?* I thought.

"You look so pretty in that black dress. Tell me you're going to the play tonight," he said in a flirtatious way that attracted me to him even more.

A big smile came across my face and I had to look away. His glare was overpowering. I felt my womanhood warm. My husband hadn't been that into my appearance in ages. It felt as refreshing as the smell of a full load of clothes coming from out of fabric softener. As I turned around toward him, the confidence that had escaped was quickly back.

Clearing my throat, I said, "I'm going to the play. I hear the story line is quite inspiring. I wouldn't miss it. And don't tell the lead, but he's my favorite singer of all time."

Winking at me, he smiled and said, "I won't breathe a word to that Maddox guy. And though he's alright, the story is powerful."

Hoping the elevator wouldn't stop, so we'd have privacy until we reached the lobby, I said, "Seriously, why are you doing a play?"

"My career needs a little boost. I've been doing the gospel thing for so long and I kinda wanna do some R&B too. I figure this play can give me a little bit of both. The music in it is real funky, but some of the songs help spread His message."

"Isn't this from a book?" I asked, wanting to see his reaction.

I thought Bryce was all that, but knowing he never really read the book would certainly put a stamp of reality back in place. Dillon had never read any of my stuff. My husband refused to read my stuff, giving every excuse known to man, and it actually ticked me off. He wanted my support, but he couldn't support me. I just knew the star before me was also the stereotypical brotha' who did not read a thing.

"Yeah, and I actually liked the book even better than the script. You know with plays, all the good details can't be captured. To get into character though, I read the book three times," he said, causing my jaw to drop open once more.

Still not believing him, I questioned, "What'd you really like about the book then?"

"Oh what, you think I'm a brotha' that don't read," he said, feeling my thoughts. "Well, I'm ready for that question. I tell everybody about the book. You have this famous boxer who, through the first part of the book, was doing his own thing. Sleeping with all kinds of women, cheating on his wife. But yet every time he won a match, he would say, 'To God be the glory. Thank you, Lord.' I mean it was like so fake, so phony, so unreal, and then God spared his life by not having him on a airplane that killed everybody close to him. And right there it was like his life changed. He realized that at the way he kept going, he'd be going to hell if he didn't get his life straight. The book is moving. And the physique of the dude in those pages made me have to work out extra hard to play a boxer. Get my abs in shape." Bryce did a cute jab move.

I was impressed. Before I could respond and tell him I was the author, the elevator doors opened and five women came on and huddled around him. They weren't groupies or anything. I could tell by the way they were practicing their lines and saying they were part of the cast. Quickly, he had forgotten all about me.

One of the ladies caught me staring. She was so beautiful. Perfect brown skin that glowed as lovely as a summer day. The dusty red hair was doubled in layers all the way to her elbow. I'd seen that lady several times in magazines. Maybe it was woman-to-woman intuition, I don't know. Either she was Bryce's girl on the side or she wanted to be.

"Who were you talking to?" she said in a smug voice, as if I weren't there.

"Lacy, I was talking to this lady who's coming to the play tonight." Bryce quickly motioned to me.

The other four girls were so nice and sweet they huddled around me, and said, "You're gonna love it."

The other chick rolled her eyes at me definitely letting me know that she was a force to be reckoned with, but she didn't have to be all bummed out with me. Bryce was nice. A little flirty, but his time with me was all innocent. Never in a million years could he be interested in me. I liked to think I wasn't as homely looking as his wife who I'd seen in magazines, but by no means was I model type material like the one standing on the elevator with us either. Plus, I wasn't here to get a guy. And isn't that funny, because my husband said I'd be interested.

The elevator door opened again and we were at the lobby. Bryce and Lacy quickly walked out first. He looked back at me, smiled, and mouthed, "Enjoy the show." The other four girls walked out in front of me as well, heading straight for a chubby guy about five eight with a bunch of badges around his neck.

After I watched Melvin hand out all of the badges except one, I strolled up to him and said, "I'm Shari McCray." I sort of whispered it so as not to draw too much attention to myself.

There were about thirty people around us. I figured I could blend in and not need to get introduced to everyone there. But Melvin gave me a big squeeze. He then twirled me around and everyone looked our way.

"Hey, y'all, hey, y'all. This is the author of that book all y'all women could not put down and you too Bryce. But you probably know who she is since her picture is on it." Bryce looked surprised as he came very close to us and smiled.

"You're the author of . . ." he said, chuckling.

"Luv Right or Git Left," I affirmed, as I nodded.

"You two know each other?" Melvin chimed in.

Twitching my lips, I said, "Yeah. Well, sort of. We were just talking on the elevator."

"Oh, that's what took y'all so long to get down here. I've been waiting on you for ten minutes."

"She's gonna be touring with us y'all," Melvin said to break the ice, as Bryce just kept staring at me with a little bit more intrigue this time.

He appreciated me. His warm dark eyes, displaying that he wanted to get to know me better. He leaned over and huffed quietly in a tone that only he and I could hear.

"Now I know why you asked me a question about your book, mystery lady. How'd I do?"

I felt grand. I had to chuckle to keep my composure as I could see folks around us grinning and talking. Bryce and I were almost lip-to-lip.

Taking a deep breath, I said, "You got me."

Bryce leaned in even closer, and said, "I like your style."

"I like that you actually read and dug my work. Now put on a great show and make the world love it more."

Bowing, Bryce said, "Yes, ma'am. Don't worry, with your story and my acting we'll take this thing far."

Chapter 4

Twinkle

I was one of the last to get off the tour bus. The cast seemed to be in such a hurry and I didn't have to get ready to perform so I had no problem letting others go before me. But when I stepped out into the beautiful night's air, I looked up at the sky and saw amazing stars shining down on me. Though my life wasn't great, I knew I had hope. God was up there. And though I felt unsure inside, sorta shaken up and frazzled about what this tour would do for me, I remained positive. Just as the stars blinked off and on, they reflected the dimness in my life that God would make bright again. I just needed to hold on, have faith, and be strong.

The first night it was amazing to actually watch the play. Bryce was a true star. The way he worked the stage and commanded the lines made his performance believeable. I was proud to have written the story. *Luv Right or Git Left* had loads of drama and tons of passion, but it also had a message that

Bryce allowed to shine through. At the end of the first performance when the cast got a standing ovation, I rose to my feet as well.

When I went into the hallway to my little table to try and sell books, I was a little down. As people were purchasing memorabilia and CDs, my books weren't moving. I knew I wasn't a big-time author or anything, but this whole thing burst the bubble in my head. As hard as I was trying to promote and pitch my novel for folks to pick it up and buy, it wasn't a go.

For the next three nights, it was the same thing. I was starting to get fed up with this, and sick and tired of watching the play. No one cared about my product or me.

The fourth night, while the play was going on, I called up my girlfriend, Josie, and filled her in on what was up with my life. "Girl, I need to take my butt home. Them bringing me on this tour is like I'm collateral damage or something. It feels like I'm bringing down the house, you know."

She teased, "Child, keep your head up. You know how black folks are. We come to a play to get a lil' drink, laugh a lil' bit, and go home to get busy."

"You are so silly. How are things with you?" I asked, hoping that being a true friend would lift me up.

"Same ole same ole. My crazy mother-in-law is still jealous as ever. Causing her son to choose her over me again. But don't worry, girl. I'm 'bout to leave his butt."

"No, what's going on now, Josie?"

"Shoot. He just got me a brand new ring. A

round three-carat stone set in a platinum band. I only had to be with the guy for five years."

"Oh my, gosh, J. That's the bomb!" I said a little too excitedly.

"Whatever, girl. I just found the receipt and it happened that he had bought his mother a ring as well."

"You're joking, right?"

"Nope. It's like she's got to keep up with me. Don't she know I'm his only wife? We'll fix that later. Enough about me. Did you meet Mr. Maddox yet?"

"Hmm, funny you should ask," I said, feeling better just at the mention of his name. "A few days back on the elevator actually."

"Is he fine for real? Does he get you hot and bothered?"

"Girl, he'll make you sweat," I said, rubbing my chest as I thought back on our encounter.

"Watch out now! I might need to join you."

"Maybe you should so you can help me sell some of these books." We laughed.

We were in Cleveland and Bryce had many fans here. Women came into the play wearing T-shirts with his face on them. He had to be the biggest gospel singer of our time. Crossing over to R&B would be easy for him, his fan base was mega.

During intermission, he surprised everybody when he came out and mingled for a brief moment. I was a little irritated because I was about to make a couple of sales to the T-shirt wearing crew. As soon as the women heard his voice, they practically threw the books down at me and rushed over to greet him.

Bryce happened to glance over and see where the ladies were coming from. When our eyes met, I made the biggest pout face I could. He had to understand his stunt to gain attention just screwed me over.

Mending the tension, he brought the twelve women over to my table. "Ladies, have you heard of Shari McCray? Well, she is the bomb. I read her novel three times. If you're diggin' the play so far, trust me, you'll get a high from reading the book."

I couldn't believe he kept ranting about how if I hadn't written the book, there would be no way they'd be enjoying the play. I didn't just sell twelve books to those ladies, I sold forty. Melvin came and removed Bryce from my table to inform him it was time for the second act. As they walked away, I knew I was never going to forget his kind gesture.

Since things picked up, I decided to stay on the tour. The next couple of weeks, it was the same. The play was sold out night after night and during intermission the paying crowd was paying for my books. During the breaks, I tried to find the time to finish the novel I was working on. However, writer's block had me held up and bound.

I couldn't focus. I couldn't concentrate. I probably felt bad for leaving my kids with my mom. And with my husband; I was still so confused and mixed-up. I felt that God had given me this opportunity so that I could seize the moment and find myself.

Going into the hotel, I saw Bryce in the lobby trying to get away from a lady. Their conversation didn't seem too friendly. She was tugging at his shirt collar, practically wanting to choke him.

Melvin came over to me, and said, "Don't worry. That's his wife, Pamela. I'm sure you've read in the tabloids that they are estranged. He's trying to get a divorce, and she's trying to work with anyone to ruin him. It's just a mess."

"You don't have to tell me," I uttered aloud, without even thinking I was alluding to my own ugly union.

"What, you're having marital problems too? A cute little thing like you should be able to hold hers down. Marriage is hard enough, but being on the road can add even more tension to the relationship if your dude isn't supportive," he said to me.

"Speak the truth again," I said, as I looked over at Bryce's wife crying.

I could tell she was in pain, but yelling and screaming in the hall wasn't helping her cause. I had no clue what caused Bryce to want out, but if I was a man she wouldn't attract me.

"Melvin, can I speak with you for a second?" Lacy, the leading lady of the play, came up to him, ignoring me, and asked.

She didn't give Melvin a chance to say bye to me. She rudely jumped between us, swung her weave in my face, and jerked him over to a secluded corner. As they walked a few steps away he held up one finger, motioning for me to wait. Standing there I overheard Lacy gripe.

"Look, Melvin, I don't even understand why his wife is here. I mean, we're together now," she said, as I swallowed hard, wishing I hadn't heard that information.

"Lacy, I can't speak for Bryce, but it sounds like you're thinking the two of you have more than is really there."

"Ugh!" she screamed, before scampering away.

Melvin stepped back over to me. "Guess you didn't know that being on tour can give you a lot to write about, huh?"

"I try to stay out of other people's business," I told him, giving him the politically correct answer. "My mind can think of enough warped things on its own."

"Your agent said something about you having to report to a conference?"

"Yeah."

"Well, that's great. We got a little down time before we head to the next city. Come back."

"I don't even know if I'm doing any good here. I'm just selling the books. You guys can do that."

"Your presence is uplifting. You're the writer of this amazing story. Knowing you're around lifts the cast. Bryce has even talked about you many times in the preshow meetings. You're wanted back."

I smiled. "Thanks. I appreciate that."

And just like the stars I saw the first night of the tour that blinked on and off, I had hope. That maybe there was a real purpose why God had me where I was. Maybe if I stuck it out, that reason would become clearer.

I was in Orlando, Florida, seated beside my agent at the big banquet that the Christian Bookseller's Association hosted annually. Looking around the large ballroom I could see that there was nobody who looked like me. You know, no black folks were in the room. But they'd added a new category: Best African-American fiction.

"I think you've got a good shot at winning this thing," Tina said to me as she looked at the other names in my category.

"Just being nominated is enough for me," I quickly admitted to her.

She gave me a look of disappointment. Her tough demeanor was good for negotiating deals, but this time it was a little bit annoying. I didn't show any kind of resentment. I just chalked up her overbearingness to her caring. Despite what she said, I was happy to simply be there. Winning and losing was in God's hands. And as the evening went on and I got to be more up and personal with authors I'd admired, I'd forgotten all about why I was there.

Until Tina hit me in the arm and said, "Here's your category. Here's your category."

"African-American fiction has been on the scene for over a decade now," the presenter stated. "And I'm thrilled that the gold-medallion award this year will have representation from that genre. As Christians we all belong to the same race, but there is nothing wrong with us branching out as authors, publishers, and booksellers to reach all markets. So with the warmest regard, I present the first Christian Booksellers award for an African-American fiction title to Shari McCray!"

"Oh my God!" Tina shouted in the room.

It was a special moment for me. And the brightness of the lights and spotlight made me blink a few times. But I felt like a star, like this was my night. Like all my hard work had finally paid off.

Taking a deep breath I swallowed, stepped to the podium and said, "It took me seven years to get this book out there. I was rejected by so many companies I just wanted to quit. But the Holy Spirit living inside me told me to keep going. I realized God had me write this book to minister to the souls of the lost. The Lord has us here to bring people to Him. The title *Luv Right or Git Left* is a message to others letting them know that He doesn't want them to leave Him behind. I accept this award today grateful that the book has done well. May we all keep leading people to Him. I thank all of you for doing your work."

I was just a little black girl going into the Christian bookstores, seeing many sections but never seeing a place for African-American titles. Standing here with this award in my hand, I felt more than accepted. The overwhelming feeling felt fabulous.

"Thank you for recognizing all God's people. Though we have different needs, we all need Him. So keep doing what you're doing and live for Christ." I got a standing ovation and the tears fell.

The next day I was on the International Christian Retail Show floor signing copies of my book. I could see other booths where authors had their lines wrapped double for people to get signatures. My line was close to empty. But instead of sulking about it, I thought about sitting at the play and feeling ill about not selling a lot of books. I was there to uplift the Lord. Wanting to be the most popular author was not my purpose. The Lord just wanted me to be the best me I could, not put myself in competition with other authors. Though maybe my publisher wouldn't see it that way, I knew God was in control. So with every person who stood to meet me I seized the opportunity to overly exuberate how excited I was about the title.

And before I knew it my line had grown extensively.

I hadn't had a chance to look up because I had to move faster with the growing line. My publicist said, "You have one more."

"And who would you like me to sign this too?" I asked, looking down at the work.

"Bryce Maddox is fine," the familiar husky voice said.

The pen trembled in my hand as I looked up to see none other than Mr. Maddox himself standing in front of me. "What are you doing here?"

"I had to come here to do some promotions with my new CD. I am a gospel singer you know. I heard all the buzz about this new Christian author. Had to come check her out for myself."

"You have a copy of this book," I whispered.

"I don't have it signed," he whispered back. "What are you doing after this?"

"Um . . ." I uttered, having a frog in my throat.

He completely caught me off guard. Was he asking for my time? Not a date for sure.

"I think I'm done. I did some interviews before this so I got a second. What's up?" I asked, trying to act cavalier.

"Cool. Let's hang out."

After speaking with folks at the publishing company and wrapping up at the booth, Bryce and I walked the elaborate floor. It was like the biggest, prettiest Christian bookstore you would ever want to be in. The booths were fabulous. Publishers were well represented. I didn't have enough focus to give to all the booths I was passing, because I was floored with the gentleman I was walking beside.

"So when do you leave?" I finally asked as any concerned friend would.

"Tomorrow. You free tonight?"

Hesitantly, I said, "Yeah."

Sitting in my hotel room in Orlando, I saw I had three missed calls: one from my agent and two from my knucklehead husband. "I'm sorry, buddy. But I'm not calling you back," I said, reflecting on Dillon. He'd made a bed with me and now he needed to lie in it; really understand how he's pushed me away.

But I did need to call Tina. However, I wasn't up for any lectures. Though she was married, she didn't have children and, in my opinion, didn't have a life outside of publishing. She was very opinionated and made the world think she had all the answers. Actually, she'd lost several great clients, which ended up working in my favor. She probably would've never picked me up, poor ole undiscovered me, had she not been a little more free with her client roster.

"Hey, lady," I said, a little woozy inside.

Something about talking to her had me on edge. I was a grown woman. Around her, I felt like a child.

"So, I'll be at your room in an hour for dinner. I was wondering when you were gonna call me back. There are so many other things I could be doing. Came down here to celebrate your achievements and I can't find you anywhere, girl."

Just tell her you got plans. Tell her you can't be with her, I said to myself. That was my problem. I felt bullied by so many people in my life: my parents, my agent, my husband. I needed to take charge and seize the opportunity to chill her forcefulness. Just when I was about to let her have it, I thought about my words and chose carefully.

Gently, I said, "I have other plans."

"What do you mean, you have other plans?" she gruffed back.

"Well, Bryce Maddox from the play is here. He wants to go over some strategies with me about how to keep the buzz going if I'm available."

"Well, I can sit with you guys and go over that stuff. I've got tons of ideas," Tina said, forcing herself on me.

I hated lying, but I came up with an excuse. Babbling, I quickly blurted, "I don't know. He seems pretty weird about other people. What do you think, should I handle this on my own?"

I thought turning the tables would make Tina think it was her idea to bow out gracefully. I held my breath as she took a second to answer. Could I psyche her into not going?

"Well, if you put it that way it is a good opportunity. They are keeping you on the tour this long. There really was no guarantee that they would have this extended period of time. I got a call earlier today that you're staying for a while longer. Whatever you're doing, keep it up and keep this strictly business. I know that he's a ladies man. But we have nothing to worry about, you're married. Whatever he's selling, Shari won't be buying." When I didn't comment, she said, "Right?"

"Please, Tina. Only business," I said as we hung up.

I was so self-conscious though. Bryce was incredibly handsome. His wife wasn't gorgeous, but the ladies that clinged to him were. I was just a plain suburban mom. I hated my look.

As the time grew closer for Bryce and me to mingle, I got down on my knees and prayed, *"Okay, Lord. I know this seems weird but I don't know if this is completely wrong. I'm totally attracted to this man. I need You to be with me through this thing. And I know that's crazy because I'm married. It should be clear You're seeing all of this. But if marriages are broken, you should get out, right? Ugh. I'm so confused."*

And at that very moment the hotel phone rang. "Hello?" I answered.

"Are you ready to meet me downstairs, pretty lady?" Bryce's sexy voice said to me.

"I'll be right down. And what do you have planned for us this evening?"

"Ha. Surprise, surprise."

He wasn't kidding. Our day was filled with pampering, with us going to a day spa and me getting my nails done. Then he took me to a hairstylist, where I got a little color and new trim. I couldn't believe all of this.

When I looked in the mirror and saw my new hairdo, I said, "So, what, I needed an upgrade to be by your side?"

"No. I just know when a woman could use the joy that only taking care of herself can bring. How are you feeling?"

"Great."

"Good. There's one more thing."

"What?"

"I wanna pick you out a beautiful dress. Every time I see you in nice suits I can only imagine you with a v-neck dress with no bra and no panties. Ooh, and some sexy pumps sashaying your body in front of me, gettin' a brotha' all hot and bothered."

Okay, wait, I thought to myself. *Cool down, mister.* But then a stronger part of me wished he wouldn't cool down at all. I wished we could quit talking and go back to my hotel room and have it out. Then I realized I didn't know this joker. What was the harm in playing along and actually enjoying myself? So we headed to the mall and he found me five perfect dresses. I didn't even have to choose. But I did wear underwear. When I came out of the dressing room, I didn't disappoint as I let my hips move from left to right.

"You're gorgeous," he said as he stood up and gave me a big hug.

"I'm tired."

"Oh, no. I'm taking you out on the town. You like sushi?"

"I think I like you," I said, flirting.

"I think I like you back." He chuckled. "I'm serious. How could a guy not catch feelings for a lady whose eyes twinkle?"

Chapter 5

Shining

As my body willingly eased into the back of the limo with Bryce, I was startled when my cell phone rang. The noise caught me so off guard I bumped my head. Bryce rubbed the top of it and I was even more fidgety. I couldn't have him touching me. Hairs stood up on my back. I really wasn't supposed to like him like that.

Looking down at the phone, I dropped it like a hot potato when I saw my home number. I hadn't spoken to my husband in over a week. Scary chills now raced up and down my spine.

Immediately, I started sweating. Then I began contemplating whether I should let it go to voicemail or whether I should answer it. When it rang again, I picked it up. Last thing I wanted was Bryce to say, "Hello."

Bryce quickly asked the question, "Aren't you going to get it?" insinuating himself into my business. And though I admitted we had a connection,

I wasn't ready to divulge anything about my broken marriage.

I couldn't say to Bryce, "Oh, no, this is my husband on the line. I'm not going to answer it, because surely he wouldn't understand me having dinner at nine o'clock with a man he knew I've lusted over for years." That's when I knew no matter how I wanted to spin this friendship, encouragement, congratulations dinner, or whatever it was, this was wrong!

The phone rang loudly once more. Instinctively I picked it up. I smiled at Bryce, holding up one finger and said into the receiver, "Hello."

"It's me," Dillon said roughly, sounding like he knew I knew it was him.

I could tell by his tone that he was a little irritated that I didn't respond in my usual way. My standard greeting for him over the years had been a friendly, "Hey, honey, what's up?" But he didn't deserve that kind of greeting from me. Granted I hadn't reached out to him, but he hadn't reached out to me either. Then I had to ask myself, *Had I even prayed about our relationship? Had I asked God to protect my husband and help him see his anger was against God's will?* Yeah, sort of, I guess. Right? I was all confused.

"What's going on?"

It was really sorta hard to talk. I mean I was out, supposedly to have a nice evening on the town with a new beau. Only to have my time interrupted by my husband calling me before the night could begin. Maybe that was the Lord's way of saying, *Shari, what are you doing?*

Bryce was so understanding. He acted like my friend by motioning with his hand for me to take my time. The door was still open and he got out and said, "I'll be back. Handle your call in private."

"Where are you?" Dillon accused in a harsh sounding tone. "I called your hotel room, your parents gave me the number and, um, it went to voicemail. I just heard a man's voice in the background. Clearly you're not headed to bed."

Well, I actually missed my husband's voice, and I was so happy he was a little agitated that I wasn't securely locked in my hotel room. In Dillon's own unique way, he was trying to say I miss you.

Carefully trying not to tick him off more or say the wrong thing, I replied by saying, "I'm just getting a bite to eat, that's all. Why'd you call?"

I didn't know how long Bryce was going to be out of my presence so I wanted to keep the call short so I'd be off the phone when he came back to the limo.

"Your mom called and I talked to the girls tonight."

I didn't respond, I just held up the phone waiting for him to continue. *"And,"* I thought.

"The girls are well," he continued. "It's not like you called to check on everybody."

That comment was a little insensitive and I felt my veins bulging out as my heart rate increased. My whole body got a little testy. He didn't want me to cut the fool with him. I was already out on my own. He didn't know he didn't need to push me too far.

"I already checked in with my mom, Bryce."

"BRYCE!" he yelled, realizing I had called him the wrong name. "I mean, what's going on, who are you there eating dinner with? I'm calling you to congratulate you on winning an award and you're calling me some other Negro's name. What's up with that?"

How in the world was I going to get myself out of this one? I knew my husband didn't come from the smartest family in the world, but he was no dummy. Surely he could put two and two together. Waiting for the bomb to drop, I sighed.

"That singer guy, are you out with him? Y'all not staying in the same hotel room or something like that are you? How did he get down there, I thought he was in the play with you? He's not supposed to be at your book conference thing."

Twenty thousand questions came at once. And if that wasn't enough tension the real Bryce walked back to the door.

"Look you don't need to grill me," I said. "I'm just having dinner with him. He came down here on his own."

Knowing inwardly that I didn't have any ties to Bryce, I didn't need to be all secretive or anything. Whatever he heard he'd just have to hear. I had no double life. I was a married woman talking to my husband. Surely Bryce would not have issues with that.

To get myself back on track and convince myself that this was no big deal, I simply said to my husband what I needed to say. "Bryce and I are friends. End of story. Thank you so very much for calling me about my award. I appreciate it. I will talk to you later. Good-bye!"

"Dang, girl!" he said as he sat down beside me. "You let your man have it didn't you? You not gone be in the doghouse mentioning me."

I'd already been in the doghouse. I didn't even know why I tried anymore. Sucking my bottom lip in, I fought back the emotion that was welling up inside of me. No, it didn't make me happy that I had to cut off my conversation with my husband. But before he could call me back and let me have it, I did turn off my cell phone. No need getting embarrassed twice in one night.

"I understand though," Bryce said as he gently stroked my hand to calm me. "I got problems in my marriage too. I'm sure you've read about it all over, heard it, and seen it. I should be served with divorce papers any day now. It's tough staying committed to one person your whole life. You can't let that person get you down so much that you don't even want to strive for your own dreams and goals. If they're constantly tearing you down, making you feel inferior, making you just . . . hate 'em. You gotta cut 'em loose."

I looked directly in his eyes, wiped the water from mine, and said, "Honestly, I hear you. I'd never thought I'd be in a failing marriage. We got two young babies; it's just not fun anymore. And I know it's not only one-sided, Bryce, I know he hates me just as much. He's jealous and he's probably turning red right now because he can't get me on my cell phone."

"Do you still love him?" Bryce asked out of the blue.

"I've got so many issues with myself, I don't even know if I have any love to give anybody."

"We gotta do something about that. What's your day like tomorrow?"

As we traveled to the sushi spot, I bored him with details about my book signing at the Christian African-American Booksellers booth, the interviews with magazines and Christian broadcasting stations.

As we got seated, he asked, "Okay, so when will the busy lady be free?"

"After four. Sorry to go on and on, it's just that no one has ever sent me anywhere. This is huge."

The waitress came and brought a menu of seafood choices, from octopus to cooked sea eel. I was excited because my husband never wanted to share one of my favorite foods, but Bryce seemed to love it more than me.

We enjoyed the rest of our evening, not talking about either one of our marriages. We laughed, giggled, and enjoyed our bliss. My depressed feeling phased away and Bryce had me glowing all over. By the time Mr. Maddox was done with me, I was beginning to look forward to four o'clock the next day.

Bryce's male companionship was uplifting. Later, however, when I got back to my hotel room, I noticed that I had eight messages. I reluctantly played them back and heard my husband's angry voice screaming into the receiver. I had to call Dillon.

"What's going on with you, Shari, out with other men and stuff? You hung up on me, turning off your phone so I couldn't get you back. I mean what are you doing? Are you throwing the towel in on our marriage? Is it over? If so, you need to tell me so I can move on too."

"I can sense you're angry."

"Oh, you don't think I have reason to be?"

Now I knew why I hadn't talked to my husband in a while. Sure, maybe he had cause to be mad at me. And as he kept lashing out at me, telling me what a horrible wife, mother, and person I was, it wasn't racking him any brownie points with me.

I didn't wanna compare him to Bryce, because I barely knew that guy, but it sure was refreshing to just go out and enjoy someone who was in tune with my feelings. I didn't have to spend the whole evening eating and talking about nothing or hating that I was there in the first place. Byrce even dressed up. My husband hated to put on cosmopolitan clothes. If it wasn't an athletic look or feel, it had no appeal to him.

"I don't know what to say. You're accusing me of doing way more than what was going on. I'm sorry I called you his name. That was unintentional. I was out with a colleague who happened to be at the International Christian Retail Show. Don't trip, I've gone out on business meetings before. It was no biggie. We were simply talking about ways in which we could partner. All I was doing with him was trying to figure out how to improve the showing at the play."

Now I was starting to lie to Dillon. We really did have troubles when I could so cavalierly make up something. He wasn't a saint either though. He'd called my bluff and what he got he got.

"You need to get off my back a little, ease up. Don't be so harsh."

He fussed more and I just held the phone away. The air cared to listen more than me. I truly was starting to hate him, as we came to no meeting of the minds. And he ended up hanging up on me, so the feeling was probably mutual. I was too exhausted to even pray for our marriage.

I took a long shower and enjoyed reminiscing about my evening out. I had good company and I had gotten an award. Things were looking up and I was looking forward to more good than bad. I finally felt like I deserved the best and, come what may, the best was coming to me.

* * *

"I'm really pleased with how well your book is doing. You're such a wonderful role model for our young people. You're doing this publishing company proud," Mr. Gayley, the vice president and publisher of my book company, said to me during a private meeting before I was to go sign at the Christian African-American Booksellers Association, CAABA, booth.

I loved getting my time with him. He was such a nice, humble man. I remember when I first sought out a publisher. Not only did my favorite agent in the world turn me down, before I landed with Tina, but I also personally talked to several different publishers. It was no problem getting the meetings. I guess since they didn't have a slew of African-American women on their author roster, they couldn't be rude to me. They just found a way to say, *No, we're not interested at this time.* The rejections came in the forms of letters, e-mails, and verbal communication; any way they could say no, they found a way to do it.

Even though Mr. Gayley said no at first, I could really sense he was trying to help make me better. And of the things that he told me to sharpen, like getting a more realistic view of my characters and having a few other plots than the main one I was trying to portray, above all I had to make sure that God was the central character. Once I implemented his suggestions, Tina had no problem getting him to sign off on giving me a two-book deal. He was kinda growing me up in the publishing world, telling me a lot of stuff that I needed to know. He was such a godly man, and with most white folks not even speaking or smiling in my direction, I couldn't say the same for most so called Christians.

Because it was a Christian company, I was limited in the drama I could put in my titles. Everyone sinned and fell short of the glory of God. Why couldn't characters? But in order to stay in their game I had to conform and play by their rules. No profanity, no sex scenes, and no gay stuff.

"Thanks for all your compliments and getting my book in the right hands so that the powers that be could read it and give me a chance to win an award. I'm just so thankful," I said, clasping my heart so he could see the sincerity. "And I should apologize to you guys for not getting my second book done yet. Believe me, my agent is on me so you'll have it soon."

"Well, I did wanna impose upon you our deadlines, and we are working with your agent to secure all of that. But we just wanted to let you know how proud we were of you. We've had to let a couple of authors go this year. One was a pastor who was stealing money from the church, they let him go as pastor and we looked into it and the evidence was right. We had to release him from his contract as well. Our motto is, 'A message you can stand by,' and no one can stand by an author who publicly is out living their own way, yet telling a message to others on how they should walk the straight and narrow. We want our authors doing and writing the same thing. We are glad you are upholding His standards. I know you gotta get down there to the signing so I'll let you go," he said as he looked at his watch.

We shook hands. I told him he would have the next manuscript soon. Thankfully, he told me an extension was acceptable. Then I was off to the ICRS floor.

Another day at the conference was even more special. Strolling alone to the African-American booth, I was able to appreciate the small things. The beautiful royal purple carpet, ushering me down each of the aisles, reminded me of what heaven would be like. Hearing my people sing praises to the King convinced me. I wanted to be fully used for him.

I had a line waiting on me. Tina was standing there along with the author relations person from the publishing company, ready to show me where to stand and start my line moving.

Tina whispered in my ear, "Look at all these people ready to get your autograph. A much longer line than yesterday. Next year, you'll be over there in a private booth. You're doing great, Shari."

Grinning at her, I inwardly was okay that that wasn't my lot this time. I was thankful the Lord had given me a larger crowd than the day before. I didn't need to ask for me. I needed to be excited about what He'd given me.

With a gracious attitude, I had a ball. I met all kinds of people. Some that had read the book and some that had not. People that were hurting and people that were healed through the message in my book. Positive words of encouragement were coming from every person I met.

I had already done interviews the majority of the morning. Then had my meeting with Mr. Gayley, followed by my signing. It was now four o'clock and I didn't have a clue where Bryce and I were going to meet. I didn't have to figure it out either, because again he was the last person standing in my line.

Tina gave me a fierce look as if to ask what's up with this. I tried to hide my excitement but I couldn't hold back the corners of my mouth from turning upward in a really big fashion. Boy did he look good in his black jacket, white shirt that was unbuttoned, brown slacks, and some cool Stacy Adams shiny, black shoes. Bryce didn't have a stomach overlaying the belt area like my husband did. His clothes fit and they fit nice.

News flash to me . . . Shari McCray was extremely attracted to Bryce Maddox.

"So did you want a book or . . ." Tina stepped up two notches and looked at both our faces.

Quickly, I stepped in to answer for him. "Or what, what else would he be over here for?"

Ironically, her protectiveness was funny. Though she and my husband had had it out a couple of times, she was an advocate of the holy union of marriage. She was not going to stand by and watch me do something that she felt was morally wrong.

"I heard you're out of books, but I've been standing in this line, so just sign my bookmark like you did for the last few people," he playfully teased.

"Yeah, she ran out of books a little while ago, but you still stayed in line?" Tina questioned, looking up out of the glasses she wore just for fashion. "Why is that Mr. Maddox? It's my understanding that you two talked last night, what else is there to say?"

Sounding real professional he flipped the script on her. "I brainstormed over some ideas in which I could improve her book sales for the play and I kinda wanna discuss some of that today. That's okay, right?"

Tina's whole perspective changed. "Oh, if you guys wanna talk about business, her business, that's fine by me. Go on, get moving. Call me and let me know you guys made it back to Texas." Tina hugged me and said, "My plane leaves soon. Keep the conversation to business."

"Of course," I told her as I pulled away.

Before Bryce and I left the convention floor, we walked down the aisles we didn't check out the day before. Looking at some of the displays, we both were in awe of all the uplifting material that was out there for sale.

Then we came to the music side. He pointed to the new competition of up and coming hot-male artists that were flying up the gospel charts.

"I don't know if I like this," he said, being totally vulnerable with me.

"Other people taking your spotlight?" I said, keeping the conversation real.

"Oh, see you got jokes."

"What is it that you don't like, except the point that you want no one to outshine you?" I placed my hand on his bulging shoulder. "From what I see you have nothing to worry about."

"Well, that's mighty kind, my lady, but I'm not sure I like this straight, rigid, Christian way of having to do everything. That's why I liked your book. It was Christian, but it was sort of—"

"What, almost secular," I cut in.

"Yeah."

"And I really struggled with that. It was even toned way down from the first version. It didn't get picked up for a long time because of that. You really can't walk the thin line; you have to come to one side or the other. Either your halo is on or it's off."

He shook his head, "I disagree. I think you might not wear it straight, but at least keep it on and God is cool."

I shook my head unsure whether or not I agreed with him. Then I stopped walking. He kept going and once he realized I wasn't beside him, he turned and came back over to me.

"What?"

"Well, I mean it's just Bryce Maddox has been this big gospel star for what, ten, fifteen years now? You can't just not sing gospel, I mean, what are you talking about? No one would let you transition."

"I strongly believe I'll have my fans cross over with me. But there's other stuff I wanna say, other stuff about relationships that's dying to come out. My marriage is over, I'm a hurting black man, I got some things I wanna say and songs that I need to write. And every time I go to write a song to God and thank Him, I just can't."

"Are you mad at the Lord?" I questioned, already knowing that if the answer was yes, I could understand that.

"No one ever asks me these tough questions like you do. I don't know, Shari, maybe I am."

Bryce walked out of the facility and for the whole two-mile walk, neither of us said a word. His hotel was a couple of blocks down from the convention center and right out front we caught a cab.

"Where are we going?"

"Let's go to Disney"

"I have on a business suit and so do you."

"We can stop off at the mall and get something new. Then go to Mickeyland. You need to unwind. Actually, we both do."

"Bryce, I just don't have it like that, where I can go to the mall and buy a new outfit just because. I'm on a budget here. Plus, you bought me stuff yesterday. No more."

"I'm the one that's kidnapping you and taking you to Disney, right?" he asked as I nodded. "Then let me do what I want."

The two of us argued back and forth because I truly didn't want him to do that. He ended up swinging the car back around and letting me go upstairs to change my clothes. Fifteen minutes later, he'd come back to pick me up after he had done the same. It was a pain, but I didn't want him feeling like I owed him something by him buying me the world.

Once we both got on the first roller-coaster ride, it was like all of our troubles, disappointments, and fears were a distant memory. We just laughed, screamed, and enjoyed the rides. It had been such a long time since I had basked in the goodness of what an ordinary day could be. The only major conversation we had was when we were getting an Italian sausage from one of the vendors.

Then he made our connection more intense by staring into my eyes and saying, "You really look cute. You know that?" Bryce said.

"Yeah, right," I dismissed.

"I noticed you've done that a couple of times. I'll give you a compliment and you'll basically call me a liar. What's going on with that?"

Sitting down and sharing fries, I admitted I wasn't truly comfortable with my looks.

"What time do you fly out?" he asked.

"Not 'til tomorrow around four."

"Good. Well, it's six o'clock now. We're going to finish enjoying this great night and I'm going to see you at eight o'clock in the morning in your lobby."

"Well, what do I need to wear?"

"It doesn't matter."

* * *

At eight fifteen the next morning, I was at the spa being pampered again, and getting my legs and underarms waxed. After that relaxing treat, I went to a hair salon.

After getting acrylic placed on my fingernails, I felt good. Bryce had arranged for us to have lunch with the Disney characters. I could do nothing but laugh. He told Mickey and Minnie how little self-esteem I had.

Mickey placed his two big white palms on both of my cheeks, squeezed them tight, and Bryce said, "I agree, isn't she beautiful?" Mickey nodded his head.

"Why are you doing all this? Tons of girls would love to be here with you, and you wouldn't have to give them a makeover. From the natural eye, I think they're the model types. So why me, why are you doing all this?"

"Because from my eyes, I see something in you that I want you to see in yourself. You're beautiful, you're powerful, and you are drawing me in. Someone true who could offer something good: herself."

"Whatever. Hand me the last French fry," I said.

"Seriously, I think our paths crossed for some reason and I know in the pit of my gut it's a good one. I'm just not going to leave you alone until I get all that I am supposed to get out of this relation-ship."

"What is it that you think you're going to get?" I kind of chuckled to him.

"What is it that you think I want?" he teased back.

A scared look came across my face.

"Oh, relax. Don't worry right now. All I want is for you to share another couple of fries with me. Sound good?"

"Yeah, sounds good."

The two of us jumped up and rushed back over to the vendor. We both had a lot to figure out in our own personal lives and our walk with the Lord. What was God trying to tell us, and could we help each other hear His voice in the other's lives. Or were we making God's voice not come through?

Riding the plane home from Orlando to Columbia after the convention, allowed so many questions to rise up in my brain. Because I saw I had a layover, I was able to extend it for six hours. Flipping my Bible to Psalms 119:18, I read one of my husband's favorite passages: *Open my eyes, oh Lord, that I may see wonderful things in Your law.*

I needed direction from above. Part of the reason why I was coming home was because I felt a little guilty about what I'd been up to. Dillon had caught me out on a date. I had to just be truthful with myself. That's what it was. I had feelings for Bryce.

Whatever passage I came to, wherever my thumb led me, and wherever the Lord guided my heart, I wanted to be able to digest the Scripture; soak it up, take it in, and use it as food for my soul. I flipped over and landed in Job. Though I didn't see any particular Scripture on the page that stood out to me, I thought about Job's story and the famous Scripture Job 1:21 from that great book.

The Lord giveth and the Lord taketh away. Blessed be the name of the Lord.

I really did need clearance for this. Was God trying to take something away from me? Was that something my marriage? Or was I totally misinterpreting all of this?

At the closing of the book, I prayed. *Father, you know my situation and I wanna do right, but I'm so confused right now. The only thing I can be grateful for is that I can be honest with You to show You just how mixed-up my brain is. My husband loves You, but I just don't know if he loves me. But the new beats in my heart are jumping for Bryce, and I don't know how I feel about Dillon either, Lord. So if I bump into him while I'm at home, I just ask that You step into that time and at least let us not go off on each other.*

When I arrived at the airport, I was able to get my bags arranged so that they would go directly to the Houston airport. I was glad to be staying on the tour. Getting a chance to roll home for a minute was great as well.

I went to the Hertz counter and got the keys to the car I had reserved for the day. My cell phone never seemed to work in the airport. When I looked down to check the time, I noticed I had three messages. One was from my mom asking me what time I would be there at their house, so she could have the girls ready to greet me. She and I talked early. She thought it was a great idea for me to come home so that I could love on my kids, even if only for a few hours. She also didn't want me being home alone with my husband. I hated that my mom thought he was dangerous, but I wasn't sure. I just hate she knew so much. Maybe precaution was for the best. The Negro could be crazy, and if I could avoid any silliness I was all for that.

The second message was from my mentor,

Mrs. Kindle. She was giving me a call to let me know her mom had had a terrible fall. I couldn't catch my breath long enough hoping she'd be okay. When I listened to the last message, it was her once more telling me she was on her way to take her mom to the local hospital. Being that the hospital was on the way to my home, I went straight to emergency and found Mrs. Kindle's car in the parking lot.

When I caught up with her in the lobby area, her face was so shiny and wet. When she saw me, new tears welled up in her eyes trickling down her worried chin. There were no words, I just hugged her. Her mom was ninety-five; I knew this was hard for her. She walked me back there to the room as she told me all about the hard fall that took place in the nursing home. Her mom had been there for two months now. Ever since her mother got Incare, her quality of life had faded.

A woman that I had always known to be strong, and encourage me in my own life's walk, was breaking. As I held her, I tried helping her hold it together. I knew it was nothing but the Lord allowing me to be here for her in this hard time.

"I don't think she's gonna be okay this time, Shari. I just don't," she finally uttered.

Seeing her frail mom, I really regretted that this was the only time I'd seen her because I'd been so busy with millions of other excuses that had come up. She did look quite worn out. *But how else is a ninety-five-year-old woman supposed to look,* I thought, trying to give myself hope that she was going to pull through.

Then Mrs. Kindle said in a weird tone, "She was tired. Earlier she called out for God to just come and take her. And though she has Alzheimers, I really believe she was in her right mind when she said that." We held hands. "Wait, I thought you were with a play, what are you doing here?" she said, putting the conversation back on me.

"Don't you worry about me. I'm just here to stand by your side right now. There's no other place I'd rather be. I got a little time to lend you."

"Matthew had to head over to the church. He'll be back pretty soon. Yeah, Reverend Kindle and the boys were up here with me early this morning. Her doctors are going to make my mom stay here in the intensive care unit." Mrs. Kindle let go of my hand and went over and rubbed her mom's head.

Lord, I prayed, *I wish there was something else I could do.*

As if Mrs. Kindle read my mind, she said, "I'm just glad you're here, dear."

I prayed for her mom, and I was happy just to meet her. Mrs. Kindle never let me get away without talking about me. I loved her for that. So I was real with her and told her everything that was going on in my crazy life. Forget about judgment, I needed to confess.

Her only advice was for me to seek God's direction and not follow my own heart. She reminded me God would lead me the right way, and I might very well lead myself astray. Quickly, I hugged her. I brushed her mom's hand and saw a sweet smile come across her face, and then I left.

Driving home, I wondered how long I'd be on this earth. And to be ninety-five! God, I couldn't even imagine. The things that could happen and all the years to possibly come. If I were to be at the end of my journey, be it immediately or sixty-five years from now, I wanted to make sure I was living holy so that I wouldn't have any regrets. And with that I could smile.

I couldn't get into my house fast enough, when my three- and one-year-old sweethearts jumped into my arms. I could barely hold the two of them, but I wasn't going to let them down. In so many ways I didn't ever want to let them go. My three-year-old talked so much I could see she was excited to see her mom and had missed me terribly. My mom was kind enough to give us some time. She was washing dishes. My husband, with nothing to do but lead a training camp, couldn't even keep the house clean.

I could tell my girls missed their house too. As they played downstairs in the playroom, my mom and I both sat in the adjoining room on the couch, folding clothes.

"You know," I said. "Has he been over to your house a lot?"

"No."

No sooner had I asked than I hear the whirring of the garage door opening up. Even though we were in the basement that was a sound I was all too familiar with. When things were great, I remembered my husband having late nights at work, and me being so excited, waiting around in my lingerie, happy to hear the garage door open so that I could give him a special surprise. But over the last few months, the sound of the garage door opening had been torture.

My happy mood had grown dim when I heard

that sound. Right then was no different. I didn't even realize that I sighed out loud, until my mom said, "Shari, what's really going on? Are you scared for your life or something?" Her question almost pierced my throat.

I couldn't even swallow it made me sick. Because truthfully, though I knew Dillon wasn't that crazy, his anger was still unpredictable.

"You're here, Mom, and things are going to be fine."

"Well, I'm not leaving you alone," she said to me.

As she folded the last pair of his socks, my husband came straight down to the basement. The girls stopped watching *Barney* and gave him an even bigger hug than they'd given me earlier. I wasn't jealous though. I actually hated the fact that they had missed their dad. He should see them more often.

Not so Dillon would misunderstand anything, I quickly said to him, "I'll be headed out soon. I just came to see the kids."

"Why'd you do that here?" he said harshly, trying to talk low so my mom wouldn't hear. "You could've seen them over at her house."

"I wasn't headed in my mom's direction. And since I didn't have that much time, she brought them up here. Plus, the girls really miss the house. They wanted to see their rooms and all that kinda stuff so we're here."

"Well, you didn't come to see me so no need in telling me what's going on now. Where's your boyfriend?"

"I explained all that. Don't be petty."

"You're lucky your mom's here," he sneered at me.

As if he had a split personality, he smiled and picked up our oldest daughter. He lifted her up over his head and placed her on his neck. Gently, he bent down to scoop up the little wobbler and held our youngest in his arms. They thought he could do no wrong.

"Mommy, Mommy, come follow us. Come, Mom, come! We're going to play monster, come, Mom, come!" my oldest said.

My mother got up and picked up some of Dillon's clothes. They made small talk and then he told her he'd see her next week. She headed upstairs after looking at me to make sure I was okay.

When I gave her the nod my husband roughly asked, after my mom was out of sight, "What, you supposed to be scared of me now?" He dropped down to his knees and set down our girls, and said, "Girls, go around the corner. Daddy will be there to play in a second."

He sung the *Barney* theme song as they went out of view. I knew it was about to be on. I took a deep breath to get ready.

"You don't have to worry about me, darling. We are over! You wanna get with somebody else, that's fine. You wanna move out that's fine. I don't care what you do," Dillon stated as he grabbed my arm and then released it.

As I watched him walk away from me and go over to the girls, I prayed, *Lord, is this Your will or am I walking my own way, headed astray. My marriage feels over and I'm numb about it, what does this mean? Help. There's no spark, no glow, and no twinkle.*

Chapter 6

Sparkle

It was so hard saying good-bye to my babies, watching the light fade from my girls' eyes as my mom drove out the driveway. Though I'd been with them for hours, I wanted to spend more time with my girls. That was a good thing. The past few months I hadn't been the best mom. I was so focused on what I didn't have that I failed to appreciate and give my all to what the Lord had blessed me with. Thankfully, time away from them changed that.

Before my mom got completely away from the house, she stopped. Then she zoomed the car back to me. When her window went down, her eyes held tears.

"How much longer are you gonna be here?" she said when I came to her side of the car.

"Not much longer." I leaned down into the car window and smiled at my babies in the back. I was so in love with them at that moment. I could've taken both Stori and Starr and eaten them as if they were candy.

My mom interrupted my thoughts of them by saying, "I'm serious. I'm worried about how long you plan to stay here. Shari, is it okay to leave you here with Dillon?" The thought hadn't even crossed my mind. He stormed upstairs too fast and left us in the basement. I nodded. It was going to be okay, but I looked up at my big old house and prayed it would get bigger. Him on one side and me on the other. If that happened, I wouldn't even have to run into the crazy joker.

"My cell phone is on. Call me if you need to," she said. "Wave at your mom."

As they did, I cried.

Walking back through the garage, it seemed so natural for me to talk to God. I was scared and there weren't any second thoughts about it. Not that I thought he would punch the wall, yell like a maniac, or throw things around the house, which had been known to happen from time-to-time, but it was the silent treatment. His disapproval of what I was doing was just too much for me to take. Now I knew I needed God's help and I quickly needed to gather my stuff and get the heck out of the way.

Soon as I opened up the bedroom door, my husband startled me.

"I heard the garage door go up, I thought you were gone," he said in a noncaring way.

"Oh, I'll be out of here in a sec. I just gotta grab my stuff." I went around him with no problem.

But then he shouted, "Hey."

I felt my heart rate increase. What was the harsh "hey" about? What did he have to say to me? What in the world did he want?

"You know you really hurt me. Going on a date with some other guy and everything. That's all I wanted to say. I just wanted you to know that. Go ahead and get your crap." Dillon then turned and walked toward his favorite spot in the house, the basement.

Though my heart rate slowed down with his intimidating presence out of the room, I felt nauseated. I didn't think I was capable of hurting his feelings anymore. His dictating ways clearly let me know I didn't phase him. However, he let down his guard and told me he was vulnerable and showed me that I still mattered.

Lord, what in the world am I doing? I prayed as I sat down on the stairs. He couldn't see me, but I knew he knew that he had gotten to me.

During the plane ride back to Texas, I realized that my husband's words were still twirling around in my brain. Though I needed a nap desperately, he had me stumped. I'd been going without much rest for the past few days, but I couldn't relax. I was so uptight, so uneasy. My husband told me I had hurt him and, though he had hurt me too with his unacceptable tyrant ways, I didn't mean to get back at him like that, or did I? Subconsciously, did I want him to hurt like he made me hurt? *Of course I did*, I thought to myself. If only I'd hurt him wouldn't he come and try to work it out, hug me, or kiss me and try to apologize for the drama he bestowed upon me.

I was as confused as the hazy fog to the left of the plane. Even though I told my husband I went out for business and that I wasn't on a date with the hunk I'd cooed over for years, he didn't buy it. I didn't either. My conscience was referring to

Bryce as the man I was intrigued with. I had to be honest with myself. I had strong feelings for another. How in the world was all this going to play out? Was there any way that the Lord could use messed-up me? I hoped I hadn't let Him down too bad.

"Wow, you look hot," Melvin said as he picked me up from the airport. "Are there anymore bags?"

"No," I said as I blushed, wishing Dillon had noticed my new hairdo. "That's all." He gave me a hug and then I hopped into the passenger side of the car. "So what did you do to my boy?"

"What are you talking about?"

"The boy got back yesterday and he's acting like a man that's got a woman on his mind. The only thing he wants to talk about is you. I've never seen him so distracted. I've been his road manager for over three years now."

"He's a nice man. We had lots of laughs. That's all. Promise you, I did nothing to him."

"He wouldn't give up any details, but something's going on there and I like it," Melvin said as he eased onto the freeway. "Bryce has been ringing my phone trying to find out if you made it in. He was hoping the plane wouldn't be delayed. He's made some special plans for you guys before the play."

"Gosh, look at me! I can't go out!" I said all giddy, like a high school girl ready for her first date.

Melvin glanced over at me before looking back

at the road. "I just told you how nice you look. I don't give out undeserved compliments. Besides, you're not getting me in trouble with the boss. The place he is taking you to is casual so you're fine anyway. And y'all won't have much time. Only an hour or so before I have to pick you both up and get you over to the Houston Civic Center. Then I'll make sure the bags get taken to your room."

Melvin dropped me off in front of a Japanese restaurant. I thought I was having déjà vu. How'd I feel about Bryce assuming I wanted to go out with him again? The thought of him just making plans without consulting me made me uneasy inside. However, the moment he opened up my car door and I saw Bryce waiting at the entrance with flowers, all of my resistance melted away like snow does when the sun shines bright. Trying to hide my excitement, I showed all of my teeth, something I rarely did because I hated them. When I noticed what I was doing, I quickly shut my mouth and looked away.

"Come on, smile," Bryce said. And before I could get all into him for not checking with me before making plans, he apologized for it and said everything right.

"You look beautiful and you smell great. You've just made me more excited about taking the stage tonight."

We were sitting on the Japanese floor. As he studied my squinted face, he read my mind once again. I was thinking, *Finally, someone else likes sushi just as much as me.* I could eat it again and again, but Dillon, being a steak and potatoes man, would never go for sushi more than once a month, much less back to back. Bryce was connecting with me in many ways. I couldn't help but feel relaxed.

"I hope you don't mind that we're eating sushi again."

"No," I uttered in such a soft whisper that I could have been on Mars and been satisfied. "I don't mind at all." I started smiling again and looked away.

He caught me that time, pushed my cheek back to face him and said, "Why do you do that? Why do you hide your smile?"

"My parents kept braces on me when I was younger and like a stupid head I didn't wear my retainers. My teeth have shifted. I truly hate my smile."

"It's not ugly, Shari, it's sexy. It's you. Plus, you learned a hard lesson, don't beat yourself up. You should've worn your retainers though. But you can get braces again or you can get overlays."

"Yeah, right, like I can afford it."

"Why do you keep making money jokes? I'm gonna fix that tonight."

"What do you mean you're gonna fix that tonight?"

"I'm gonna fix that tonight, pretty lady. You watch me." Bryce might not have realized what he was doing, but he fed me raw fish.

With his skin as the extra sauce, the raw fish and rice tasted mesmerizingly delicious. It was so good that I sucked his finger as it exited my mouth. When his eyes appeared as if they wanted to devour me, I realized how much I was turning him on. I couldn't hide my smile then. The twinkle in my eye proved I had the hots for a man that was not my husband. *Lord, help me.*

After I made sure my books were set up nice and neat, I felt a little hungry. So I went around backstage to the greenroom. Before I could enter the door, I heard fierce yelling coming from the room.

"You haven't returned any of my calls and I don't understand what's going on!" the familiar voice of snooty Lacy screamed out.

It didn't take a rocket scientist to figure out who she was talking to and I didn't even peek into the room. Yet I was correct when the next voice I heard was that of Bryce's. It was five minutes away from show time. The backstage hallway was completely empty. Most of the actors were on the side wing waiting for the curtain to let up because the first act was a big musical number including the whole cast. The two leads were back here in a heated discussion. I know I should've walked away, but I was frozen solid when I heard Bryce speak.

In a voice fit for a doctor telling a family there was no hope for their loved one, he said, "Look, I'm sorry. It's over, okay? I don't want to hurt you, but that's just the way it is?"

"You're just saying that 'cause you found some new floozy to mess up your mind."

Okay, I started sweating then. Did she know about us? And was there even an us to know about?

"I tried to cut ties with you before this play even started."

Lacy ranted, "You said you were going back to your wife not going back to some other—"

"Don't even go there," he said, cutting her off before any negative, nasty words could come out of her mouth.

"I don't know what I'm going to do." Lacy changed her voice to that of a pitiful one. "If you leave me, I can't make it. Anyway, no one knows you like I do. We'd have nothing standing in our way once you get your divorce."

"It's over," Bryce said with force as I heard footsteps toward my direction.

Bryce was probably headed toward the stage. I couldn't have either of them catch me listening in. The desperation in Lacy's voice was truly a lady in love with a broken heart, and a part of me did feel for her. But I wasn't her doctor and I wasn't trying to make her feel better. She wasn't a nice person to me or others. Whether Bryce and I got together or not. He didn't need to be with her.

"Please don't leave me, please."

"You gotta let go of me," he yelled as I saw his foot inch out the frame of the doorway.

I stepped into view, and said, "They're waiting for you guys onstage." *What a quick save,* I thought in my mind.

"Great." Bryce looked at me, and said, "Just in time."

He left the two of us alone. Lacy fell to the floor, water all over her face. She clutched her knees up to her chest and rocked back and forth. She appeared in a trance like his words and the separation had really destroyed her. I did completely feel sorry for her at that moment. No woman should be so down that when a man says it's over she can't go on. I went over to a table with scarce appetizers on it, from where the cast had gobbled them up before the show, and grabbed one of two napkins left.

"Here," I said to her. "You've gotta get back in makeup. We need you on stage."

As if she wanted to harm me, she uttered, "You."

I guess I gave her enough motivation that she stood to her feet quickly. The diva got all up in my face waving her hands around. It took all my composure to give her the benefit of the doubt.

To take it up another level, she started spilling out false accusations. "It's because of you he doesn't want me anymore. Look at you, you can't even compare to me. I know he's interested in you. But I swear, it's going to wear out and one day you'll be just like me. Enjoy the ride while you can, because it doesn't last long. And he won't even pull over and let you out. You'll feel like he's going ninety miles an hour and then he'll open the door and push you."

Lacy didn't grab the napkin out of my hand. She rolled her eyes, grunted at me, and grabbed the last one left on the table. But she wasn't hurting my feelings with her ugliness.

She walked out saying, "I don't need anything from you."

Leaning back on the door, I sighed. She vented words of a sore loser. But Bryce and I hadn't even committed to anything. Did she really sense I was taking her guy's interest? Plus, Bryce belonged to someone else anyway. She didn't need to get upset with me.

For me, the night was starting out like any other.

Nothing spectacular in terms of my sales numbers; four or five books sold. Leading up to intermission, Mel frantically came over.

"Come on, you gotta grab your stuff," he huffed, out of breath.

"What do you mean my stuff? All my books?" I asked with a dumbfounded glare.

Motioning for me to hurry, he said, "Well, just one book should be good I think. Also, get your purse or your personals. I gotta take you backstage. We don't have much time."

"What for?"

Mel placed his hand on my shoulder. "Bryce needs you onstage. Come on, come on, come on! Girl, you 'bout to be large, come on!"

I got the point then. Bryce wanted to introduce me. I hustled up my black Brighton bag. I had just splurged on it at the airport. Then I picked up one copy of my book.

"There isn't much time." He grabbed me by the arm as we went to the left wing of the stage.

Bryce was on stage talking to the audience. He looked over at Mel in the wings, and Mel nodded. As I stood there able to see the packed audience from behind the curtain, I remembered that Bryce had given me a hint he was planning to do something special for my career. People had given me praise before, but never had the star of a play taken time during intermission to say jack about me or my work. Whether his gesture helped or not with sales, I was impressed by the action it required for Bryce to even do this.

Bryce motioned for me to join him on stage and without hesitation, I did. *Lord, thank You,* I thought. Holding out his hand for mine, the butterflies came as we stood there connected. He mouthed that it was going to be okay and then he squeezed my hand.

He looked into the lights and said to the audience, "How many of y'all out there like to read? Shine the lights on the audience and turn the house lights up please."

I couldn't believe all the hands that were up when we could see all the folks out there. It had to have been all twenty-five hundred people with their hands up. If even a tenth of them bought the book, I'd be really doing something.

He continued, "Well, this play, I'm sure y'all heard, is based on a book. But you might not have heard, and you probably definitely didn't read it in the program, that the author is traveling with us for some stops. Ladies and gentlemen of Houston, I'm proud to introduce to you tonight, Ms. Shari McCray."

Folks started clapping. Bryce let go of my fingers to applaud me as well. I was blushing and felt overwhelmed.

"This sista' can make the pages come to life. You need a copy of her title, *Luv Right or Git Left*. Again I say, you need a copy. The play doesn't even begin to touch the surface of the message that God has laid upon her heart to share in the pages of her novel. We make it a little funny up here, but in her book she keeps it real. You gotta love God, man. And if you gonna say you're His child, you gotta do it all the way or you'll get left behind. I don't want y'all just raising y'all's hands saying you read. All y'all folks that really read, give her your support and make her sold out. Don't just buy one for yourself. Buy two more as gifts."

A lady shouted out, "I know that's right!" The audience chuckled.

"So help the sista' out. Would you like to say anything?" he said, looking over at me.

"I'll say a little something," I nervously whispered over to him.

"I'm gonna buy a book 'cause she's fine!" a man blurted out from the audience.

I touched him lightly on the arm and took the mic. "I'm just so thankful right now to be before you guys. I know it's intermission and I don't wanna take a lot of your time 'cause some of you are ready to get to them chicken wings." I got tons of laughs. "Seriously though, there's a big message in the book. Life is tough and sometimes we wonder where in the world is God in the midst of all our problems, when we're the ones that walk away from Him. My book is about a character that is loving all the wrong things. He's loving and seeking earthly fame and fortune. And to you that might be a big house, big car, a big job, and there's nothing wrong with that. But when loving things of the world take over your heart and cause you to sin then watch out."

As I talked I got choked up. Where was I in my walk with God. Was I loving worldly or heavenly things? Certainly I wasn't sinning, but was that what I was headed for. I shook out the negative thoughts I was having.

After a pause, I said, "But the character learns that he needs to love God and realizes that once he follows Him everything will work out. We all got issues. We all got trials, but I know a God up there that can solve all your issues and get you through all your tribulations. Give the book a try and get blessed."

"Amen sista'!" another lady shouted out.

"How much is the book?" somebody else yelled out.

"Regularly fifteen ninety-five, but today we got it for thirteen dollars!" I handed him back the mic and gave him a light hug.

Bryce said, "Clean as you all look I know everybody in here can afford that."

I couldn't hold back the tears when I got back to my table that had been empty for a week and saw a line longer than the one for the chicken wings. People didn't just want one book. Like Bryce encouraged, folks were walking away with three and four. My hand was finally tired from signing. What a joy it was to be able to have support. I had two hundred and fifty sold before intermission was over, I only had six left. It was amazing. It was unreal. Then I thanked God, because it was for real.

When the play was completely done, I had another long line. Yet, I only had six books to sell. Twenty-five people walked away with flyers saying they were headed to Borders, Barnes & Noble, Wal-Mart, or whatever black bookstore they could find to buy my book. Others said they were going to e-mail me and let me know what they thought. It was really a blessed time. I felt better about that signing than I did about getting an award. God had to be doing something, because too many great things were happening. And I wanted it to stay that way. Ever since Bryce had come into my life, my dreams were coming true. Was that a sign that he was right for me?

As I signed the last book, I thought, *Lord, let me love the right way now. Even in my own life, help me to do it Your way and not miss what You're trying to tell me.*

The next two weeks were more of the same. I was riding high. I went from selling two hundred and fifty books a night to five hundred plus. It was unbelievable.

Bryce and I were having more and more one-on-one dinners. I was really starting to see the brotha' was deep. He cared for his children and was so torn about the separation. He listened to me as well.

Though I hated I didn't see my girls daily, I was happier than I'd been in years. Making something of my life was fulfilling. And my mother was pleased to see me finally fully utilizing my talents. I talked to Stori and Starr before they went to bed each night though. But I was missing them. But for a woman who'd been overwhelmed with motherhood, this break was mentally healthy. If I was going to return home a single mom, taking time away from the girls to blow my name up as an author was crucial. I'd be able to support myself.

In the next few cities we went to, people started to hear about the novel and I didn't have to wait until intermission to talk about my book. Bryce had me onstage at the beginning of every show. I gave my testimony and encouraged folks that if they had a dream they could reach it too.

My agent, Tina, couldn't believe the success she was hearing. So when we got to her town of New York City, she came and couldn't believe her eyes.

My books were flying off the table. Like the play, the book was a big success.

We were backstage in the greenroom after the New York show and Tina was just acknowledging my praises when all of a sudden Bryce came up beside us, wrapping his arm around me saying, "Oh, yes, she is the bomb and I can't wait to read her new book."

All of a sudden the pressure was on. That's when it dawned on me, I hadn't written a word. Just then I felt the creative juices flowing. I was ready to produce. Though I hadn't had a lot of quiet time with God, I felt so close to Him. I could feel Him breathing into my soul what He wanted me to write down on paper.

"Well, she better get to writing it soon," Tina replied with one hand on her hip and her neck stretched out looking me eyeball-to-eyeball. "Or the publisher might have to drop her."

I didn't speak. I just looked at her like, *Come on. You gotta step in and help me out with them.* She caught my vibe, and said, "But with all this good press the play is giving her, I'm sure dropping her will be the last thing they'll do. But you gotta get to writing, Shari."

Looking more pitiful than a kid that got in trouble stealing out of the cookie jar, I said, "I will, I will, I will. I'm planning to do a little creative stuff tonight."

Tina sternly said, "Good then."

"I'm awfully proud of her," Bryce said as he stroked my back.

Just the very touch of his hand made me feel warm in places that had been cold for months. Bryce and I had spent time together, but we'd managed to keep physical advances from entering those moments. Now, I was so flustered that I immediately looked into Tina's eyes for advice.

She noticed that I had the hots for this guy so she said, "Excuse me, Bryce, let me borrow her for a second." And pulled me over in a corner. "What are you doing?" she questioned me.

Of course I said, "What? What do you mean?" as if I had no clue to what she could be talking about, trying to avoid a big confrontation.

"I mean he's a star, he's a hottie, he's fine. But girl, he's married and so are you. I know you and Dillon have been having some issues."

"Issues? How about I'm ready for a divorce."

"Well, you're not divorced."

"Why do you care? I can't believe you're saying this to me. It's not like you really like Dillon anyway." Tina stood before me with her mouth open, not believing I called her out on what was true.

Tina asked, "What would make you think that I don't like your husband?"

"What would make me think that you do like him? He's always held up info you need back from me. His mind has been poisoned against you by other authors that have had bad experiences with you. And he's been a little verbal with you before because you know sometimes you're mean to me."

"Oh, I just tell him to get over it."

"I know, I know, but I mean he's my protector."

"We always get into it," Tina boldly admitted.

"So I know you don't like him."

"Well, that's pretty strong of you to say. My philosophy is if you like him, I love him for you. But right now I know I love the institution of marriage

and I don't want you to get yourself into some-
thing—a big old mess. You're a Christian author.
Christian. That stands for a whole lot of things.
Your morals don't need to go out of the window."

Just as she was talking to me, I could see Bryce
still standing where we'd just come from, making
eye contact with me from across the room. The
goo-goo eyes and crazy faces were so silly I just had
to laugh.

When Tina looked over her shoulder and noticed me eyeing Bryce down, she said, "Okay, I see
I'm not getting through to you. You need to think
about what I said. And if my voice of reason in
your head is not enough, pray, girl."

"I hear you. Nothing is going on with me and
this guy. He's just a good friend that believes in
me. Something my husband has never been able
to do, and I don't know how I'll repay him. He
made me blow up overnight."

"No, he didn't make you do anything. Let's get
it straight right now. The Lord allowed him to
help you," Tina said as she hugged me good-bye.

Though I heard what she said and it did make a
lot of sense, I still felt that I needed to do something to thank Bryce for all he'd done. Bryce wasn't
pulling my chain that day in the Japanese restaurant when he said he was going to make my name
household. Everytime the play got a great review
there was also a mention about me and my book. I
was about to be featured in *Essence, Ebony, Jet,* and
Upscale; an author's dream. Yeah, I knew deep
down I had to do something to thank him.

Later that night, I pulled out my handout tape
recorder to start taping a chapter of my new book.

I didn't get too far because the phone startled me. Dillon hadn't called and I felt like I needed to get ready for his negative spirit.

"Hello," I said groggily, looking at the clock as it read 12:05 AM.

"Oh, you're asleep. I need to let you go." The husky voice was a pleasant surprise.

"Bryce? No, I'm up," I said, faster than a deer gets out of the way when he sees headlights.

Though I was asleep, my voice sure perked up. I was excited. That feeling of excitement was unexplainable. He wasn't my man, but there was a connection that I'd been suppressing for weeks. Something that made me get so excited when I knew he reached out to me.

Bryce asked, "I don't want you to take this the wrong way or anything, but I'm having a major problem and I need to talk. Can you come up to my room?"

Everything in me wanted to say no because I knew that was wrong. My mouth ended up saying, "Yeah, sure. I'll be there in a few minutes."

After I hung up the phone, I immediately felt horrible. Agreeing to go to his room at twelve o'clock in the morning. What kind of signals would I be sending? But as I took each step forward, I did not retreat. In a matter of seconds, my mind switched from sweet thoughts of us sitting in chairs to thoughts of us rolling around in his bed with me giving his loving.

About ten minutes later, I felt my little teal jogging suit was cute enough to prance off in. As I approached his room, I shook my head hard as if I was a wet puppy trying to dry off. *What am I doing? This is crazy!* I said to myself as I stared so long and hard at the letters "Penthouse Suite" that they became a blur.

Lord, I silently prayed, *I don't know what to ask of You. Bryce and I are just friends but why do I want something more and why does it seem fitting? Now he wants to talk to me. Just go with me into this room, and if I'm not supposed to go in help me walk away now. Because I am so weak I need Your power to guide me through. Thanks, Lord. In Jesus' name, amen.*

I took a deep breath and decided I was going back to my room. I could call Bryce on the telephone and we could talk about whatever in the world was going on with him. We didn't have to have a face-to-face conversation to get to the root of his problem. He had come to the right one. I was ready to listen, ready to keep him encouraged. I did owe him something. Inspiration was what I was ready to give him, but I could do that with distance. But as I turned to go away, my elbow brushed the door. I couldn't get away fast enough; it opened and Bryce was standing there in the cutest long-sleeve silver blue silk PJs I had ever seen.

He said, "Dang, I was wondering what was taking you so long. Come in."

But I didn't go in. I just stood firm looking at him. What I saw before me wasn't even something I could stay away from. However, me just looking wasn't adultery. But the more I checked him out the more I saw his deep pain. He didn't have his normal wide grin plastered across his face. He did need my help. Something serious was going on with this guy. This wasn't about me, this wasn't about sex. This was about something heavy going on with him. My friend had lost his sparkle.

Chapter 7

Glowing

"Come on in, beautiful," Bryce said as he took my hand and ushered me into his suite.

Being a huge star did have its advantages, not that I was complaining at all about my room at the Ritz-Carlton. But this particular pad was laid out. It was three times the size of my room and he had converted the space in the corner into a mini-recording studio. I walked over looking as goofy eyed as a child seeing Mickey Mouse in person for the first time.

His warm breath on my neck made me shiver as I heard him say, "You like?"

Deep inside I thought, *Ooh, there is so much I like Bryce Maddox, and that's what scares me. Why in the world am I here?* Coming into his private space was wrong and I couldn't imagine anything going right because I was ready to lose myself to whatever he wanted to do. But then it dawned on me, something was weighing him down. What was the major thing he needed to talk to me about? When I turned to find out, our lips were real close.

Ignoring the attraction filling the air however, I said, "Let's sit."

I walked over to the conference table and pulled out a chair for me and him. I motioned for him to sit. After he did, I joined him.

"What's going on? It's really late. What's on your mind?" I was getting a little irritated after a few minutes passed and he just stared into space.

It seemed like there was nothing wrong because he wouldn't open up and just talk. I had to ask him millions of questions. He called me up here. He shouldn't make me jump through hoops for his agenda. But this was a good thing because I was feeling too connected to this guy and needed something to put distance between us. Maybe the Lord was at work, because again I was getting a little fed up.

"Maybe you just need to sleep on it and things will seem better for you in the morning. I'm a little tired. I'm sorry I gotta go."

When I stood up to head toward the door he gently yanked me back toward him. "I'm a failure."

Those three simple words put together wounded my heart. The way he said it to me made me know he meant them. Placing my hands on both sides of his cheeks, I massaged them a little.

I said, "Are you kidding? You're the most successful man I know."

Then he turned his head away from me and walked over to the hotel window. I knew this was major. The man was severely depressed. Leaning next to a chair he looked abandoned.

"Seriously, Bryce, this play is successful because every night you pump up every actor. You give the crowd a show. You're a leader and we're all soaring because of that. This play is now selling itself with record numbers in terms of black plays. Your album is also selling like crazy. You're the bomb. Why would you feel otherwise?"

"I can't write a gospel song," he turned and said to me. "Like, I don't have my skills anymore. The words just won't come out. It's like before I've always been able to hear from God and right now He's telling me nothing. I guess it's because I'm just not living right. Maybe it's because I left my family. I don't know. It's just not working out. I can't write," he said as his fist pounded on the table.

He went over to the keyboard and slammed his finger and the chord was awful. As if to send a sign to both of us that, yes, he was no longer a musical genius.

"You know we all fall short though. I mean, we all have thoughts and we all want God to suggest, and honestly," I said, going over to put some ice in two small round glasses, "I'm having more problems." His face lit up like that was the coolest thing he'd heard in a while. It's funny how people never want to be alone in their misery.

"Okay, my brotha', you're smiling too happily over there," I said as I opened up the bottled water and poured some in both glasses.

Bryce walked over to me and picked up his. "Now, don't get me wrong. I'm not trying to say I'm happy you're struggling too, but the creative bug seems to have left you as well. So I figured maybe we can help each other get bit again."

"Have you prayed?" I asked as I put down the glass that he'd just picked up and held both his hands tightly.

I could tell by the blank look in his eyes that he couldn't even recall the last time he asked the Lord to help him with a new song. Then he started to tear up as he realized he'd become that removed from God. To restore healing, I began.

I prayed, *"Father, Bryce and I come to you right now. We ask for You to speak to us and give us direction. Your expectations are so high and we certainly don't want to let You down. Lord, help us, help us please."*

After the prayer Bryce hugged me. "Okay, okay," I said pushing him away because the hug was feeling a little too comfy. "What you're thinking right now, this whole situation with God. This frustration that He's not speaking to you, that He's not directing you. That's it! That's a song! That's something! Come on, come on work with me!" I said as I moved my arm in a circular motion round and round hoping he would get my vibe and work with me.

"Okay, I'm feelin' it. Give me a second." He walked over to his keyboard and started playing a beautiful chord.

After an hour of messing around with words and notes, he had the first verse of a song called "Please Talk To Me."

He sang, "Please speak to me, please speak to me. I don't know what to say, sing, or do. Please speak to me."

"I love the chorus!" I said to him as I ran over and choked him around the neck.

Before I realized what was happening, our eyes were locked on one another's. Though I was sure

God wasn't speaking, Bryce's heart was speaking to mine. Mine was answering back. There was something there. Something that was growing more powerful by the second.

"Um, excuse me, I gotta go to the ladies room," I said.

I took both of his hands from around my waist, smiled larger than I thought my mouth could, backed away, and then bumped into his bed. Course I was embarrassed. After a quick laugh, I turned around to head to the restroom.

Quickly, I splashed water on my face. It was so late there was no makeup anyway that could run, and the warm water made me realize I needed to get out of there. I sat on the toilet for a bit, soaking in the strength to leave. My mission was accomplished; I'd helped my friend. He was on the way to writing a wonderful song for the Lord. Yup, my work was done. I needed to go.

But as I opened up the door, I heard voices. *How long had I been in the bathroom,* I wondered. And who was the female Bryce was talking to? *Well, obviously he was talking to Lacy,* I thought. I couldn't let her see me in his room this late at night. Then of course the green-eyed monster rose up in me, because I wondered what the heck she was doing coming to his room at night. But when the voices escalated I didn't have to eavesdrop. I clearly heard this wasn't a girlfriend pleading for another chance. This was a domestic dispute about two times uglier.

"You told the boys you were gonna call them. Your youngest son cries himself to sleep every night because you never do. If you were a gospel singer doing a play about living God's way, your

real life is sure far from it. If the walls could daggone speak, the whole world would see what a hypocrite you are! I hate you!"

Peeking out of the bathroom I looked down toward the keyboard and there was the lady I remembered seeing when the tour first started out,
pounding her fist into Bryce's chest. He let her.
She was crying.

He asked, "Why'd you come all the way here?
How'd you get a key to my room?"

"I'm still your wife you jerk!"

Cracking the door, it made a loud squeaking
noise. He looked up and spotted my face. Bryce
wore a look on his face that said he was sorry for
all this. I waved motioning it was okay, but our sub-
tle gesture wasn't enough to keep his wife from
figuring out something wasn't right. She quickly
turned around. I jerked back into the bathroom
and shut the door, like I didn't want to get caught
doing something wrong. Unfortunately, I didn't
shut it softly. I kind of slammed it by accident, and
I heard footsteps storming over there to me. She
quickly opened the door and spotted me.

"Who is this lady, Bryce? It's three o'clock in the
morning? You got some trick up in here! You better sweat too heifer," she said as she looked at the
water I had splashed on my face, but was not dry,
and misinterpreted it.

However, I didn't correct her. I let her vent.
This was a mess. She went on for another minute
or two calling me everything but my name.

Then I said, "Listen, you've got it wrong. We
were just working on a song. I'm not trying to take
your husband." Even as I said it, it didn't even
sound like the truth and I didn't even know if it

was the truth. What was I doing? I came out of the bathroom and stood beside Bryce.

"Who is she? Tell me who is she!" she yelled at him.

"Pamela, calm down, baby, calm down," he said to his wife.

"I'm gonna find out. You don't have to tell me, I will find out who you are."

"Seriously, we're just friends. I mean, I'm nobody. I'm married too. I hope you guys . . . this is . . . this is nothing. Bryce, I'll talk to you later," I said, all mumbled up.

I opened up the door and closed it behind me. Staring at the "Penthouse Suite" letters, I wondered what kind of mess I'd just got myself into? I didn't know if I wanted them to work it out or not.

Lying in the comfortable king-sized bed, it was ironic that I couldn't get comfortable at all. Mid-August was brutal and though the air was on, my body didn't believe that. I kept playing back last night's events. Seeing Bryce's angry wife's face in my mind made me so unsettled.

Looking at my clock, it was five something in the morning. I walked over to the curtain. Pulling back the sheer white fabric, I looked out on the gloomy city lights. Pounded again by the question, where in the world was all this stuff with Bryce going?

Because I wasn't in the cast, I didn't have to do sound checks, rehearsals, vocal practice, or anything like that. All I needed to do was eat breakfast, lunch, and dinner with the crew if I so desired. We had to show up an hour before showtime. Because I got no sleep, showing up before showtime was the only thing I could do and we didn't have to worry about a bus this time. Our theater was right across from the hotel.

"Ah, so there you are." Bryce came over to me as if nothing had happened the night before.

I just kept stacking up my books and ignored him. Maybe he'd get the picture that now was not the time to discuss anything with me. He had issues much deeper than I wanted to fool with. With a fresh outlook on things, it was now time to cut whatever it was we'd begun.

"C'mon, c'mon don't be like that. I need to talk to you," he said as he placed his hand on mine.

Quickly, I yanked back saying, "Bryce, what are you doing? There's nothing for us to say. Your wife wants to work it out with you. That's gotta be worth something. I wish my husband cared. I wish he came to my hotel room. Dang it, save what you can."

"Pamela doesn't hold my heart anymore. She can't inspire me, she can't liven me up. She just drags me down and wants to cause problems. The only thing we did last night after you left was argue more. Honestly, she's not happy with the fact that I don't wanna be with her anymore, but that's just the way it's gotta be. And after she left, a couple of hours later, I think it was actually five something, all I could do was think about you."

Wow, both of us were up at the same hour. He seemed to be genuine. But was it right for me to be taken in by his advances? Was I really ready to give up my marriage as well?

He touched my back and said, "I went over to my window and thoughts of you dominated my mind. As the sun rose everything started to light up. Then it dawned on me that's exactly how you light up my world; slowly, but wholeheartedly. After thoughts of you made me happy, I went back to the keyboard and finished the song. All because of you, I was able to get over a stumbling block that had been in my way for months. I played it for my boy, Mel, this morning. He thinks it's jammin'. And I want us to celebrate."

Just then Mel came around the corner and said, "There you are, Bryce! Come on, man, no time for the lovey dovey stuff. I gotta get you backstage in wardrobe."

"Are we on for a date or not?" Bryce asked as he was being dragged away by Mel.

Against my better judgment and everything I decided to not mess with anymore, I said, "Yes, sure why not?"

Bryce let go of Mel's grasp and jumped up in the air as if he had just won a prize. "Sell your books." Then he blew me a kiss.

I reached my hand up and gently pretended to catch it. I brought my hand to my lips. Bryce showed all of his pearly whites. We were too silly and it felt good.

When he was completely gone, I sank down in my chair and prayed, *"Lord, maybe it's a good thing that our marriages aren't working out. I'm starting to envision a life with this man. Is this possible?"*

Opening my eyes, I was startled to see Lacy angrily gritting her teeth in front of me. "Yeah, you better pray. You need to ask the Lord for forgiveness and help."

"Lacy are you threatening me?" I stood up and

said looking her eye-to-eye without flinching one bit.

"That man is married and so are you. Both of you are confessing to be Christians, but are sinning and stuff."

"You know nothing about my life and what I do behind closed doors."

Rolling her eyes and neck, she said, "I know you were in his room late last night before his wife kicked you out."

"What were you doing? Spying on us?" I said to her.

"So what if I was?"

"Well, it's quite pathetic if you were. I'm not doing nothing wrong anyway, not that I owe you any explanation. The guy was married when you went out with him too. And plus, me and him are just friends."

"Save that bull for somebody who'll believe it," she said, purposely flicking my books across the desk messing up the pretty display I had just took my time to create.

"Ay, wait a minute," I said, furiously coming from around the back of the oblong table.

"You better get out of my face, Shari."

"You better fix my books back!" I said without moving.

She nudged me back a little and I pushed her back farther. Seeing that I was no pushover she started trying to recklessly fix my arrangement.

"Nah, that's alright. Forget it," I told her, knowing her half-effort wouldn't get it right.

"I'm so much better than you," she told me as I turned my back to her to straighten the table.

"You profess to be a born again Christian. What a crock! Yeah, I'm in this gospel play. I sing the songs and I act the part. But I haven't really given my life to Christ. I don't wanna be a hypocrite. Folks like you mess it up for nonbelievers. Your walk leads people to hell faster than mine would. They know I'm a sinner, but you . . . you saying the right things, but doing more sin than me. I was attracted to Bryce Maddox because I believed he loved the Lord. Now, I see he's just like every other Negro in the street. You can have him." I turned and she looked at me like I was worse than trash. "But don't get too comfortable with the thought of him being yours. Just when he gets tired, like I told you before, you'll be just the next lady he'll dump not the next lady he'll keep."

I dismissed her venting knowing she was still jealous. How could I be leading people to hell? She was crazy and needed to accept Jesus so she'd have her name in the Lamb's book of life, not be worried about what I do.

After another outstanding performance, Bryce and I found ourselves eating Chinese food in a New York music studio. This one was far superior to the sweet little one he had set up in his room. Listening to his first few recordings was so fun at first. But when two o'clock rolled around and I found myself still listening to the exact same thing over, and over, and over again, I realized the record industry wasn't for me.

"I need a female background vocal. Will you sing with me on the track?" he asked.

"No, I don't have that great a voice," I said, walking toward the door.

Faster than I could think, Bryce tugged me in

front of the microphone and started singing *"la la la la la la la"* to help me warm up my unused voice. It was another long nighter. At four, after we were satisfied with the vocals, we warmed up the left-over Chinese food and talked.

"You're looking sad," he said, picking up that my vibe had changed. "Something's going on with you. You're thinking really heavy about something, what? Talk to me."

"Nothing crazy, just something Lacy said that rattled me earlier, but I'm fine."

"Lacy? I'll tell her to leave you alone. She's just fishing for info to use against me. She's upset that we aren't close anymore. She needs to chill. You know what I'm saying."

Passionately defending her, I charged, "No, I don't know what you're saying. How hot and heavy were you? Women just can't forget."

"What, you want me to tell her business," he said, looking guiltier than strictly admitting it ever would. "I was a little wild with her. It was wrong. But it's over now. She whines and expects way more than I ever promised. She can't do anything for me."

I heard everything he was saying and somehow his words were just as stale and yucky as the old Chinese food in my mouth. Spitting it out, I said, "Ugh,"

"You want some of mine?" he said, thinking I was only talking about food.

"No," I told him, ready to call it a night.

He took my food and walked it over to the trash can. Then he came back over to me and literally took the couch. I was ready to be rid of him.

"Your face is so pretty," he said as he stroked my cheek. "You smell so good."

"It's late," I said nonchalantly to him.

He gave me a hug. With our tight embrace, I felt him growing below. My resistance of his care-free attitude about Lacy being sad, went out the window. I knew I couldn't contain the moisture I was releasing. I felt my skirt sticking to myself.

He nibbled on my ear and said, "You want me don't you?"

What I wanted was self-control, self-restraint. It felt real to say, no, that's not what I want, but as my tongue made its way to his mouth, the upright position we had on the couch turned into a laid down one. I knew he was right. I wanted him desperately.

The passion was shining all through my body, ready to burst out and show him just how much. There was no way I could stop the craze, no way I could hold the desire in. No way I could tell him no. But somehow, someway I did. I thought he'd be angry when I got up, leaving him on the couch alone with his pants unzipped. But he tucked in his business and stood up beside me while he fixed his pants.

He kissed me on the forehead and said, "Another time. I like you way too much to rush anything. Let me get you home."

"I like you too," I told him as I huffed, battling the spirit and my flesh. "But thanks for understanding that I just can't."

"Shari, I respect you and I'll take you on a safe date."

"Cool, yeah," I told him, really thinking that

Bryce Maddox was for me. That thought alone made me beam brighter than the sun that would be up in another few hours. Everything felt great.

When I got back to my hotel room it was about six o'clock in the morning. As I swiped my room card, I couldn't even get the green light to come on as I frantically tried to open the door. My telephone was ringing and because of the early time, all I could think was that it was an emergency. Finally, the key worked and I grabbed the phone before it stopped ringing.

"Hello, hello," I said as I sat on the bed and tried to catch my breath.

"Where have you been?" my mom yelled back in an angry voice that made me take the receiver from my ear.

"Mom, is anything wrong?" I said as I held my chest hoping her answer would be no.

"Your husband is trying to get in touch with you and he called me saying he's been calling your cell phone all day. He doesn't have your hotel schedule. So he didn't know which city you were in."

She was really bummed with me. Okay, I was out of pocket, but no biggie. There was nothing major I'd missed. Plus, it was the start of football season and the last thing my husband would have time for was me. Add on the fact that we had an estranged relationship, what was there for us to talk about? Surely nothing that would involve giving him numbers on where to find me on a constant basis. My cell phone was enough. But since my mom had the number and still couldn't find me, apparently by the heat in her tone she was not happy that I wasn't available the first few times she called either.

"I called you ten times. It got to a point where I was setting my alarm clock every half an hour to try to get you girl! Where have you been?" she huffed.

Why didn't she get the fact that I was a grown woman? Anyway, I said, "Mom, I was in the studio recording a song."

"Recording? Did you say recording?"

"Yes, ma'am, I did." Taking off my shoes.

"I'm sure he's gonna wonder what's going on since I didn't call him back last night. But you didn't call him back last night 'cause I couldn't give you the message 'cause you were nowhere to be found. You're a writer, Shari. You're not a musician. In the studio? I mean come on, that just doesn't even make sense. Girl, where were you and who in the heck were you with?"

"Mom, first of all I'm separated, so calm down. It's not like I'm committing any crime. If I was out on a date, which I was not so don't even scream anymore in my ear. Hold on." I placed the phone down and took off my shirt. "I'm back."

"Is he in the room with you? What are you doing? All that wrestling going on?"

"Mom, I'm changing my clothes. I've been working all night. And yeah, I have skills other than just being a writer, okay? And sometimes to deviate from my stress it helps to get the creative juices flowing."

"Alright, creative juices." She kept badgering on about something, although I really wasn't listening. I was so tired, so sleepy, and a little curious as to what Dillon wanted from me. It had been a couple of weeks since I'd seen him and he hadn't dialed my number once. I looked over on the desk and glancing at the charger where my cell phone was placed, I saw that I had three missed calls. Before picking it up, I checked to see that there were two missed calls from him and one from my mom.

Cutting her off, I said, "You called me on the cell too?"

"Yeah, 'cause I just thought you weren't picking up your husbands number because you recognized it. You know how you do sometimes, when I called you, and you didn't call me back . . . I kept calling the hotel's room to see what had gone on. I didn't know if you had lost the phone or something had happened to you on the road. I mean you are a million miles away, you hadn't called to check in on the kids all week. You're just out there."

"How the heck often would you like for me to call them, Mother?" I said in a smart tone.

"Don't get sassy with me, girl. I'm just saying. You are still married and you do have responsibilities here. So you don't need to just be missing in action."

"Mom, I left my cell by mistake on the charger in my hotel room. I was working. Nothing else to discuss."

"Working? Are you getting paid for this music recording you're doing or is this another pipe dream your chasing?"

I could just see this star up in the sky shining so bright and her with her hands around it choking all the light out of it. She so didn't understand me.

I guess she heard the hissing in my voice because she calmed down, and said, "Listen, I'm sorry. I've been sounding a little forceful, but I was worried."

"She was worried!" I heard my dad yell from the background.

"Ma, you gotta tell Dad I'm okay."

"He knows. He hears me talking to you. I guess it's just I don't want you to throw away your marriage just because times are tough."

"Mom, you're the one that said he was crazy. Besides, I needed a change."

"Yeah, I'm glad you both had some time apart. Dillon's been over here a couple of times this week to see the girls. We've talked since and he's sorry about some things too. But he can't be the only one who tries to get things right."

"Well, it's one thing to actually change and another to just say you're gonna change. He doesn't wanna go to counseling because he's too afraid the Christian coach really isn't so Christian behind closed doors. But I hear you, I hear you. Thanks, Mom."

"Will you call him right away?"

"Mom, it's six fifteen!"

"Six eighteen," she said, straightening me out.

"Okay."

"Good, call him. Your husband can be found at odd hours. Unlike some people I know."

"Ma, I thought you just apologized for being really strong?"

"Yeah. Just take care of yourself and be careful. Dillon told your dad about the singer guy you like, and frankly the whole situation scares me a bit. Shari, you're gonna get yourself into more trouble than you know or can get out of. Just think about it."

"I'll call him, Mom."

After hanging up with her, I jumped in the shower and the hot water melting on my face felt wonderful. Every muscle in my body relaxed. It was like the shower took me away. But as soon as I turned off the water, the cold air hit and reality sorta set in and allowed me to realize it wasn't going to be easy talking to Dillon. If he asked any questions, assumingly out of line for a separated man to ask his wife, I'd let him have it. Dillon couldn't run me. Plus, that overbearing Dillon was why I was gone in the first place.

I had been way too easy for far too long allowing him to talk to me any kinda way. Now that I was away and had some independence, and quite frankly had a man who knew how to say the right things to me in the right tone, I didn't need to hear special words out of his mouth. I didn't need to go backward. When the damp towel felt cold on me I couldn't put off avoiding the call any longer. Reluctantly, I called Dillon. On the first ring he answered as if he'd been waiting for me to dial his digits.

"Hello," he said in a real, real tired voice.

"Sorry, did I wake you?" I said, trying to set the right tone as I talked nicely and keenly.

"Naw, naw. I gotta get up. I can't be late for training camp."

"Yeah, that's what I figured. How's it going by the way?" I asked, truly concerned.

"Good. Things are looking good. The first game is next week and now we have this big family dinner and coach asked me if you were coming," Dillon said, trying to make me feel guilty.

You couldn't tell him I was on the road promoting my book? That I do have a job? That I am capable of doing something other than being a wife? I said to myself, wanting to say it to him. However, I knew that was a little strong. To keep the peace, I said nothing.

He said, "I know I probably should've told him that you were busy doing your own thing. He just went on and on and on about how it'd be good to see you. Plus, with the recruits coming in, coach knows you would be good at helping us work the parents to get the kids to commit. I . . . I don't know. I just want to see if your schedule is clear. Coach thinks it would be great if you could come. You don't have to."

Talking again to myself, I said, *I know I don't have to. You could at least open up and say you want me to, dang it.*

"It . . . it would mean a lot to me. Quite frankly, I miss you and I've been doing a lot of praying too and I'm sorry for a lot of things. I know it might sound a little mushy but I might as well tell you my heart. I'm just so screwed up right now. I've got nothing else left but to be honest. You're in one place and my kids are someplace else. I've done a good job with our home. But if you could just do me this favor. Let me know if you can't."

"I respect that," I said as I heard words from my husband that I hadn't heard in a long time. "I'll do what I can to get there. That's all I can promise."

"Alright, well, I won't keep you."

"Okay. Talk to you later," I said as I was about to hang up.

"Wait, Shari?" he said, before I put down the receiver. "I love you, bye."

When I heard his phone click, I just held on to my receiver. I couldn't put it down. Those words from my husband sent a shock through my spine, giving me a tingly feeling all over. What was happening? Because of those three little words I was glowing.

Chapter 8

Darkness

I can't believe I left the last few days of traveling with the play to come home to this. Riding in the car with Dillon to a dinner with the football coaches and their wives was like me riding in a car alone. The only faint sound was that of the Christian radio station playing lightly in the background. I let my husband's words of "I love you" and "I miss you" convince me to get on a plane to be with him for this event and I just felt stupid in doing so.

Lord, I prayed as I held my head back on the headrest with such frustration, *I thought his words meant something. I thought it was a sign that we were supposed to get back together. I thought Dillon really cared about me, but look at him. Clearly, it isn't this way at all. I put on a new sexy dress, stiletto heels, a new perfume scent, and my hair is the bomb. Nothing's catching his eye. What the heck is up with this, Lord? I think if You don't do something, I think we are seriously through.*

In the darkness, I didn't realize I was talking aloud a little. But through the mumbles Dillon couldn't make out what I said. However, he knew by my frustrated tone I wasn't happy.

He asked, "Everything alright?"

Not wanting to start something, but having to be true to what was going on inside me, I voiced, "Those are the first words you've said to me all night."

It was on from there. He shook his head and then slammed his fist on the leather steering wheel. Scared, I jumped.

"You're the one that's been over there like you don't want anyone to touch you or anything."

"Where did that come from?" I said, getting comfortable.

As the interstate lightly lit up, the fierce look on my face let him see that I wasn't playing. I wasn't happy. Nor was I going to have him brush this off on me so easily.

"You know what? I don't even want to go there with you, Shari. We got this dinner tonight. I'm not even trying to get frustrated. Let's just drop it."

"No, no we can't drop it. You told me you missed me. I came all the way here because I thought that—"

"You thought what? You don't think I missed you because I'm not forgetting that there is all this stuff between us?"

"In order for it to work we're gonna have to talk. You don't have to treat me like I'm still on the tour." Taking my hand I placed it on the back of his neck. "I'm right here, baby. I got dressed up for you and your not even getting turned on. What's up with that?"

"Many nights of being excited, when I thought

about my wife, and having to either calm myself
down or work it out myself. This ain't Burger
King; you can't have it your way, Shari. Nor is it a
puppet show. You can't pull the string."

"Ooh, look at you," I said, twiddling my fingers
up in the air as if he was scaring me with his talk.
"What's up with all the analogies? Why can't you
just talk to me?"

"Why you makin' such a big deal out of everything?" he said in a louder tone. "We've got problems. The first minute I see you they aren't gonna
be solved. That doesn't mean I don't miss you,
that doesn't mean I still don't love you. We have
much to work out and it's hard for both of us. So
let's just drop this until we can talk about it, and
don't go—"

Scratching my head with disappointment, I said,
"Embarrassing you tonight?"

"Yeah," he said, not backing down in his tone.

"I don't even know why I bothered, Dillon," I
said harshly as I turned toward the passenger window and wished I was anywhere but in the car with
my bullheaded husband.

Twenty minutes later we were in the conference
center parking deck, and my husband didn't even
help me out of the car. In the day, his chivalry was
a huge attraction. Back then he was a first-class
gentleman all the way. Now he's merely a jerk. But
as soon as he got in the room with his peers and
his boss, the brotha' flipped his nice-button switch.
Instantly, he became the most attentive husband
in America.

Though I smiled and played the same role he
did, inside my head was shaking, my eyes were
rolling, and my mind was saying how phony this

was. Football was cool, and I know that thanks to the sport my bills were paid. But dang, every time these stuffy coaches got together it was the same old conversation. There wasn't anything else. The wives were here this time. I was tired of hearing about the strength of the offense and the weakness of the defense.

When the coaches came up for air from the recruits, the coaches started caucusing about what players were academically enabled. Now it was really boring. So when I noticed no one was paying attention to me, I said, "Excuse me," and went to the ladies room.

This was a new venue and I was confused about where the restroom was located. My search was taking way too long because it felt like I was about to drip between my legs. Finally, I made it to a restroom on another floor. I opened the door and walked into a wall as I tried to find the switch to turn on the light. My trouble symbolized the icing on the cake for this dreadful evening of mine. Seeing the frustration roll down my cheeks as I finally found the light, I was able to see my mascara doing zigzags underneath my eyelids.

My phone rang loud. The ringing startled me. Yet, I was so happy to see the number of my girlfriend, Josie.

With despair in my voice, I said, "Gosh, I'm glad you called."

"Shari, what's going on? Why you sounding pitiful and sad?"

"He won't even talk to me," I said as I leaned up against the bathroom stall door. "I came home because he said he missed me, but that was a sham."

"For real?"

"Yeah, and I think it's the end of our marriage, girl. Dillon just doesn't do anything for me anymore."

She was not judgmental. I missed my girlfriend. I spent the next five minutes quickly giving her the update because she wouldn't let me off the phone before she asked about my other little friend.

"Bryce is fine, girl. I came so close to giving him some."

"Shari! I've never heard you talk like that or feel this way for another man," she said.

"He's just too sexy, Josie, and it doesn't look like I'll be getting busy with my husband, so . . ."

"Whew! I hear you big baller. Just be careful."

"You're right. I'm taking things slow. Thanks, girl, you got me smiling. Enough about me, what's going on in your household?"

"That's why I called you. I have a sister-in-law working my nerves. Check this out, girl. I let her and her son come and stay when her own brother is completely against it. Now the heifer has the nerve to tell her brother what time I come in."

"What? She is spying on you. That's crazy."

Josie went on to tell me that she went skating while her husband was out of town. This wasn't a big deal though, because grooving on wheels was something she often did when he was in town. It was a great way to stay fit and enjoy life.

"Oh, I went off on him, girl. I went off on her butt too; up in my house keeping time on me! I told her look, while she's up in my house she's gonna respect my daggone privacy. If my husband wanna know where I am, he can call me. I got a daggone cell phone, and I don't have no problems telling him the truth. I don't need no watchdog or babysitter."

She'd told me that they were also paying her sister-in-law to stay there because she was supposed to be watching the kids. Unfortunately, everyday she came up with some excuse as to why she could not watch the kids. To add insult to her mooching, the chick asked Josie to watch her son on weekends while she went to party. Yeah, she needed to be dealt with.

Josie continued, "I can pay for after school care. So she don't have to worry about watching them and stuff. And then she tried to get smart with me, telling me that this is his house too. I told her, 'Look, her brother ain't the only one paying these bills, my name is on the paperwork just like his. I'm still contributing to this household I was gonna be comfortable in.' And if she didn't understand that, she can have her bags packed and in the daggone streets; she would understand it then. Needless to say, she got her stuff and left. She's looking right now for somewhere to stay. My husband is pissed, but frankly he can follow her."

"Oh no, girl. I'm sorry."

"Don't be sorry. I feel relieved. Somebody had to put her in her place. Nobody's gonna walk all over me. I had to stand up. She has such a jealous spirit. Now that she's gone, I may have more in-law drama because, of course, his mom hates me even more. I have no peace of mind."

We ended our conversation and she gave me hope that I too needed to have backbone. Though I dreaded going back to the table, I was ready to handle the pressure. I guess I'd been in the ladies room longer than my husband thought was proper. Immediately upon my return to the group, I got the evil eye from Dillon. I really didn't care.

To add more intensity, silence accompanied us on the ride home as well. In the darkness of the night, my husband didn't try at all to work things out with me. So as he slept, I got online and made plane reservations to leave for the West Coast. I smiled after I got confirmation that I'd be on the first plane out to San Francisco, getting to finish the last three play dates.

The next day I prayed on the long plane ride, *"Lord, is it the right thing that I'm going back out to this tour to finish what I started. Something's telling me it's a little more. There's something missing. Keep me from harm's way like I know You can. I do pray for my husband. He needs to be more real. The lifestyle I see him lead, it just doesn't match one you intend for a godly husband. And my girls are perfect ladies. My mom did want me to spend a little time with them before I took off again. I love them a lot, Lord, and one good thing about my time away is now I realize just how blessed I am to have them. Thank You for that. Thank You for making me see the glass as half-full rather than half-empty. I don't feel so negative anymore. I wanna get it right so much lately, that I've tried too hard and I'm basically getting it wrong. I want to follow Your lead from now on, Lord, and I can't see my world without You. In Jesus' name I pray, amen."*

The next two days the Lord led me to just do my part. I stayed connected to Him through prayer. Selling books out front and being in my room writing was what my time consisted of.

I did run into Bryce once, but kept walking. He called my phone a couple of times, but his phone calls didn't get returned. I hoped the brotha' would get the message. And I had hoped I knew what I was doing, because a whole other part of me wanted to call him quickly and tell him how much he'd been on my mind. But that was the weaker side, the side I was leaving now. The Holy Spirit gave me strength to abstain from dialing his digits and I was excited about that. Both of us were still married and until both situations were dealt with, there was nothing else we could do that would be pleasing in God's way.

We had one more night to go before the whole play tour was over, I was pretty much home free from my feelings running wild and getting myself into deep trouble. Staying away from Bryce proved to be the right thing to do when a lady came up to my table after the finale and went on for about ten minutes on what my book had done for her life.

"I moved out of my shacking up situation because of this book, girl."

"Really?" I said, a little shocked that she had just picked up and moved out.

"Your book clearly told me that I wasn't doing it God's way. Fornication isn't His will. Ever since I went on my own, it's like my world stopped dying. Now that he wants me back I don't even know if he's the one. He couldn't see it when I was there so why should I think he really changed? Girl, give me a hug, you changed my life!" the lady said in an exciting way.

Mel came up to me after she walked away, and said, "Lots of folks have been telling us your book has been blessing them. Everybody's been asking when the next one is going to drop. You are large, girl."

"No, no, no," I said humbly.

"Yeah, you're getting bigger and bigger!" he said. "Oh, I talked to your girl."

"Who, my agent?"

"Agent, publicist, manager, whatever you want to call Ms. Tina. She tried to get a hold of you yesterday or something, but you jetted on all of us to head home."

"What? What's going on?"

"Naw, you sold almost one hundred thousand copies on this tour."

"What? Now I know I didn't sell that many books."

"Okay, you're right. You didn't. You sold more like two hundred thousand copies. While you were on the tour, books have been flying off the bookstore shelves." I clutched my heart. "This is big right. Well, let's go celebrate. It's time to escort you into the finale cast party."

"No, I wasn't in the cast," I said as Mel put his arm around me, trying to lead me to the temptation of being with Bryce.

I knew as soon as I saw him, I'd go crazy. I'd want to be with him. However, Mel did not take no for an answer though.

"You are a part of this tour. Cast and crew alike."

While going to the cast party, I had to be around a whole bunch of drunk folks. It was interesting to me, even though they were doing a gospel play, most of their lifestyles were far from that of Christ. But how could I talk? I'd been flirting with everything I had, but he was a married man and I was a married woman. I couldn't judge anybody. We're all on the wrong path. But I couldn't think completely then. My flesh was leading and my spirit was stronger. I told him again that I wasn't going as he persisted.

Seeing some folks in the cast sharing and sniffing an illegal substance, and another group practically dancing nude, I wondered how I ended up in the cast party anyway. I guess I talked myself into believing that just because you're in the house doesn't mean you can't stay strong.

As soon as I found a seat, I saw the eyes of the man I knew I clearly missed. Bryce was talking to Lacy. She had her newly polished nails all over his waist. But they were in a little heated debate as he tried to get away, his frown told me he was agitated. He didn't see me, which was a good thing because the brotha' and I didn't need to talk. Old school music was playing. When I listened a little closer, I could make out the O'Jays singing.

I got very hungry seeing the spread of food. It looked delicious. There was only one problem stopping me from going over and piling up my plate, I had to cross Bryce in order for me to get there.

I just kept looking at the lobster, then I heard a "What? What, you're ignoring me? It's her you want, huh?" I knew Lacy's voice. "That witch is married."

Okay, how much of this was I supposed to take? I knew she was talking about me and when I heard "oohs" and "ahhs'" from the crowd and the O'Jays last note stopped when the DJ stopped the music, I realized I should've stuck with my first intuition and not have come here in the first place. Something in me gave me the strength to keep walking. As soon as I picked up the glass plate, Lacy came over and knocked it out of my hand.

"You know I was talking about you!" Lacy screamed and spit in my face.

When I looked in her eyes, I saw that they were big and puffy. Seeing she was still in pain, I wondered if I could walk away and be the bigger person? I looked down at my hand and saw blood. She'd actually cut me when she knocked the plate out of my hand.

"I'm bleeding!" I yelled out, showing her what she'd done.

"I'm sorry but Bryce just wants you. I'm gonna tell you what he's gonna do. He's going to dump you like he did—"

Just then Bryce cut in front of her, and said, "That's enough, Lacy. You're drunk and you're making a fool out of yourself. That's enough." Bryce rubbed my back and ushered me away from the crowd. "Come on. Let me take care of your hand."

He led me into the hallway. Using a handkerchief out of his suit pocket, he wrapped it around my gushing red index finger. He was overly attentive.

"Thanks, but I'll be okay. You need to work that out with her. She probably has a lot more issues."

"Let's not even talk about her. I missed you. I've been calling you, but you've been avoiding me. I didn't know where you planned on going since the play's done."

"I need to take a vacation and just get away from everything before I go home. I'm so close to Napa Valley that I've got to go," I said as I backed away from him.

He pulled me back. He kissed me like I hadn't been kissed in a long time. While the hairs on my back stood straight, I didn't want the moment to end.

Then I pulled away. "I've gotta get back to the hotel."

"It's too late to be going home by yourself. Let me walk with you."

"What about the cast party?" I said, just before he kissed me again.

"Does it seem like I care 'bout the cast party? The only thing I care about is being with you." When he kissed me again, I knew we had to go together.

Three glasses of champagne later my shirt was off, and he was halfway done having my bra unbuttoned. This wasn't my plan, but Bryce and I had a connection that couldn't wait for a hotel room. He was teasing me and having his way with me in the back of the limo. It was one AM and we wasted no time heading to the winery less than an hour away.

I hadn't made any arrangements or anything for where I was going to stay, but he told me not to worry about a thing. And a good thing about the play tour was that our bags had to be packed at the end of every performance. So all we had to do was scoop up our stuff and keep moving.

"You want this, don't you, baby?" his husky voice breathed in my ear.

I wanted something like pure sex but I didn't know if that was the actual answer. I didn't stop. I couldn't stop. And when he made me squeal with his finger, I wanted more.

I finally told him, "Lets get there. Talk to me."

"I want you, baby, can't you tell?"

I couldn't explain what I was feeling. Part of me was having issues with this. My mind started playing tricks on me. I saw my husband's face replacing Bryce's. Quickly, I went to the other side of the limo. Like a scavenger searching for food, I reached for my garments.

"You're okay, Shari, trust me," he said, finally realizing I was having trouble with this whole thing.

As I rocked back and forth, I wondered what I had really gotten myself into. This was feeling too good, but feeling so darn wrong at the same time. What in the world was next? He put his hands around me and laid my head on his husky chest and sang a sweet love song in my ear until we both fell asleep.

"You're room is ready," was the next thing both of us heard from the limo driver.

"A'ight, man, we'll be out in a second," Bryce said as he noticed I wasn't fully dressed. "We're here, beautiful."

He kissed my brow and the passion for him rose again. Yes, he was charming, but nothing he fed me felt like a line. Hand in hand we exited the luxury vehicle staring each other down.

"I'm glad we are doing this," I said as we made our way to the grand antebellum entrance.

"I plan to make it a time you won't forget." He sat me down in a cushy-faux chair and checked us in.

"It's just how you asked on the phone, sir," the owner said. "This way."

Following the owner up to our suite, and getting instructions about how to work the fireplace, Bryce tipped him and closed the door. Candles were all over the room burning brightly and a sweet song was playing softly in the background. I couldn't see much, but I could see him taking off his clothes and that bronze brown chest with muscles everywhere.

"Close your eyes," he told me.

As I tasted the juicy cold strawberry and sweet whipped cream dabbled all across my face. He licked off the remains. I reminisced on the unbuttoned shirt in the limo and without looking touched the bare chest in front of me. Opening my eyes, I saw love and desire illuminating from his. When he kissed me, that confirmed what I thought I felt. He blew out the last candle and we made slow gentle love in the darkness.

Chapter 9

Falling

*H*ow *do you know when you might be in love with someone?* I thought to myself as I ran my fingers down Bryce's back after our paradise moment, I felt more than good. But for the cool morning, the guy on top of me was relatively silent. If I had my way, he would've said, *I'm so glad we're together. Girl, you've got me hooked.*

I had so much to lose by joining Bryce in this act. Being married I was used to not using protection so I didn't make him put anything on. However, none of the consequences particularly mattered when he found my spot and made me join him in moaning. It was so pleasurable I could hardly stay still to let myself enjoy it.

Our time lasted for hours. Laying my head on his chest felt so comfy, I felt secure in his arms. Though I didn't have all the answers of what was yet to come, I didn't need them because I knew that with Bryce, everything would be okay. Things wouldn't be easy, but the enjoyment felt solidified that none of this was wrong. Soon it would be completely right because of how we felt for one another. Even though he hadn't openly come out and confessed his undying love and affection for me, the physical way he set me on fire told me more than a few words ever could. As I pulled up the crisp white sheet, to take off some of the September chilled air, Bryce sorta shook me off him and rolled over.

"Whoa," I said, playing with his belly button as I tried to lean him back my way. "I want you to hold me."

Harshly, he said, "It's five something. I need me a couple of hours of sleep before I head back. You need to do the same."

"You can sleep with me in your arms," I said as I continued trying to turn him around, but he didn't budge.

He just tugged his arm away from mine and ignored my request. He didn't have to say, "I'm serious, leave me alone darn it." Because seeing his body language said more and hurt me to my core. *What have I done?* I said to myself as the distance I felt between us was so opposite to the act we had just performed. My mind kept playing tricks on me, I heard my unsympathetic husband say, "Was it ever worth it? Putting our marriage on the line, pretty much destroying it, by being with another man when it's clear he doesn't even care about you."

And then I imagined hearing the callous voice of my mom, "I didn't raise a tramp. No protection, Shari. I hope you don't contract some disease from that user."

Josie's words came to mind, "Now we've been

through a lot and seen a lot of jokers. Have fun, but be smart, and girl don't fall in love. You know whatever he says he probably doesn't care about you."

"He does care." I started fighting the voices back by saying it aloud.

I was kicking off the covers. My fist was hitting the air. I guess I was asleep myself and didn't even realize it.

Bryce woke me, and said, "Who cares? What are you saying? Did you hit me?"

Both of us were out of it. He wiped his eyes. I saw him glance my way and I grabbed the covers. When we sat up in the bed, I had to ask him some questions.

"Wait a minute, you really do care about me, right? We're gonna be together, I mean as a couple and stuff. This just wasn't a one-time thing. Tell me Bryce this was real. I know you have kids, I have kids too, and we'll just be a big happy family together."

"Calm down," he said as he put his arms around me and I wiped up my sweaty body with the cover. "You're talking crazy, girl."

He reached over and gave me a kiss on the cheek. Then he stood up and I watched his bare body walk across the room to the minibar. He pulled out a chilled bottle of water, unscrewed the cap, and smiled at me as he handed it to me. He held my other hand in his.

He said, "Now let's talk about what's bothering you."

It was now seven thirty and I was hoping I'd mis-read him a bit earlier. Either way, I had to talk to him. I didn't wanna walk away with guilt on my conscience. I needed some kind of understanding.

"Was it good," I asked, wondering why he'd stepped back.

"Yeah, baby, it was real nice. Want more?" he asked as he lunged toward me.

Touching his muscular mocha chest, I sat him back down. "I'm in love with you. Not just physically though, Bryce."

"Wait, wait, wait," he said, standing up again, and I could barely concentrate by the view before me. My mind was all messed up.

"You ain't talkin' about being tied down or nothing like that? You're not freaking out about nothing like that, are you? I hope you're not trying to say I misled you."

He kept on and on. I guess there was something in my body language that told him that what he suspected I thought, was correct. I did want more. If he didn't, he'd misled me. I couldn't even look at him. It wasn't because what was before me was so enticing, but it was because what was before me clearly wasn't mine.

"Are you saying you don't want an intense relationship with me?" I asked, holding back tears.

"If I had to answer that right now, the answer would be no. I mean we're still married. And not to each other."

"I'm starting to feel unwanted," I said.

"You're just like Lacy. I can't believe you're all whiny and possessive and sh—"

"Wait," I said, cutting him off. "Don't curse at me. I'm nothing like your costar. I don't know what the two of you guys did together and what she accepted, but I don't know why you thought I'd be cool doing this and then accept merely a friendship. Of course I'm upset. For me, it's a little bit deeper than that, Bryce."

"Well, you should've told me something in the beginning because I never sent love signs. For me it was just sex. I was just being a man," he said, shrugging his shoulders like I had a problem he couldn't fix. "I'm gonna go take a shower. I suggest you finish that cold water 'cause you have some cooling off to do."

I sat up, grabbed the bottle and vented. "You did show me signs. Saying all the right things, being more attentive than any man I'd ever met. Helping my career to rise. I thought that you loved me. I thought that the way you pursued me with genuine zeal was real. I just gave you everything. I don't give my all to friends."

"We were just satisfying each other, but being a couple? Honestly, Shari, it's way too early for any of that. I am certainly not looking for that right now. We won't even see each other. You're going back to your home and I've gotta go back and work out this mess with my wife, because I'm trying not to have her take me to court. And me loving you? You're talking crazy."

He abruptly left the room, went into the bathroom, and shut the door. When I heard the old, steel handle lock, I plumped down on the bed and just wept. My life felt over.

Lord, I prayed. *"I'm sorry. I'm so sorry. What have I done? How did I fall into this mess? Lord, why do I feel so worthless? So confused?"*

When I heard the water turn off in the bathroom, I stayed on my knees believing in God for a miracle that somehow He could turn this whole thing around and work it out. I didn't budge, my knees were clutched together. I did look up though. I wanted to be facing Bryce as soon as he exited out of the bathroom, but my actions didn't faze him. In fact, they set him off even more.

As I could no longer concentrate on my prayer, I had to block out his words, "Oh, so you think pretending like you're praying is gonna affect a brotha'? Girl, your married behind just slept with another married person. Don't act like you're all Christ-like up in here. I been through it all when I was in the bathroom, and it seems like it's gonna be best to cut this completely off now. I don't want you calling my phone trying to find my house number and calling me there. We don't even need to be friends. We're through."

He gathered his clothes quicker than a track gold medalist runs the one hundred meters. It hurt that he wanted to leave so bad. He made a call.

"What?" He paused. "Mel, are you sure she followed me with a PI? This is crazy."

I didn't understand what he was talking about nor could I take his woes. My tears grew as I quickly got off my knees and went into the bathroom. This time I was the one who locked the door, wishing I could lock away all of my doubts, thoughts, problems, and uncertainties at the same time, but this was my reality. I had to face the music of the song I had written for myself. I didn't think anything was going to help me. But I turned on the hot water and, for almost thirty minutes, I stood in the shower and let the water and steam relax me the best it could.

* * *

When I came out of the bathroom, I found a note and four hundred dollars in cash. The note read:

> *Hey,*
> *Sorry you got the wrong idea. It was great for me. I'll miss your friendship. But I'm out.*
> *B.*
> *P.S. Here's money to pay for a taxi back to the airport.*

No verbal good-bye, no "I'm sorry," and no thoughts about what we did. He was gone. It wasn't a joke and it certainly hurt worse. Getting a much colder shoulder than I ever got from Dillon. Though my marriage was rocky, at least it was stable. Dillon might not want to cuddle after sex, but he'd never left me. Now what was I going to do? I got back up in bed, balling up in a knot.

The next time I looked at the clock, it was 5:50 PM. I'd slept the day away. With all the traveling and emotional stress of the last twenty-four hours, it was no wonder I was so out of it. But after taking another shower, I checked my messages on my cell. Though I didn't want to set myself up for a let down, a small part of me believed that Bryce was coming back. That he couldn't just leave things like this. We had something special. Our time together here couldn't be over.

"No," I said out loud, wishing I was drunk to numb the pain.

So I picked up my cell, entered in the codes, and listened to four messages.

"Hey, Shari," the country, sweet voice of my grandmother played. "I miss you, baby. I'm just touching base with you. Sally May, you know my friend up the street, said her granddaughter saw your book in the store. Ooh, you're making me so proud. Alright, I'm just touching base. Call me, sweetie. You know Grandmamma loves you now. Bye."

Hearing her voice made me lie back on my pillow, wishing I could lay my head on her bosom. She would stroke my face and tell me everything was gonna be alright. Wishing she could make me some of her sweet tea as well, though it was ice cold and not warm, the love she put into it made it right on point. But I couldn't have any of that to drink. This time I had gotten myself in so thick that it would take more than her tea to get me out of it. But I was certainly thankful for hearing her voice. Somebody loved me and that felt good. I knew my streak of hearing good remarks wouldn't last long.

My agent, Tina, came on saying, "Where are you, where are you? This is ridiculous that I can't get you. I need that book and I need it now. I'm going to call your house because the play is over and I'm sure you're there working on it. Now, you need to pick up the phone and at least tell me something! This unresponsiveness is going to make me want to drop you."

I immediately wanted to say something back to her like, *I can't be available to you every minute you call.* But I knew there were two problems with that. One, it was a machine so I couldn't respond to a taped message, and two, if I did tell her that, she'd put me down for sure. Or put me at the back of her list and not do everything she could to move me forward. Though she was a strong Christian woman, at least she cared about making her authors large. I'd watched her tick off publishers when they didn't pick up books she thought they should, but her harsh tactics made them rethink their decisions most of the time.

Anyway, I wasn't in a position to want her to let me go. So I figured I'd let myself cool down and hope and pray that she really didn't follow through and call my house. I had no idea where my husband was. The last thing I wanted to do was have him find out that I was supposed to be home when I was actually clear across the country.

Then the sweet voice of my best friend, Josie, was next to leave an urgent message. She sounded to hyped. I heard loud music in the background.

"Girl, I met this good-looking man. He has kids, I have kids, and girl, he's up in the skating rink flirting something awful. Call me immediately. I need you to talk me out of this before I do something crazy. You're the one that never acts on an impulse. You been with fine Bryce Maddox all this time and haven't moved forward. If you can do that, I know I can tell this man to leave me alone. But, girl, looking at his abs it's hard. And plus, my husband is still acting crazy about his trifling sister. Ring me up for real."

Josie gave me way too much credit. She really didn't know as much as she thought she did. Usually, I was the level-headed one between the two of us. But now I needed her more than she knew, because when I revealed what happened, she wouldn't condemn me. She was my true sister. She certainly was gonna be surprised. I needed to call her fast, because this was a mistake that only one of us needed to make. It doesn't feel good after a few moments of greatness.

My heart stopped beating for a long second when I heard Dillon's voice last. "Shari, I've been thinking about you. I'm sorry I was a jerk that night at the dinner. It seems like I can't ever tell you how I really feel when you're right in front of me. I just let our entire problems crowd me, my heart longs to say, I don't know . . . I miss you. Tina called. She said something about you should be home, so hopefully you're on your way. It's pretty sad our relationship is so strained. I really don't know what to do. I'll be looking forward to getting this back on track. I'll be home late. Hopefully you'll be there waiting up for me. I'm sorry I hurt you. Alright bye."

Hearing the caring concern in his voice, I just shut my phone off and wept some more. "He misses me," I said out loud as I wiped my tears with the sheet. Then I let the cotton material go and thought, *This is the very same sheet I just gave it up to another man on and now I'm crying on it about my husband.*

The next hour I ate food brought up by the owner of the hotel. I booked a very expensive red-eye flight straight home to Colombia, South Carolina. I gathered my personals, called a taxi, and as I waited for it to come, I said a prayer. *"Lord, again I'm sorry. I broke my covenant and I regret it so much. I asked You to work on my husband's heart and now I am the one needing grace. I asked You to help make Dillon not throw away our marriage by his harsh actions, and look at me now needing forgiveness. It's just so crazy. Help me connect my thoughts to Your thoughts and come to the right conclusion. Do we even have a chance? Please show me the way. In Jesus' name, amen."*

As I checked out, the owner's wife touched my hand and said, "I'll be praying for you. It's not my business, but a lady claiming to be your guest's wife showed up last night. I've got my own problems so I'm not judging; I just felt you should know."

It was like a frog jumped in my throat leaving a big uncomfortable lump. This nightmare was worse. I didn't tell her that I was self-destructing, but I knew the puffiness in my eyes gave away the fact that I needed direction. I wanted to tell her I would be alright. However, I didn't even know at that moment if that was true. I had fallen for a man that played with my emotions to get what he wanted. I didn't want to let her know that I had fallen into depression, but when she let go of my hand, I had somehow felt stronger.

I knew I needed to shake off the past and look toward how I was going to put all the junk of my life together and make something out of it. Okay, so what. I had chosen a few wrong paths. I had basically gone astray from the Lord. Now that I was aware of that, I could change. I wanted to change. I had to get my life right. As I boarded the plane to fly back to my real world—my kids, my husband, my parents, my writing career—I knew all of that was important to me. Clearly, I wasn't perfect but I knew the Lord wouldn't give up on me, so why would I be trying to give up on myself? As I nestled under the covers to shrug off some of the chilly air on the airplane, I took comfort in knowing that the only way I could walk right was with God. I didn't know where He'd lead me, but this time I knew—wherever He'd lead, I'd follow. That was the only way to ensure a safe journey. Giving into my flesh would only lead me to a place of pure heartache, desperation, and disaster. No more.

As I gazed out at the clouds lit up by the airplane's lights, I felt as safe as in the arms of God as the plane soared perfectly through the air with no turbulence and no bumps. I hoped to parallel that peace by getting to a heavenly place on earth one day soon. I was already beating myself up enough. I would get it right so that I wouldn't be left behind. As an old gospel song goes, *Nobody told me the road would be easy, but I don't believe He brought me this far to leave me.* Somehow, someway, things were gonna be okay.

Walking into my house, it was so quiet I could hear a pin drop. I knew I wasn't the only one there. I'd seen Dillon's car in the garage, and at the airport I had gotten to see on ESPN that the Gamecocks had won their game the night before against Ole Miss. Heading up to our bedroom was a natural thing for me, but it wasn't like I planned to sleep in bed beside my estranged husband.

However, something was drawing me up there. Maybe it was that I just wanted a hug. I certainly wasn't in a rush to tell him about my meaningless affair. Maybe subconsciously, me wanting to be with him was a sign that I did want to salvage our marriage. But when I saw the sight of Dillon as I opened up the double doors, butterflies were in my stomach. My husband was sprawled out across

our king-sized bed with two little ladies nestled be-
neath his big body. He hadn't had a ménage à
trois experiment with two young girls, no. The
sweetie pies were our daughters. Somewhere along
the road he had gotten hooked up with my parents.

Without me, I could clearly see my family was
just fine. I clutched my chest overcome with emotion upon seeing the sight of them more than okay.
Their dreams must have been peaceful because all
three of them were grinning wide like circus clowns.

I felt a knife in my heart because I wasn't a part
of it. Instantly, like someone had unlocked a cham-
ber in the depths of my spirit, I knew I wanted to
be . . . I wanted to be their mom again. I wanted to
be his wife again. There had been so much damage done.

As I noticed my youngest daughter's leg hanging off the bed, I gently placed the adorable little
limb under the covers, kissed her forehead, and
looked at my husband, admiring how much he
loved them. He was holding our family together.
As I tried to place my bag down gently, I saw his
eyes open.

"You're back," he said in a pleasant voice, without moving his body.

"Yeah, and it looks like you've got company."

"I was reading them a bedtime story and the
next thing I know we were all just knocked out. I
got back about eight and your mom was here with
them. She said they really missed the both of us."

"For real?" I said as I walked closer to the bed.
"They—they missed both—both of us?"

My words couldn't even come out of my mouth.
It seemed too good to be true. I hadn't talked to

them as often as I needed to. Yet, the Lord had allowed them to still love their mommy who'd let them down.

Without waking them, my husband came over to my side, placed both my hands in his and hugged me so tight. He didn't say anything. He just didn't let me go for about two minutes. And in that embrace, his thoughts connected with mine.

Finally clutching me tighter, he said, "I'm sorry for so much, Shari."

I didn't pull away, want to leave, or be sarcastic, but water dropped hard like pellets from the sky. "I'm sorry too, for more than you know."

"I was wrong for not wanting you to do the tour," he said as he looked me in my scorned eye. He gave me a sense of self. "I'm proud of you. I'm sorry I stepped in your way."

Immediately I turned away, unable to face him. His instincts had been right. He had been trying to protect me from things at the time, but I had been to pigheaded to see. Everything that glitters isn't gold. If he only knew what I was doing out on that tour. Oh, Dillon, was so right. But how could I tell him what I'd let myself do? How could I have screwed our marriage over? I just couldn't.

"Hey, hey," he said, sensing something was wrong.

He was being more attentive than I'd ever seen him be in so long. Gosh, he was making this hard for me. I had messed up and yet he was acting like the husband I needed, the husband I wanted, and the husband I'd longed for. Was it too little, too late for us though?

"Mommy," my oldest daughter said with glee as she sprang out of bed.

I needed that diversion. Family time took over.

Both Dillon and I rolled around in the bed with the girls. After about two hours of catching up with them all, my husband confessed he had to go down to work, to watch the film of their game against Ole Miss.

"Sorry I gotta leave so soon," he said.

I would usually be uneasy about the head coach making them work on Sundays, but this time I was not. Even I was changing for the better, or maybe I just needed to have time to think about what I really wanted for my marriage.

"If you're tired it's no problem. I'd already arranged for your grandma to watch the girls. She said she wasn't going to church today. Said she's been praying for us a lot. She even asked about our sex life. She is so funny."

I almost choked when he mentioned that word. Playing off it, I said, "I bet she was. The girls are fine with me. Thanks though for being considerate. I may take them over to see her anyway."

"Yeah, she'd be excited to see you back." He kissed me on the cheek, swung the girls around, and told me he'd be in at about 7 PM. The house was unusually clean. It was obvious that my mom had arranged for a maid service to tidy things up. It was funny how she wasn't sure about my marriage either, but she certainly wanted to make sure that my husband was well taken care of. I called my grandmother and told her that the girls and I were coming over for a meal. She was delighted to hear that I was back. She said she couldn't wait to talk to me about some stuff. She was such a wise lady.

When the girls went to sleep, I placed my cell phone that was out of power on the charger, and as soon as I did that it beeped to let me know that I had a message or two. When I saw the number of Bryce pop up, I wanted to puke. Oh, so now that it was another day, the brotha' was having remorse for treating me so badly. Well, I was back with my family. There was nothing he could say to make me want him again. Sitting in my husband's base-ment recliner, after walking around with the phone in my hand for five minutes trying to decide whether or not I was going to hear what he had to say, I fi-nally entered my code and listened to my message from Mr. No Good.

Bryce's voice was high pitched and panicky. "You gotta call me back. This is not the end. My wife hired some private investigator. This is not a joke. Seriously, call me."

Though his message was kind of sketchy, I could fill in the blanks. I remembered the call he had with Mel that now made sense. The owner of the bed and breakfast told me someone had been asking questions. Wow, could what we had done in private possibly going to be made public?

"Oh my, gosh!" I screamed.

It took me three calls to reach Bryce and, when I finally did, what he told me was mind boggling at best. "She hired a PI. There are pictures of us in bed from a window. They are very, very explicit. There are also pictures of us in the hotel room making out and pictures of you coming out of my hotel room. We're gonna be on that new show, *Cheating Spouses*. It's on cable. I don't know when it airs or if she'll sell to the tabloids, but I just thought I'd tell you. Look, I'm sorry. I just wanted us to have a good time."

"How in the world could you not have known

she was capable of this? I'm messed up for life here," I said angrily, before hanging up on him.

My actions were leading me down a path so deadly that there'd be no way I'd be able to escape the madness to come.

When I got to my grandmother's thirty minutes later, she gave me the biggest hug. I was literally shaky. I wished I was her baby granddaughter again. Unfortunately, I was all grown up with big people problems.

"Baby, what's wrong?" she said.

"Talk to me, baby," she said as my girls banged on her piano thinking they were playing better than ever.

My tear ducts released more salt water. She took one of her hands and wiped my cheeks. "Baby, I know you've been through a lot, and I will talk to that husband of yours. The one I helped you get."

"It's not him," I said. "I messed up this time, Grandma."

"What've you done?"

Falling to my knees, I placed my head in her lap. Before I could tell her about my conversation with Bryce, I thought, *Yeah, I wanted to have passion, pleasure, and a whole lot more than any romance novel. Now look what all that's gotten me.*

"Grandma, I cheated on him."

"Baby, do you love this other guy?" she asked, trying to understand.

"No, I had deep feelings. Found out the guy took me for a fool. It was only once, Grandma, really. But one time too many. Grandma, what am I gonna do? When my mom finds out she's gonna kill me and then Dillon's gonna divorce me. The world's gonna hate me."

"The world?" she said in her sweet country voice. "Yes, Grandma. It's gonna be on TV."

She started stroking my hair and trying to pick me up off the floor, but my body wasn't letting me leave the secure position. "Yeah, you messed up. That happened. But you gotta find a way to get on up. Through Christ, get on up. We all fall short, but my grandbaby ain't no habitual sinner. You gotta stop lusting. You gotta stop lying. You gotta stop crying and you gotta start praying. Do all of that so you can stop falling."

Chapter 10

Night

Gosh, I was so depressed after seeing my precious family. My two girls and my husband. I could knock myself in the head for practically ruining it. I had what most women dreamed of—a man. Even though he was often times anal, he was a man that cared for his family and worked day and night to provide. His one hundred and twenty thousand dollar a year income paid the bills and even a little extra. I didn't need more. God had given me a husband that supplied my needs.

I used to get so mad at Dillon for having sex with me and then falling asleep, or leaving the room and going to the living room or something, but at least he stayed. At least he was there. At least he cared. Bryce got what he wanted and was gone. Oh, how stupid was I.

I turned on the guest room TV because I couldn't go to sleep. But after getting in the bed, I curled up in a knot and just held myself. I still felt so numb over what I'd done with Bryce. Yet, I longed to make things right with my husband, but how could I tell him of my infidelity. I certainly couldn't blame it on him.

Though I never thought it would happen, somehow that night I fell asleep. And I thought I was dreaming when I felt a strong hand rub my thigh. Letting out a sensual moan, I guess I enjoyed my thoughts. And I wasn't thinking of Bryce. Oh, no. The kiss I was imagining with my husband was mesmerizing.

But then I heard his voice. "I missed you."

I realized I wasn't dreaming at all. Dillon was on top of me saying sweet things and touching me with his finger in just the right places.

"I'm so sorry," I uttered, kissing him back.

"I'm sorry too," he told me. "I never should have hit you. I have such a temper and I'm working on that. Shari, thanks for coming home to me. I love you and I want you so bad."

As he lifted my T-shirt, I wanted to tell him all about Bryce. But at that moment when he was making me feel all good inside, Bryce who? Most of our married life I pursued him. For Dillon to wake me and desire my loins, made it a moment of pure ecstasy.

Our usual fifteen minute interlude was now turning into an hour. He almost had me sore. I could only thank God for this second chance. While my husband shouted my name, I thanked God just the same. I had done something wrong. I had cheated, but not because I wanted to hurt my husband, but because I thought I really didn't love him any more. However, this new feeling this magical night, this complete oneness, was a gift from God. Our time together solidified that I had something special. My marriage was like a precious diamond. Yeah, sure it was rough and dirty at first, but once dusted off and clean, boy could it shine.

When the lovemaking was over, I didn't know what I expected. Actually nothing, I wouldn't have been surprised if Dillon would have gotten up and went back to the bed with our girls. He did get up and I heard a little water running, I heard the toilet flushing, and then I heard footsteps trotting downstairs. I rolled over trying to get some sleep. But before I could, my husband stood before me again with two cups of ice-cold water.

"Here, baby, I brought you this," he said, handing me the glass and kissing me gently on the forehead. "I thought so many times, Shari, how I would tell you I'm sorry. I know I was such a jerk, and I prayed for you to come home."

"But you don't understand, we need to talk."

"We will. I do know that there is so much about you that I need to understand. I'm just so happy to have you back. I really wasn't asleep when you came home yesterday. I was with my girls only half-dozed, in protector mode."

"Why didn't you say anything," I said, after enjoying the nice cold beverage and then placing it on the night stand.

"Honestly, I was getting up my strength. I didn't know how to tell you how much I missed you, how much I wanted to be with you, and how proud I was of you and all."

He bent down and kissed me. Our physical time together was over but he bent down afterward and gave me more love. Boy, was I surprised.

"What was that for," I said.

"I just want to treat you better. God's giving me

another chance and I'm just thankful to have it before it was too late for us, you know. I hope that it was good for you."

"Yeah," I said, unable to keep my breath as I thought about it. "It was great."

"Well, here," he said as he held out his arms for me to nestle by him. "I want to hold you. I've got to be at work by five AM workouts, but until I leave I want to feel you next to me."

I wanted to tell my husband about everything, but all I could do was look into his eyes and apologize again. "I'm glad I got a second chance with you too. But I don't deserve one."

"Shhh," he told me. "Neither of us deserve anything. We didn't do any real damage."

Oh, if he only knew how untrue his statement was. The guilt I consumed made me feel as uptight as if I were behind bars versus laying comfortably in his arms. As I stared out the dark window through the crack in the blinds, I prayed, *Lord, You've given him back to me. You've got to help me keep him.*

The next day, I was awoken at 5:45 AM to two little girls who were on a weird time schedule. Before I left they used to wake up after nine in the morning. I should have known, my mom loved to start the day early.

"Mommy!" Stori said, looking like she'd grown an inch in the two and a half months I was gone.

They were so excited my heart was filled with joy. How could I have wanted more than this? The pair was so perfect, their love so pure. I was blessed to have them, and as I held them both as if they were just born I was finally happy to except, without limitations or boundaries, their love. Also,

I could give it back tenfold. I squeezed them tight and smothered them with kisses.

"What's it going to be, oatmeal or grits?" I asked, reluctantly letting go.

"Grits, Mommy," Stori said, naming her favorite. "Come on," my oldest daughter said as she pulled me out of bed.

It took me no time to fix their sweet buttery grits. After getting them settled, I carved out time to work on the book. Opening my laptop, I just stared at the two of them as they watched TV. The purple dinosaur was entertaining them. Starr was walking, but just barely. She was so cute trying to keep up with her big sister.

How had I missed this all along? How could my eyes have been so closed to the greatest gift God had given me? To be these girls' mom, how could I have wanted more? I hadn't known I was being so stupid. Thankfully, I was dumb no longer. From that moment on, I knew I'd always be thankful, grateful, and ecstatic over the fact that they belonged to me. Yeah, I knew they were still the Lord's and He had kept them all this time, when their mother couldn't love them in the way that she should have, but now I'm ready to assume my earthly duty. And until they were back in His arms, I would love them so much.

Gosh, I was so happy that one thing in my life was finally in perspective. "Mommy, Mommy come dance with me," Stori said as she turned.

Who cared about a deadline? I was already behind. *Dance with the child already, why don't you,* I thought to myself. When I danced with my girls, I felt so free the creative bug was on its way back to me. Before I could sit down, I started typing. I got a call from Tina and she wasn't too happy that I hadn't gotten anywhere on my book.

"You are so far behind, Shari. This is unacceptable that you're still at the preliminary stages of your book. What are you trying to do here? Give up the deal?"

"That's so crazy to ask me. You know if I'm late there has to be a reason. Speaking of what one of us has done for another, I stayed with you when all your big authors left. And I talked to others, convincing them that I had gone to bat for you time and time again, put my reputation on the line with these people, and why is this just about you, Tina," I said.

I couldn't believe I was standing up to her. I'd never really talked back to her. I only wish she wasn't old enough to be my mom, but she was older, so I just respected her. She'd only picked me up because a friend of hers had said she should, and now here I was after feeling bruised and beaten by her for so long, I have finally found the courage to speak up.

"You know what. Is this about me or is this about you?" I said in a harsh tone.

She was silent for a while. I knew she was obsessing, trying to figure me out. I didn't need anymore drama in my life, things were already crazy enough. I certainly didn't want to lose her, but she needed to treat me with respect. Her yelling and talking at me was not tolerable. She needed to understand she worked for me, and that I was going through something. I was dealing with a lot and she needed to be supportive. Yeah, I understand she had gotten me the contract. But I had to pay her fifteen percent for negotiating the deal.

Agents tripped me out anyway. They get paid for getting their friends to pick up people's work. Or they get companies that already like certain authors to get signed to another deal. Yeah, right. A homeless person could go in and negotiate deals under friendly circumstances.

So what if the words used to cool down my publisher, because the book is late, got a little hostile. Every deal wasn't going to be easy. Tina needed to mediate with them and work the delay out for me. She needed to earn the money that I would have to pay her eventually, once I turned in the book.

"All right, I hear you. I'll talk to them. Just get cracking." Wow, I didn't believe Tina was losing her bark and not biting my head off anymore. "Do you think you can give me a timetable at least? You know what . . . don't even give me that. I'll just push them off a little longer. You know what, you need to handle your heart. Right now your editor is saying so many great things about you. The sales numbers from the play have been out of this world. You get to work and I'll do the same. No need to worry. I hear those girls in the background. How are they?" she said, changing the subject.

We chit chatted for a little while. I was so thankful that I have gotten the courage to really tell her how I felt. Because of that I had a little breathing room. But the pressure really wouldn't lessen forever, I still had to produce for my publishing company. I still had to write the manuscript. I still had to fill the blank pages on the screen. I felt a little bit more confident about knowing the Lord would give me what I needed to say in His timing. Now wasn't the time to concentrate on any of that. I was with my girls. I couldn't just step back into the house and go to work. No, today was their day.

I had been with their dad the night before and it was magical. Just as I thought about Dillon the phone rang again, and it was him.

"I was just thinking about you and the great night we had," I said, seeing his number on the caller ID.

"Well, I was just calling to tell you I'm going to have to work until about nine. Sorry about that, honey."

"You know what, do what you need to handle. I'm fine." As soon as I hung up the phone, my girls pulled me back over to the TV.

We watched *Sesame Street*. It was such a relaxing, awesome day. Before I knew it, it was night.

I hadn't gotten much work done, but I'd had such a productive day. I'd made my man happy. I had straightened out some things with my agent. And I had spent so much great time loving up on my kids. Yep, I didn't have life all worked out though, and I still had to do the book. I knew I had to come clean with Dillon somewhere along the way. Also, I still had to give my girls a bath. Yep, I had issues to get to, but right now I was going to soak it up to give me strength to face the things I didn't look forward to.

As the next day dawned, I hoped Dillon would get home. We'd had such a great time together and he was just so sweet I wanted him near. I picked up my cell to call him and noticed I had two text messages. He'd sent over loving notes. I was giddy. I started worrying so I dialed the ten digits that equated to his cell number and I got his machine. There wasn't a need for me to leave a message, he would see that I had called.

Still unable to sleep, I got up and checked on the girls in their respective rooms. Gosh, I wished I could rest as peacefully as both my angels were. My little one was curled up in a nice snuggly ball. I mimicked her position when I got back to my bed, but the perfect slumber they had was hard for me to get.

Ten minutes later when my phone rang, I quickly picked it up and said, "Dillon, Dillon are you okay, honey?"

"Girl, this ain't Dillon," my girlfriend Josie said in a voice that made me really nervous. "Are you sittin' down, girl?"

"I'm laying down, but I can't sleep."

"And I figure that your husband ain't home."

"Yes, and I'm really, really worried he said he would be home hours ago. I know they were going to have a late night but I didn't think this late. Something is going on."

"Well, I hope he ain't seeing what I'm seeing right this second."

"What, girl?"

"I got the *Shining Star* magazine."

I laughed. "You've got the tabloid?"

"Yes, I had to go and pick up some milk and I saw your boy on the cover and it said, '*Wife catches him in the act,*' so you know I had to buy it. Shari, your picture is straight up in there."

Feeling my heart pulsate faster, I said, "What do you mean my picture is in there?"

"Well, you didn't tell me about your little rendezvous. You know I feel slighted, but we'll get to that later, you got bigger problems. There is a nude shot of you in bed. Of course they placed a black stripe across your special places, but I mean there is no mistaking this is you. It doesn't list your name, but it says it's the Christian-fiction novelist who wrote the book that the play was adapted from."

This was bad. I felt myself dropping the phone. Shucks, actually, bad didn't even begin to cover how awful, how humiliating, how utterly terrible this whole thing was. I picked up the receiver.

I said, "Just when I was getting my marriage back on track, Josie. Oh my, gosh, Dillon and I were together last night."

"What? Oh, yeah, you've got to tell him before he sees this. Your butt will end up dead somewhere. Girl, men kill over this kind of foolishness. One thing to do it and nobody knows, but the whole world's gonna see this, even your mama."

Going over to the window with the phone gripped in my left hand with my right one opening up the blinds, I knew she was right. I was staring out at the road, hoping that my husband's car would pull up so that we could talk about this whole thing before he saw it from someone else and would then make his own horrible assumptions.

I wished the news wasn't true. However, it was Josie. She was listed in my will to raise my babies if Dillon and I were ever gone. If she'd seen the pictures, I could only assume Dillon had as well.

Sucking in my emotions, I stopped staring into

space when my girlfriend said, "Hey, are you there? Talk to me. We need a plan."

"Yeah, I'm here. You know what, I just don't think he's seen this," I said, trying to be optimistic. "Dillon never looks at tabloids. He thinks they are trash and, I mean, he's never in a grocery store. I think I'm fine."

"Well, you need to talk to him."

"Yeah, thanks for the warning. Josie, I got your message about the stud at the rink, but take it from me, cheating ain't worth it." I took a deep breath. "I see some lights."

"What, you see him?"

"Yeah, the way he's flying down the street it would only be him coming toward the cul-de-sac like that. The boy better slow down. My daddy thinks he's going to one day keep on past the house and head into the woods or something."

"Alright, you straight?"

"Yeah, I'm straight."

"Call me if you need to, girl. I know it's not going to be easy for you to tell him, and I really wish no one knew, but it's out now. Do damage control for real."

I heard the garage door open. I could only pray for the strength to be able to talk to Dillon about my mistake. I hoped that he'd forgive me. I made my bed, and as bad as I didn't want to lie in it I had to.

As soon as Dillon hit the bedroom door, I knew something was wrong. He had much attitude, slamming the bedroom door a little, not even speaking, and no kiss on the cheek. He placed his leather bag haphazardly on the floor and even kicked it on his way to peel off his clothes.

"I was really worried about you," I said when he wouldn't acknowledge me sitting up in bed, wide awake under the light. I really did believe a magazine was the last thing he was frustrated about, but I made the mistake of asking. "What's wrong?" He bent down to his bag and pulled out a copy of *Shining Star* and threw it at me.

"What the heck do you think is wrong? Like a fool I laid up with my wife last night, talking about how much I missed her. All the while she'd just come from posing for some filthy magazine. Her little butt was with some other Negro. How dare you ask me what's wrong."

I rushed over to him touching his shoulder, but he jerked away. "Get off me. I don't have no time for your lame excuses."

"How'd you find this?" I said as the tears started to well up in my voice.

He pushed me back a few feet. "Don't even insult me by asking how I found this crap! You need to talk to me and tell me if what's in here is real. What the heck is up with this? Photos don't lie though, so don't even fix your lips to tell me some story. You know what's in here, right? Don't look all innocent! Don't look all like you don't know you're in bed with that Bryce singer dude. I should have known when you were out with him. I should have known." I couldn't fight back the water from flowing more intensely.

I wasn't innocent and there was no way that I could act like I was. I was sorry and there was no way I could act like I didn't care.

"For you to come home to this house and not even mention to me you knew the stuff that was going on. Having me pour out my heart to you, telling you how sorry I was, and you never once told me anything about you and another man. I'm a fool," he said as he grabbed his silk PJs and headed out of our bedroom.

I wanted to tell him not to leave. I wanted to share. I had to apologize.

Dillon returned, and said, "Can you believe one of my players brought this trashy magazine to me and asked me what was going on with my wife. I'd never, never been more humiliated. I want out of this marriage. I'll sleep in the basement and tomorrow I'll get my stuff. I won't be here for a while until we figure this whole divorce thing out."

"Please let me explain, please let me tell you it didn't mean anything."

"You think I'm still crazy, please," he said harshly, before disappearing for the night. Dillon was gone.

He was only two stories below physically, but emotionally I knew he was worlds away. I went back over to the window to shut the blinds. I couldn't feel anything. I was numb all over. My insides were gloomy, disheartened, and dark. Finally giving in to defeat, I just cried throughout the rest of the night.

Chapter 11

Galaxy

Awakening to the startling sound of the hard-falling rain, it frightened me. With what little energy I had left, I pushed myself off the floor in a panic. After I took the girls to day care the next morning, I was so burdened that I'd cried 'til I'd fallen asleep. Looking at the clock on the microwave, my heart skipped a beat when I noticed it was almost two hours past the time I was to pick up the girls. I jumped three feet when the cordless rang.

"Hello, hello," I said when I noticed on the caller ID that it was the day care center.

"Ms. McCray, is there something wrong?" the new girl annoyingly asked. "We are about to close and you aren't here, so . . ."

"So sorry, I had a little problem. I'm on my way though. Be there in fifteen minutes," I said quickly as I hung up the phone, knowing though I'd have to pay a fine, they couldn't leave my babies.

I had to get myself together. Dillon had just

walked out on me. I had to be a mom and hold back the tears that were still falling.

I prayed, *"Lord, I don't even know where to begin. What do I say? Where do I start? It's clearly my fault. My infidelity caught up with me. However, I should have told him. Though I tried to speak up, I knew I didn't try hard enough to spill the beans. When I first came back, but we were growing so close together, I just couldn't do it. But is this all my fault? Bryce was saying all the right things. Dillon was doing no right until now. Looks like now is too late. Lord, help us. Without you guiding me, I'm at the bottom. I am trying to look up so I can see some light. Help me see Your light."*

Leaning over the island in my kitchen, I reached for a napkin and used the hard tissue to dry my face. Thankfully, the prayer spoken provided me with a spot of nourishment needed for my badly frail body. All of a sudden, I believed that God heard me and He was going to walk with me. I believed that I had hope. It wasn't like I felt any better for committing adultery. And it wasn't like my husband had forgiven me. He was still gone. However, despite all that was wrong, despite all the things I needed God to fix, I felt Him beginning to fix the one thing that meant everything—my perspective on Him.

I wanted hope. I wanted joy. I wanted peace, and not worldly happiness, but spiritual happiness. That serenity took me to a place that calmed me down enough for me to grab my keys, play Yolanda Adams gospel song, "Still I Rise," and drive on to the day care to pick up my baby girls.

"You were late, Mommy," Stori said to me as she sobbed. "Why? We were last."

"Mom is so sorry, baby," I said as I buckled her in to the car seat. "I'll take you to your favorite restaurant and let you have fun on the play set."

"Yeah, McDonald's, Mom! You can be late tomorrow too."

Twenty minutes later, I was cutting the chicken nuggets into tiny pieces while sitting at the booth.

Stori ate her French fries and then reached up and hugged me tight around the neck. "You are the best mommy, the best."

After they were fed, I let them play in the ball pit for about twenty minutes. They enjoyed tossing the balls around so much that they didn't want to get out. Thankfully, the long school day and playtime wore them out. When we got into the car they both dozed.

After carrying the babies to their beds, I checked my messages. I had hoped my husband would change his mind, come back to the house, and let us be rational adults that could talk about why all this happened. Wishful thinking though. I did, however, have a message from my mentor. It had been awhile since I talked to Mrs. Kindle.

In her sweet, yet concerned voice, she said, "Hi, just checking to see how you are doing. You've been in my heart and on my mind. Seeing your name everywhere. Give me a call."

She saw my name everywhere, *oh my, gosh,* I thought. This was just great. I've not even had a chance to tell her of my indiscretion.

Quickly, I looked for my phone book. Before the tour, I had known her number by heart. What was that saying about me? The lady that spiritually feeds me, I had forgotten her number. Clearly that wasn't a good sign. After locating the digits in my office drawer, I dialed the number, remembering I could have redialed it through the caller ID.

I really did want to have this conversation with her. I had done such wrong. I was embarrassed. I certainly was trying to avoid talking about it, but she had seen my name everywhere. She probably knew, though she did not come right out and say it. Good thing was, no matter what I did, she always made me feel loved.

We talked small chitchat for a while and she hadn't broached the subject. I didn't want to spill the beans if she didn't know. I could see my pastor being so through with me if she told him, and then him not wanting his wife to have anything to do with me. Or being mad at her for not counseling me enough. He'd hate that her mentee committed a sin so bad that all the world knew about it.

However, sensing my tension, she said, "Is something wrong, Shari? I haven't heard from you and you seem preoccupied."

I said, "A lot is wrong. Your husband is going to hate me. You might too. I made the terrible mistake of having an affair and it's being displayed in the tabloids."

"Shari, that isn't what either of us would want for you. But we don't condemn folks. You know my husband's cool."

"Yeah, but he is a pastor."

"Your pastor, and he is the first one that knows none of us are going to be perfect until we get to heaven. Like me, he'll just be worried about what this is doing to you and Dillon. Does Dillon know?"

Replaying his exit again in my frazzled mind, I said, "Yes, ma'am, and he left me."

"Oh, I'm sorry, honey. This isn't what you wanted is it? I know you guys were having problems before you left to go on the tour. I just wouldn't have thought this would have happened while you were still a married woman," she scolded as nicely as she could.

Not getting offended, I said, "I feel so bad about it. Not that it excuses anything, but it was just a one time thing. I let it go that far because I honestly believed it was more, but the guy didn't care about me. Looking back now I realize it was all a mistake. Then, I didn't think I wanted the marriage, but when I got back, Dillon was different."

"Different how?"

"Like he wanted me. Acting like a godly man instead of being all crazy. He was ignited again. We were putting the pieces of our marriage back together. And now it might be too late."

"Oh, honey, it's never too late. We've got to pray on this thing. We've got to trust God that He can fix it."

"But if Dillon and I don't find our way back to each other, I don't know what I'm gonna do."

Confidently, she said, "Well, you just said he was acting like a godly man. So though he's probably upset, that doesn't mean God can't work it out. If He can change the hearts of kings, then He can change Dillon's heart. Shari, I love you. Know you can call me for anything, especially for encouragement and prayer. A spiritual covering can keep you from doing something regrettable."

"I hear you now. I was just so caught up, there's

really no real explanation. I was lost and going down the wrong path."

"Well, I hope you are now found. It surely sounds like you are headed the right way. You are willing to fix your marriage, and your husband changing is a good thing. Because the vows you guys made to God are covenants, there is a spiritual bond there that can see past the pain. Plus, your beautiful baby girls need you both. Let's do lunch soon, and stay encouraged. Do all the things around there that you need to do, Dillon will be back trust me."

"You believe that for real, huh?" I asked, unsure myself.

"It's going to take him some time. Remember his pride is hurt right now, but yes I think he'll be back. Like I said, get your house in order and trust God to do the rest."

"Thank you," I said to her.

"Alright, get you some sleep and turn on that alarm."

I laughed, "Yes, ma'am."

I wanted to say, Mom, because she surely acted like one. Also in some ways, she was closer to me than my own biological mom. I wanted to fix that to. God knew what He was doing when He gave me her as a mentor. She understood me, but she also wanted to help me. The balance of listening and giving out advice was just perfect. I did need to get myself in order. Right now, I couldn't have a marriage if I didn't have a healthy me. Again, I saw hope in a hopeless situation. I didn't know what tomorrow would bring. All I knew though was that with God by my side, tomorrow was going to be a day I could get through.

*   *   *

The next week not much had changed in terms of my circumstances. My marriage was on the rocks. My husband had moved out and hadn't even come by. Granted it was football season, but he hadn't even seen the girls.

During that time of isolation, my writing was evolving. I had drafted a whole outline for my new book. The thought of writing about an author having problems in her marriage was so real to me. The story line just flowed. It was fiction, but it was my life. The thoughts poured out on a draft page, and the complete story looked like it was going to bless many women. My point, cheating isn't as good as it seems. My purpose would be to make many women not want to cheat. But for them to put into their marriage the same fight and extra energy that they put into being in an extramarital affair.

The phone rang and I was shocked to see that it was Mr. Gayley my publisher. "Hello, sir."

"Hello, Shari," he said, not sounding warm at all. "Let me just say we've talked to your agent and this isn't a call I wanted to make."

Where was he going with this? I felt like I was on oxygen and someone had taken off my mask. I had to brace myself. I knew what he was about to say wasn't good for my career.

Clearing his throat, he said, "Listen, you are one of my favorite authors. And your first work was a huge success; from a play to an award. But all this recent negative press you've been receiving is a direct reflection on our publishing house. I'm not judging, but as a Christian company we simply can't condone an author tied to this type of scandal."

As hard as it was for me, I said, "I understand."

"We're releasing you from your contract. You don't have to worry about paying back the first half of the advance you were paid upon signing. You'll continue to receive royalties on your title, *Luv Right or Git Left*. We wish you the best, and I know with maybe a secular company you'll have a place for your writing to soar."

After the call ended, I was sad. However, I knew I had done wrong. And just like someone who had murdered someone, they'd have to pay. Why didn't I think my sin would be any different.

The next day, after Tina and I talked, I was motivated to move on. I was a writer and I was sent here to write from my pain. Though a Christian company didn't want me, didn't mean I couldn't tell a story with a message. And even if I had to self-publish, I'd live to write—to bless—at least one.

So I got excited about getting to the manuscript. In my dark period, the bright spots were my book and my girls. They kept me going. However, as pumped as I was to get to the novel, when I sat down to pen it, I had writer's block.

Figuring I needed some girl time, I called up Josie. She agreed to meet me for lunch. Things were still crazy with her as well and she wanted to share. Maybe we could help each other.

I was so excited to see my girlfriend. Seeing her outer appearance, I would never have been able to tell she had something negative going on in her life. She was the bomb. Her short sassy haircut, cute adorable clothes, and the confidence to make any other female nearby hate her. We weren't seated for five minutes, when gentlemen sent drinks over to our table. A waitress whose name badge said Cindy, handed us two apple martinis.

Cindy said, "The nice-looking gentlemen at the bar said they would love to come join you ladies."

I was so ready to say, *No, no send them back uh, uh I'm already having enough problems in my marriage as it is.* But I didn't have to say anything 'cause my girl handled it. She looked at the fancy glasses as if their contents held poison.

Josie handed the drinks back to Cindy. "Tell them thanks, but no thanks. We are married women. They should enjoy the drinks for us. Plus, it's the middle of the day. What kind of women do they think we are anyway?"

I let out a fun chuckle. Josie had such a lovely personality. She knew I was stressed and she made certain our time together was free from tension.

Seeing I was into her silliness, she said, "And where are they anyway?"

Cindy turned around and pointed to two handsome guys, one looked mixed and the other was dark chocolate. Both apparently in their midthirties. Both dressed in nice suits. Clearly they had professional jobs.

Josie grabbed the waitresses arm as she was about to walk away. "Wait a minute. As cute as they are, maybe I should reconsider."

We both laughed as I knew her enough to know she was joking. She did give them a sly smile, kind of a thanks, but no thanks look. Then she shook her head at them and the waitress took our order.

When Cindy left, Josie said, "Dang, girl, you're pulling in the men now, huh. Getting us drinks and all. Dillon better watch out."

"Don't even try it," I told her, " 'cause you are the cute one."

She flicked her hand like I was full of it. "See, I know you are not having a pity party. What's going on with you? I've called you so much. I couldn't believe you called me today to go out to lunch."

Dropping my head, I said, "Dillon found out and left me."

Never did I ever think I would see Josie be quiet. However, she didn't say a peep. She looked sadly at me like she did when we were in college and her mom called saying her dog she'd had for years was dead.

After a long pause, she clasped my hand and said, "He'll be back."

She came around the table and gave me a hug that I desperately needed. The strokes she gave me were confidence for me to hold it together. I loved that she cared so deeply.

"How did he find out? Did you tell him?"

As I looked over the menu to find out what I wanted to order, I said, "He saw the magazine himself, girl. Thankfully, you called and prepared me. A football player showed it to him."

Smiling, she teased, "I saw the magazine and let me just say, somebody was having a whole bunch of fun. He needs to try to get back with you so you can sex him up like that."

I took my napkin and swatted it at her. She was so crazy, but boy did I appreciate her take on it. She was honest.

"If Dillon knew men were sending you drinks in

the middle of the afternoon, he would get his act together. He'll be back."

"Enough about me, even though I'm sorry, sorry, sorry that I had such a pity party and didn't call you back. What a horrible best friend I've been."

"Are you okay though?" she said, really into me.

"But I've been writing, girl. So honestly, I want him back, but I'm concentrating on getting my life together. So if I have to be on my own, I'm ready. I got to write this daggone book and get some dough."

Cindy interrupted, "Okay, you ladies know what you want?"

After we ordered, I said, "What's going on on the home front?"

"That's why I've been trying to call you. She not only moved out, but she's been bashing me with the mother-in-law."

"I thought she left."

"She did, but he told her she could move back. But I came home and found she had fed her son and left my boys starving. She had no reason and no excuse. The wench was just hateful. I told her to take her crap and go. I wasn't going to let him tell her to stay this time. If he did I'd be gone with the kids."

"Oh, Josie."

"Girl, please, my life is so much better now. Maybe I can get my marriage back on track without the sabotage."

"How has he been since she's been gone?"

"Well, she's just been gone a couple of days and it hasn't been roses. I know he is sulking a little bit 'cause he feels he let his little sister down, but he'll be alright trust me. I've got more respect for him now that he took my side when his mom went off on him. You know how much of a mama's boy he is. We're good."

My heart felt full hearing that. Her husband had been such a jerk. Calling his mom late at night and talking for hours, when he should be in bed with Josie taking care of business. Or he never gave her compliments on how lovely she was, yet would get jealous when other brothas noticed. She deserved better.

I lifted my water goblet, and said, "Okay, well, here's to the fact that at least somebody's family life is going right."

"Seriously, I feel you'll be alright as well."

"Girl, I'm at the bottom now. It can't do nothing but get better. I mean, what else can go wrong?"

Just when I said that my cell phone rang. I quickly picked it up so as not to disturb the other patrons in the restaurant. The brotha's at the bar smiled in my direction. I guess letting me know my mishap was okay.

"Get that phone and don't be distracted," Josie said as our food came at the same time.

I was thrilled to hear my father on the other end of the line. "Hey, Dad!"

In a deflated tone, he said, "It's not good."

"What, what do you mean?" I said, feeling my heart race faster than a gazelle runs on its turf.

"We took her to the hospital." He paused and I was so scared.

"Who, Dad?" I clinched my bosom.

"Your grandma. I'm on my way up there right

now and wanted to know if you could meet me at the hospital."

My mom's mom had been in and out of the hospital for the past two years. I knew my mama would be upset that her mom was sick. I felt bad that I hadn't called her in ages.

"Dad, it will take me a while to get to Orangeburg," I said, thinking through where my maternal grandma lived.

"No, no it's my mom," he said as I held the phone.

Now, not that I wouldn't be upset if my maternal grandmother was in the hospital again, but I guess I kinda prepared myself that her life was coming to an end. However, I wasn't prepared at all for my dad's mom to be sick. I couldn't lose her. She was my babies' nana. I was just with her. She just talked to me.

"What's wrong with her?"

"I'm not sure what's going on, just meet me at the hospital. All I know is that she is in intensive care."

"I'm on my way."

Josie picked up on the conversation. "You get over to the hospital and see what's going on with your grandma. You want me to drive you?"

"No, you have to get back to work."

"Alright, go take care of that. I've got lunch." She touched my hand. "She'll be okay."

"Yeah," I said, barely able to stand or breathe.

Driving eighty-five miles in a fifty-five mile zone, on my way to the hospital, I couldn't believe that just when I thought things couldn't get worse they were. I prayed all the way that Grandma was fine.

Forget about my marriage, forget about my book, forget about my reputation, I just needed the lady who'd consistently connected with me all my life to be okay.

When I located the waiting area of the intensive care unit (ICU), my dad was in there alone. He was looking out the window, shaking. Putting my arms around him from behind, he turned around and fell into my arms sobbing. Never had I ever seen my dad lose it. Yeah, he had shown lots of emotion before, when he would spank my butt when I was young. He even shed a tear when I got married, but nothing like this. I was glad my brother agreed to get my girls. Not that he couldn't be here, but I knew how my dad felt. This lady lying in the hospital was both our hearts.

I had to hold it together for him, even though I didn't know what was wrong. Clearly it wasn't good, with the way he was reacting. Just the thought of losing my grandmother made me cry with him. We were both a mess.

My eighty-eight-year-old granddad came out from behind the steel doors, and said, "She's talkin' y'all. Wants to see you, son. Go on in there."

Dad wiped his eyes, and said, "I'll be right back."

Only two people at a time could go back there. Being that his brother was already in there with my grandmother, I had to wait. But that gave me time to talk with my grandfather and figure out what in the world was going on.

I threw up my hands with an unsure look on my face.

My granddad said pitifully, "She had a stroke. She's real weak. They say she's going to be fine, that's all I know. She won't look the same, now that she can't move part of her body. I remember when Caroline up the street had a stroke, then she had another one and died. I hope she's going to be okay."

"She is going to be fine, so you don't need to worry." I knew I needed to keep my granddad lifted up, but I was honestly trying not to hear stories about folks dying. I had a lot of hope. I left his side, walked over to the window, and just looked up, though I didn't say a word inwardly, I was praying for the Lord to fix this. The brightness of the cranberry sun made me believe she was going to be okay. Though I didn't want this, He was God and He was in control. He had my grandma and whatever happened she was going to be okay. I just needed for me to be okay with whatever happened, and that part was harder.

The hard waiting room couch had become so comfortable over the past couple of hours. As I waited for my turn to go in and visit Grandma. I had fallen asleep and dreamed of the day my girls would have a piano recital. Having my grandmother sitting right beside me squeezing my hand and saying, "I'm proud," throughout their performance. And I could see the tears falling from her eyes from being proud.

I woke up sweating. It was a lovely dream, but I wanted it to be our future. Grandma had to be okay. I needed her.

"Oh, there you are," I heard the familiar voice say as I turned from gazing out the window to my husband's eyes.

As my tongue slowly slid across my teeth, I wondered what I was going to say to him. I was an emotional wreck because I wanted my grandmother to be okay and also because my marriage was in shambles. There he stood before me though, and I didn't know how to receive him. I didn't want to mess it up by uttering the wrong thing. He didn't reach out to hug me and I took my cue from him and stayed my distance.

Though my husband would never appear in *People* magazine's most beautiful issue, I was certainly attracted to him at that moment. What had turned me off months before, his weight and lack of dressing, now seemed to be a Dillon of the past. There he stood before me a toned two hundred thirty-five pound fine man, dressed smart-preppy casual in a dark brown suede jacket, new blue jeans, and some dope pointed-toe shoes.

"How did you know about Grandma?"

"Your dad called and asked me if I could pick up his sisters from the airport and bring them here."

"My aunts are here?" I asked with excitement.

"Yes, and they should be right behind me somewhere. They had to stop off at the ladies room." He looked concerned. "How are you holding up?"

I was so taken aback. Just hearing my husband ask me those words meant a lot. For some odd reason, I couldn't show it on the outside. I stayed strong and kinda acted like I didn't care. Call me crazy, I don't know why I did that, I should have jumped into his arms and apologized profusely. However, the ICU door opened and my father came out toward us. Therefore, I was saved from expressing anything personal.

"How is she?" I asked.

He shook Dillon's hand. Looking back he smiled. "She is going to be alright, why don't you two go in there."

Dillon said, "Your sister's are here. They should be up in a minute."

"Thanks for getting them."

"No thanks owed," Dillon said. "I'm family."

He said he was family, did that mean he was trying to save our relationship or was I having wishful-thinking thoughts racking my brain. Dillon motioned for me to enter first. I felt secure facing this with him.

When I saw my grandmother, I couldn't hold back the falling water that dripped from my eyes when I saw her frail body laying there. She was awake and, though her left side was drooped, she was smiling.

"Y'all came to see me, Shari, baby?"

"Shh, Grandma," I said, wanting her to save her energy. "Don't talk."

"Shh, yourself," she said, getting a fiery spirit. "I'm fine, girl. What's she talking about, Dillon?"

He smiled at her. Then he pulled up a chair and grabbed my grandmother's right hand. She squeezed it tight.

He wiped her brow and said, "Oh, we don't pay her any attention. We know you're strong."

"That's right. I'm gonna be around for years. Y'all might make it to heaven before me," she said, making us laugh.

After fifteen minutes the nurse came in and said she needed to change grandma. Dillon and I slid out of the way. We weren't ready to leave totally.

However, my spunky grandma, with what strength she had, pointed toward the door motioning for us to leave. "Now, y'all know I need my privacy."

I got up, kissed her on the forehead, and said, "We'll be back."

"Now, I love y'all. I need for y'all to love each other and take care of them pretty babies, them my baby girls, I . . ." She was becoming emotional.

I just couldn't take it any more. Dillon grabbed my hand and tugged it gently outside. The embrace he gave me in the hallway took me to another world. A world where I had a husband that loved me. A world where I knew he would lead me into a safe place. But when he pulled away, and said he would talk to me soon to see how she was doing, I knew that world didn't exist.

Watching him walk pass the ICU desk as he thanked the busy nurses scattered around, I knew I was letting a gem get away. Sure we had problems. Sure it wasn't easy. But he sure had a lot I loved, that I respected. When I pulled back all the crud of vain things, I could see the goodness and all the things that attracted me to him in the first place. And the one whole good thing about Grandma being in the hospital was that I realized life was precious and you shouldn't take anything for granted.

We had to make every moment count. But I couldn't apply carpe diem because my feet were frozen. I couldn't go after him. Something inside told me to give him space. As I started praying the more I realized that something was the Holy Spirit that I had to be sensitive too. I didn't want a quick fix, a Band-Aid type of approach. No, I needed true healing so that the scar would not even be left at the end of the day.

When I got to the waiting room, I saw my mom seated with my aunt, Velda. Aunt Velda was considered to be a very charismatic Christian. My other aunt, Regina, had a sassy style and she was a divorcée. Deep inside, I believed she was lonely. My mother had never been great friends with them. I remember going to visit their places a couple of times with my family growing up, but I could also remember my mom keeping her distance. I used to always feel that she was so standoffish and I hated that, but as I grew older I learned that my grandmother and her daughters were a little messy. And sometimes I worried and tried not to make any waves. Just steer clear of the water, and my mom was smart in that respect, but funny when she asked me to please take my aunts to dinner.

My mom said, "They want to visit with their mom, then go. They are really hungry and your dad doesn't want to leave. Can you do that for me? I'm going to go home and get your girls from your brother, so I can't."

"I'm not doing anything up here. Yeah, sure," I said.

Being concerned, she said, "When you want to talk we can. I know some stuff is going on with Dillon. But I love you. I'm here for you."

Fighting through the silence, I hugged her and said, "I love you, Mom."

She appreciated the closeness, which was weird because all growing up it was like she was never a big hugger, but right then and there, the smile she displayed as we embraced, told me the gesture meant a lot to her.

My mom left, and my aunts stood up and hugged me for a minute before they went in to visit with their mom. I sat there alone, gazing out that same hospital window. All of a sudden the hospital staff started rushing toward the ICU. I stepped into the unit and saw that my grandmother had all of a sudden become critical. I dropped to my knees and looked up to the sky and prayed to God for help.

Chapter 12

Breeze

I felt like I was the one that needed to be admitted to the hospital as I stood there trembling, watching three nurses and two doctors flee into my grandmother's room. They ran past me so fast I felt the air change. My aunts and I tried to go in too but other nurses, not working on my grandmother, tried to clear out the ICU area.

"You guys have got to let them do their job," a sweet black nurse said to us.

"Yeah," Granddaddy said in his tired frail, but strong voice. "Ain't nothing we can do. If it's her time, we just need to be prepared. Y'all come on out now."

I was so unstable at that moment. No one had to tell me to get out twice. I fled around the corner and was stopped dead in my tracks when I saw my uncle, Phil, a forty-two-year-old junky, being hemmed up on the water fountain by two thugs. Normally, I would keep myself out of other people's business, but my grandmother might be dying. This was her son, even though he was a big part of why she had so much stress. She needed him around.

Phil was my crazy uncle still living at home with his parents. If my granddad had his way, Phil wouldn't be there. Some days they would come home and another big item in the house would be missing. Turns out Phil would have stolen it to hock the item for drug money.

Quickly, I stepped in between a guy who wore a do-rag with holes in it and my uncle.

"Step back, this is a hospital first of all. And his mom is in there fighting for her life. Have y'all lost it," I said, letting my pain make me bolder than I normally would be.

"Ah, sorry," my uncle said in a panicked voice. "I gotta get back there now. I thought she was going to be okay."

"Now you see how crazy this is. You understand what I'm saying," I said to him. "All those medical people that just ran down the hall, they are going to see your mom. She is not doing well, get in there. She needs your support, not more of your ignorance."

Yeah, my uncle was older than me, yeah he should have been wiser than me, but he wasn't and from time-to-time I just had to step in and tell him what was up. I didn't know if he ever listened to me or not when I would say get your life to-gether and stop stealing. But this time I knew he heard me. His blood-shot red eyes watered up. He ran toward the ICU door to head inside and left those guys without saying a word.

One guy looked at me and said, "Shorty, you don't know what you just did."

Then I realized I had stepped in a little too

deep, and trying to pull myself out of my jam I said, "I'm sorry. I'm sure whatever you were talking to Phil about is major, and I'm even going to make sure he get's you what you need. But please respect our family. This is a hospital. This is not the time. Besides, police are all around here for one, the rest of my family is here, and my grandma needs him more than you do."

They didn't look impressed. One of them flashed his gun. I had to make them understand I meant no disrespect. I prayed, *Lord, help me think like these nuts and say what I need to say to squash this.*

"I'm sure you have a grandma. Can't you respect that ours is fighting for her life, please," I pleaded.

One said, "Alright, Shorty, just tell him to call me though. If I don't hear from him tomorrow, I'll be back."

I nodded. "I'll tell him he needs to call you." They left.

Before I could get myself together and go back in, I ran into my father and my youngest uncle, Sam. Sam was seven years older than me, and boy was he a cutie. When he graduated from high school he actually came to live with my family, and I used to kinda think he was my older brother, just for play, but I've never really gotten that crazy thought out of my mind for some reason. Back in the day, see, all the other girls loved me 'cause they wanted to go out with him, so I became instantly popular with my own crowd. He taught me things that helped me with all my problems. And he played the big brother role when it came to my dates. I loved Sam. He lived so far away with his family and I was so glad to see him, though certainly not under these circumstances, we just hugged.

"What's going on with Mama?" my daddy said to me as he got back from getting food with Sam in the cafeteria.

I huffed, "I don't know, but I don't think it's good."

"What do you mean, she was fine when I left," he said as he threw his hands in the air in defeat.

I said, "The doctors just went in there . . ."

Before I could finish, they both took off. They said a few words to my aunts. Then the ladies came toward me.

Aunt Velda said, "We are just hungry and need to get out of here. There is nothing we can do. Let's go."

Though I wanted to hang at the hospital, I walked them both to my car. I was happy to see them consoling each other. There was a big rivalry with them as sisters growing up. They were only two years apart, but my grandma told me stories of how they had competition between them about everything. That was probably why I was very nervous bringing up my girls, they were only two years apart. I certainly didn't want Stori and Starr bickering for years and years.

Now, my two aunts appeared not to have drama anymore. Of course, they were heading into their sixties and going through a crisis, but they both were too beautiful to me and my grandmother to bicker.

We couldn't even make it into the doorway of the restaurant easily because the wind kept pushing us backward. The physical experience mirrored how I felt; a strong wind blowing me over. Finally, pulling it toward us together, we opened it.

As we sat in the restaurant, Aunt Regina said, "Come on, Lord, and work with me. We can't lose Mama."

Aunt Velda shook her head in disagreement. "I just think it's her time. I'll miss Mama, but it's time for her to go and be with her Mama."

I waited for Aunt Regina to say, "Oh, girl, where is your faith?" But she didn't. Both their eyes just filled with water. Their despair was evident.

Instead she echoed, "Yeah, I miss our talks already. You know we talked every day for at least an hour."

It was like they were giving up. I had to be the voice of faith and reasoning. God could do anything but fail.

I said, "What are you guys talking about? She is going to be fine."

Aunt Velda said, "No, sweetie, when we were here in May for her birthday, she was frail and tired looking then. I knew this was coming."

"Yeah, I know it's about to be the end," Aunt Regina chimed in.

The waitress came over and took their orders, I couldn't eat a thing. I was so shocked hoping they were wrong, and food was the furthest thing from my mind. Plus, I felt nauseous. I tried to settle down all the thoughts wrestling within me. I didn't need to add to it with food making me even gassier. I would vomit for sure then.

"You know what dress we are going to put on her?" Aunt Regina asked her sister.

"There is not really much stuff in there. Phil sold all her nice stuff," Aunt Velda replied.

I listened to the two of them go on and on about all my uncle had taken: TVs, radios, appliances, jewelry, and then clothes. My grandma was going through more than I knew.

"Not just clothes either. Did you hear about the check book," Aunt Velda asked her younger sister.

"Uh-uh, what happened with the checkbook?" Aunt Regina said, shaking her head in despair.

"Dad is mad. Phil has been forging checks lately. The strung out junky practically wiped out all their savings account."

"Take me back to the hospital right now," Aunt Regina stood up at the table and said. "I'm going to kick his tail."

I couldn't tell if she was joking or serious. The only good thing in all this is that it kept my mind off my husband and the drama that he and I had. Well, until I got quiet and my aunts were served. They studied me.

Aunt Regina pried, "So you know I got the scoop, right?"

"What scoop?" I said, just hoping she wasn't talking about what I knew she was talking about.

"Baby girl, there are newsstands all up in New York. Last week every corner I turned on had a spread about my niece. And you know how people are? I'm always bragging on my niece, the author, the one that was on tour with that singer guy. Well, my friend that was jealous, her relatives are worthless, quickly showed me a picture of my niece and that singer guy in the sack."

I looked over at my other aunt, Velda. She didn't blink. Obviously, because she didn't hit the roof, it was safe for me to assume she knew. What was I going to tell them?

Aunt Velda said, "You might as well go on and admit it. You been in the magazine, no need to deny it, or be ashamed of your mistakes. We all sin. Plus, Mama told us about the problems with you and that Dillon of yours."

I was so upset at the lady I'd been praying for most of the day for God to spare, that I almost wanted to rescind that offer. My mother always told me the three of them gossiped. Honestly, it never bothered me. It was fine when they were telling other folks business, but now I needed to go to the hospital and check my grandma. How could she tell them my business? I thought she and I had a special bond. I couldn't even look at the two of them.

"Don't get to rolling your eyes at us," Aunt Regina said to me. "Sweetie, we know you all got issues. Every marriage does. We just want to school you." I still didn't face them. "Don't want to talk to us. Well, alright, just listen to what we've got to tell you. You know I'm divorced, been that way for fourteen years and, girl, all my friends were like he ain't loving you right. Leave him. He ain't doing that. Leave, go get you somebody else. Well, I got rid of him and I'm still by myself. My same friends that were trying to get me out of my marriage thought that was the worst thing for me, ain't no where around. They wanted me to be miserable and I'm worse off by myself. You got two kids. Trust me when I say you need to work it out."

Aunt Velda agreed, "And, honey, though I'm still married, I consider myself married to the Lord. Kurt he's a good man, but most times he doesn't satisfy me either. I am not talking about in the physical way. I'm saying he's not the nicest

man. So I think, *Lord, I serve him as unto You.* When
I look at it from that point of view, I don't need
any love back."

Maybe that was why I was so unhappy. I expected too much from Dillon. If I let the Lord fill
me, then I'd serve my man gladly and wouldn't have
pushed him to a point of anger. Keeping my eye
on God was the key. The wisdom from my aunts
helped me see, though I wasn't perfect, God still
loved me.

As we rode in the car and got closer to the hospital, it had been about thirty minutes since we
talked about my own marriage troubles. Aunt
Regina wouldn't let it go though, she brought it
up again.

"Honey, I know you, and it must have been
something that happened with your man that
made you feel like you needed to be with another.
Again not judging, but you know that was wrong?"

"Yes, ma'am," I said in a depressed tone, feeling
like what she asked me was a question more than a
statement.

"Good because now that you recognize that, the
issue is what's going to happen now. Dillon picked
us up from the airport and he looked like he was
through it. We're just gonna lift up this whole situation because God can bring y'all back together."

Aunt Velda said, "Yeah, he's probably hurt now
that she made him know he's not the only fish still
swimming in her ocean. But I'm not sure we want
to pray to get him back. I know he's got a temper.
Mama told me. He needs to take a long hard look
at himself."

Aunt Regina said, "Both you guys have got to
make the marriage work. Both you guys have got

to do a little bit of giving, a little bit of loving, and a little bit of forgiving. And you'll find your way back to each other."

Aunt Velda was in the backseat and she placed her hand on my shoulder. "Is that what you want?"

As I drove into the parking lot, I said, "Yeah, that's definitely what I want but I . . . I don't know if that's what he wants."

"God changes and controls the minds of kings. He certainly can with your husband as well. Keep lifting it up," Aunt Velda said, seeing that I truly wanted to reconcile.

Getting out of the car, I hugged both of them. I hated that we had to head on upstairs to see their mom lying in the hospital bed helpless. But the time together was valuable. Something I would treasure forever. The wisdom they shared with me I knew I would use.

My intuition kicked in and I felt good about Grandma. The breeze was lighter, not so strong. The wind had settled down, which kind of made me think she was now okay and that the angels hadn't come to float her spirit home. Besides, all three of us had cell phones and none of them had gone off, so she must still at least be with us.

Thankfully, when we got to the ICU waiting room Phil was smiling. Then my dad came out of ICU and told me my grandma was asking about my girls. I wasn't going to bother her, feeling she needed her rest, but he insisted.

He pushed my back through the door and said, "No, get in there. She's asking about those babies. Tell her the babies are fine. Then come right out. She's real weak."

"Yeah, for sure I won't tire her out," I said.

With every little step I took, my heart started beating harder and faster. It was sheer anxiety, worse than a person trying to get out of a burning house. I didn't want to go in there. I didn't want to see her suffer. I wanted her home.

When I opened the door, there was a lady from my granddad's church in there trying to talk to my grandma. My grandma wouldn't respond to her though. I didn't know what that meant. So the lady talked to my granddad and held his hand real tight. Then she grabbed his shoulders and then kissed him on the cheek. I did see my grandma stare. The woman left when she saw me in the doorway, because only two people could be in the room at a time.

Grandma lifted her head up and with the left side of her mouth, she asked my granddad, "Love me, love me."

He was watching that lady leave, but he turned around and came to my grandma's side. He reached for her hand. Then he kissed it.

He said, "Course, I love you."

I pondered on what that whole scene meant. My grandmother was clearly jealous, *Saying alright now. You got a lady don't be looking nowhere else.* That was hilarious to me. I couldn't believe I was a part of that whole thing. What was I supposed to do with all that information. It was like I was literally a fly on the wall. Guess I'd have to store it away for another day. A story of undying love that maybe one day I might tell in a book or something.

When grandma spotted me, she said, "Where are the babies?"

I held my heart, saddened that she wasn't as strong as she was when Dillon and I had visited her earlier. Hopefully, she just needed to get some rest. I hated that my babies couldn't come up and see her, but no children were allowed in the ICU.

Coming back to reality, I said, "They're fine, Grandma. They said get some rest. They will be feeding your cat."

She smiled and closed her eyes. "Love."

"I love you too, Grandma, so much," I said as I went over and stroked her head. "I'll see you soon."

When she didn't respond, I realized she was asleep. I escorted my granddad to the waiting room and he filled the rest of the family in on how she was doing. We all were exhausted, but we were all thankful she was still with us.

She wanted to see the babies. How in the world could I make that happen? Then I quickly thought of showing her a video tape, which was perfect because we hadn't done an updated tape in a while.

I told everyone I'd be back soon, headed over to mom's house, got the camera and brushed the girls' hair. Stori and Starr said something cute for their nana. My oldest daughter started by saying, "Night, nana. Love you, bye. Now I'm going to feed the cat." Then Starr came toward the camcorder with her arms wide and, if you were watching it looked like she wanted to hug you, which is hopefully the feeling my grandma would get, she said, "Nana." Oh, this was perfect.

I told my mom what I was doing and that I would be back soon. She thought it was a very cute idea. It was weird having her support, but I loved it.

I kissed her on the cheek and said, "I'll be checking in with you from the hospital, okay?"

"Tell Daddy I'm cooking a big dinner for every-body."

My mom was so sweet in my car, I played back what I had recorded and it looked so adorable. I couldn't wait for my grandma to see it. My babies were so blessed to know their great-grandma, and I know she would be equally blessed to see them say how much they loved her.

When I got back to the hospital parking lot, I could barely open my door. There was that strong wind again. So strong, so heavy it tried to keep me from going inside. Every time I walked two steps forward, it knocked me in the opposite direction. What the heck was up? What in the world was going on? After about ten minutes, I made my way up the elevator and when I saw tears coming from my family, I knew the strong breeze I felt was that of heavenly angels carrying my grandma's spirit up to a higher place.

The camcorder fell out of my hands. I didn't care if it broke or not. I didn't even look to see. I covered my face with my two hands and wept.

My dad came over to me and said, "She's in a better place. You gonna be alright. You'll be fine."

The way he was saying it was like he wasn't really talking to me. Seemed more like he was trying to tell himself he was going to be alright. However, his shaky voice didn't really sound like he felt al-right to me, whether he believed he would be or not. Everybody was somber, but Granddaddy. He was the head of the family and we needed his strength. Hopefully we could soak a little from his unphased stance. I thought it was odd though that the first time we got the word she was gone and no tears did he shed. Part of me was upset.

"Y'all need to stop this crying. She's in a place where we all better hope to go. She told me for weeks she didn't feel good. She's fine now, shoot. We got some planning to do. Come on, ain't nothing we can do at this hospital," he boldly said as he left the waiting area.

As my dad helped me gather up my camcorder, I said, "Mom said she's making dinner for everybody."

"Such a godsend," he whispered, before crying. "My mom's gone."

I hugged him and tried to give him hope. "Yeah, I know it's tough dad. Like you just told me, she's in a better place and she loved you. You know you were her favorite."

He smiled slightly. We both knew they were all her favorite in reality, but I knew my dad needed to hear that. The doctor came out and stopped us from leaving.

While my dad and grandfather talked to the doctor, I watched my aunts wipe their faces. My uncles, Sam and Phil, were still consoling each other. When I stepped outside of the hospital and felt that the wind had stopped, I could only hope the pain I was feeling would dissipate as well.

My mom insisted on keeping my girls at her house when my brother brought them to the family gathering. I was supposed to go back to my house and pick up clothes and then come back over there so I wouldn't have to be alone. But I took the time by myself to let out all the pinned up tears that just came streaming out.

My granddad was right, my grandma was in a

much better place. That still didn't mean I wasn't going to miss her. That still didn't mean I wasn't going to feel bad because she was gone. That still didn't mean I couldn't be sad at least for a moment.

I got down off the bed needing to do something more constructive with my emotions. Once on my knees, I prayed, *"Lord, I know You know what You're doing up there. But I certainly wish You would let me in on it. This just doesn't seem right to me."* In the midst of my prayer, my body started shivering as if God was saying, "I need to shake you up young lady because you're not the one in charge. I don't need to tell you anything. Just trust me. Just know that I've got this."

Something in my spirit clearly showed me my grandma's face, and she had an enormous smile on it. She was perfect. She looked young. She was floating. Most importantly, I clearly saw she was okay. Though there weren't any wings on her back. I could see a glow all around her. I saw no image of her new big mansion, but I knew she was at peace.

I felt comfort. I jumped to my knees and sprang over to the window. As I saw the trees shaking from the fall breeze, I knew God did have this. I ran a hot bath. Put in a few drops of oil and got me a big cold glass of ice water. I found my tape recorder that had been just a little rusty, pulled out my new outline and just let the creative bug bite. I was so relaxed, so on fire, in an hour I had talked two chapters. I knew to be able to do that with such ease that Grandma hadn't left me. She'd always be there.

Not only did I have the Holy Spirit, but I had

her spirit, her legacy, and her love still all over me. I was fired up. I started thinking about her and what she really meant to me. Before I knew it, not only was I writing my book, but I pulled out the song-writing skills I had developed with Bryce and wrote her a song. The lyrics rolled:

> When I think about my grandma and what she
>   meant to me,
> she was loving and gentle and she loved to fix me
>   tea.
> She cared for my babies and she sang me all her
>   songs.
> I'll miss my grandma, but she's with God.
> She gave me love. She showed me peace.
> She said have hope, feel sweet release.
> I'll miss my grandma, but I'm thankful she's with
>   God.

Before I could create anymore, my phone rang. It was Mrs. Kindle. Gosh, she always knew when I needed her.

"Hey," I said, sounding like things were good.

"I've been thinking about you, lady. How are you?"

"Actually, Grandma passed today, but I'm good now."

"I'm so sorry, my mom's not doing too well either."

As I thought about her sweet ninety-five-year-old frail mother in a nursing home, I said, "Are you serious?"

"Yeah, she fell out of the bed again today and they got her in the hospital. She's got a pretty nasty cut on her head too. We can't live forever, so we've got to get it right so we can get into heaven and hear the Lord say, 'Well done.' How is your marriage going?"

"The same. Not great. Dillon came to the hospital for support. He wasn't rude to me or anything, but he was there for family then he left. I don't even know if he knows that she's gone."

She asked, "You haven't called him?"

"No, you think I should?" I asked, really unsure as I slid on some baby oil.

"Yeah, you should. The good thing going on with me is that my boys are doing well. My oldest has a promising superintendent's job. My younger son is exploding with his whole music business. He's got all this new equipment and some new clients. We'll see what happens with his tracks. He is so inspirational."

"Oh my, goodness," I said as I thought about the song I was composing for my grandma. "Do you think he will work with me? I've got a few dollars I can give him to lay some tracks."

"Perfect, he'll work with you. Call now. I think he's home," she said before giving me his number.

Soon as we hung up, I was dialing her son. He was so excited to get my call. He had me sing it. The rest of the song spilled out:

> *I remember when I was really young.*
> *I spent time at her house and we had so much fun.*
> *And when I became a lady, she was still by my side.*
> *Telling me, with Jesus, I could fly.*
> *She gave me love. She showed me peace.*
> *She said have hope, feel sweet relief.*
> *I'll miss my grandma, but I'm grateful she's with*
> *God.*

"Alright, I recorded you on the phone and I'm going to work on the music," Harry told me. "Then tomorrow you can come in and lay the tracks."

"Really," I said, so excited.

"No problem. Anything for my mom and the song is tight. You need to sing this at her funeral."

"Oh, no, I couldn't do that. I'll be too emotional. There is no way I could sing over her body."

"The way I'm hearing the music . . . trust me, you will want to sing this for her. You'll have everybody in tears."

"Starting with me," I said, still doubting, as we finalized plans to meet the next morning.

When I hung up the phone, I heard the garage door go up. I knew it was Dillon. I wasn't ready for a confrontation. I didn't know what to say in order to avoid one. I didn't have time to put on any clothes. So I sprayed Bath and Body Works ginger scent all over me, grabbed my fuchsia robe, and headed down the stairs. He came inside and I wasn't able to read his mood.

"I was just about to call you," I said, breaking the awkwardness.

"Yeah, I checked in with your dad. I heard the news." He came walking toward me and placed his arms around me. "I'm so sorry, Shari. I know how much you loved her."

Darn it, I was fine. I was okay with it. I was cool. But being in his arms, having his sympathy, knowing I really would miss her, I fought hard to hold back the emotion from flowing out once again.

"No, I'm okay," I told him. "I know she's not suffering anymore."

"I'll be here with you through this."

God was really great to me. He'd already allowed me to express my thoughts through music. He helped me be productive with my writing and now He walked my man back into the house to be supportive.

Being in Dillon's arms felt right. "Thank you, Dillon."

"I'll miss her too."

"She loved us both. She'd want us to be here with each other."

Dillon smiled. At least he didn't disagree. He followed me over to my parents house and when we got there it was a zoo. It was ten o'clock at night and the adults were bickering like first graders about what color the dress was going to be, what kind of coffin they were going to buy, who was singing a song, who was doing this, and who was doing that. They just couldn't seem to agree on anything.

My grandma had too many strong-willed kids. Though I longed for a son, I thought maybe my two girls needed to have a will with it clearly spelled out, so the two of them wouldn't have drama, issues, or trouble once I was gone. Just seeing my dad and his siblings go crazy let me know I needed to get my house in order, because tomorrow wasn't promised. These folks were fools, nothing got settled.

Even the next morning they started the day doing more of the same. I cut out to go to the studio.

The time with Harry on the keyboard was magical. I could just see all the times I was with my grandma. Every note he perfectly created moved me. The song was the bomb, I left there with a CD of a instrumental track and a vocal one.

When I got back to my parents house and heard more arguing from my family, I just played the music. My recorded voice carried throughout the house. All the adults wanting different things for their mom quieted down. The song helped them understand that this wasn't about them or what they wanted. But this last good-bye was a collective effort that we all had to work on to get closure.

"This has got to be performed," my dad said with excitement.

None of his siblings gave any arguments. In fact, they swarmed me sharing his sentiments. I wanted to argue, but time passed so quickly. We were on one accord. We loved on each other and got to the service.

I wasn't comfortable about singing, but when I stood in front of grandma's still body all my doubts were washed away. I sang the song with power, passion, and ease. The closing lyrics were:

See now she's with her grandmas. I have peace because she is there.
One day I will join them, we'll be with God.
We'll be with God. We'll be with God.
We'll be with God. We'll be with God.
For now I will miss her, a lady I held dear.
Sweet peace precious grandma. Go be with God.

"You did great," Dillon said to me as he rubbed my back when I set back in my seat. "She'd be proud."

My babies really didn't understand why their nana was laying there peacefully, not moving. Why those men in dark suits closed a steel, gold lid on her. Though my dad, aunts, and uncles were strong, I knew their hearts were wounded. Later when they lowered her sweet body into the ground and the wind started swirling again, we all felt refreshed and revived. We rejoiced. My grandma was caught up with Jesus in that sweet breeze.

Chapter 13

Dream

"It was real," I said to Dillon a week later as we sat atop a revolving restaurant in Atlanta, Georgia, the night before South Carolina played Georgia. "I can't believe you rented a limousine to take us from Athens to Atlanta. Wow!"

"This is so unlike me," he said. "That's what I want to change. I had to look within to what drove my wife into the arms of another."

"Shh," I said, placing my finger over his lips. "It's just us, baby, we gotta be real with each other, we gotta talk about this. I was wrong to do what I did."

I shook my head and looked away. I didn't want this to turn into a nightmare. Actually, I still couldn't believe he asked me to come to the game. We hadn't talked and I'd been writing, but I certainly missed Dillon. So, I didn't want to talk about such deep issues right now. I only wanted to enjoy my husband and continue feeling like the queen he had made me feel. But he persisted and as I listened I was actually surprised at what I heard.

"The night before your grandma died, Shari, I was in agony wishing I had you by my side. Mad at myself because I allowed you to slip away. I was angry at God for not keeping us from this situation. It's around the clock work for me because it's football season. When we had free time, I just stayed in my office. There were times when I cried."

I hated hearing he personally had been dealing with a lot. I could only imagine how I reduced him to nothing around his players. A jock letting his woman get out of control, I felt bad.

He continued, "I also talked to a few of the Christian coaches and it was interesting. Coach Nixon, you know the defensive coordinator, said he really hated that our business was out like this for all the world to evaluate. I was just ranting and raving kind of going off saying my marriage was over. Though I was saying it, in my heart I didn't feel like I truly wanted to lose you. I know my hard ways turned you against me in the first place."

This was so amazing hearing him take on a big part of what was wrong with us. Admitting his faults meant more than he'd ever know. God was doing something.

"Another coach told me what gets him through life is knowing that when he's wronged he is not supposed to respond naturally. He is supposed to respond supernaturally. I was angry at my wife, myself, and God."

My husband went over to the window and looked out over the capital city of the peach state of Georgia. The serene view was beautiful. I couldn't believe we were having this deep conversation.

He turned back to me and said, "When I saw the whole situation from God's perspective, He clearly showed me what I'd done to you. Not being there like I needed to be and not loving you like Christ loves the Church."

Trying unsuccessfully to hold back the tears, my husband got up from his seat, came over to me, and kissed my tears away with his sweet lips. He gently grabbed my hand and led me toward the empty dance floor. Then he held me in his arms as we enjoyed each other over the sweet music of Luther Vandross. The communication between the two of us was genuine. I didn't want the night to end, but I knew I needed to get my man back up to a hotel near Athens, Georgia, so he could get ready for a victory the next day.

After dancing to two more songs, I starting feeling dizzy, I didn't know if it was the actual room or if it was really me spinning. When the twirling did stop, I knew something else was going on with me.

"Suddenly," I said to my husband, clutching his arm "I feel nauseated."

He tried helping me over to my seat, but I dashed to the ladies room. I made it just in time before all the delicious dinner came up in the wastebasket. Moments later as I dabbed my mouth with water to relieve some of the distasteful duck, I looked in the mirror and saw how flushed I looked.

I said out loud to myself, "You've been awfully tired lately. What's going on?"

I didn't even notice a lady coming out of the stall. I thought I was in the restroom alone. She stared at me and chuckled.

She said, "It looks to me like somebody is expecting."

As she quickly washed her hands and gave me the eye like uh-huh. I shook my head no, and left. I thought, *No, no I can't be.* The last time I had sexual relations was with Dillon. However, a couple of days before that I was with Bryce. We were so tipsy there was no condom used. I could not be one hundred percent sure this baby was my husbands. Therefore, I couldn't be pregnant. That would be a cruel joke and I wasn't laughing.

When I got back to the table my husband had already paid the check. "Shari, I need to get you to bed. Everything with your grandmother and keeping the kids has been stressing you out. You need to get some rest. You don't have to go to the game tomorrow if you don't want. You can take a taxi to meet us at the airport after the game."

"Thanks," I said, realizing if I was with child I might be taking him up on his offer to rest in the hotel.

"Plus, I'm dying to hold you all night," he told me.

I was hoping he wouldn't pry and ask if anything else was wrong with me. I didn't know if my mind was playing tricks on me or what. The whole limo ride back to the hotel, I felt sick. Thankfully nothing came up. But before getting in bed, I took a nice hot shower and when the water touched my chest my breast felt tender, so tender that I had to turn to the side. My husband made good on his promise as he held me in his arms and he drifted off to sleep. His sweet snoring that used to annoy me was comforting. This is where I wanted to be; his wife, with him on the road during football season.

Everything I held dear was in jeopardy. With my

butt safely nestled in his stomach, I thought about the whole pregnancy thing. And with everything happening with grandma, and Dillon moving out and me losing a publishing deal, I realized I'd missed a cycle.

I couldn't sleep and tried not to wake Dillon. I moved from under his arms and called downstairs to the front desk and asked if the hotel store was still open. My heart hurt when the guy said no, I didn't know what I was going to do. I had to find out certainly, but I couldn't get caught leaving the hotel at weird hours of the night. All kind of South Carolina alumni might be roaming the halls. I'd just have to bear it.

As I slid under the covers once again, Dillon said, "Oh, you feel good."

He bit my neck. That one innocent kiss led to a night of passion. I was so forceful, like something inside of me wanted to make sure that if there was a baby that it was Dillion's. How crazy was that, because if the baby was there the father was already determined. However, my psyche was so screwed up that none of that mattered. During our love-making, I wanted my husband to know how happy I was to be with him again.

I said, "Oh, that feels good, Dillion."

He shook me and said, "What feels good? Are you dreaming?"

I tried to wake up. I was losing it in a good way. I had drifted off to sleep and dreamed about my man. That was a good sign that things were going to be okay. Dillon placed his hand on my stomach and I believed it had to be okay. So I told him what I suspected.

"What do you mean you think you may be pregnant?" he shouted back at me in disbelief.

I didn't know how to respond to his question. He was being facetious. He had heard what I said. I did not stutter. I made it plain. So in reality, I knew that he didn't need for me to repeat what I had just told him.

Based on his frantic actions, the way he coupled his head in his hands, started twitching his feet, sprang off the bed, and paced back and forth, I knew this wasn't good news for him. I could have hit myself in the gut at that moment for even telling him before I completely knew. Now I had opened up a can of worms that I could not close the lid on. I had to watch Dillon distraught.

I finally just said something. "Well, what's the big deal?"

As if I didn't know. I brought that one on myself. When he looked me dead in the eyes, I saw rage flare.

"I'm probably not even the father," he said in a mean tone, reminding me of the Dillon I wanted to get away from months back.

I was so mad at that moment that steam was coming out of my ears. If my hands had a mind of their own, they would have placed themselves around his throat and squeezed until he apologized for being a jerk. Was that thought unrealistic or was I the one that was the jerk. Didn't he have a legitimate question because I had been an unfaithful wife.

Dillon and I had never talked about the particulars of my infidelity. He didn't know that a condom wasn't involved. Yet, his statement revealed he knew that Bryce being the father was a possibility. He yanked the comforter off the bed, got a pillow, and didn't even say good night. Thinking harder on all this, I realized I had no right to be mad. Everything he was thinking was justified.

The next day, I felt worse, but sucked it up to go to the game. Carolina won the game beating Georgia 40–3. I hoped, as we flew back on the plane with the team, my husband would be in a good mood. First of all, they were underdogs, and to practically kill Georgia was huge for my husband's career as a defensive coach. The Gamecocks had been winning all season and mainly because the defense was awesome. Dillon was coaching his tail off.

When we flew in silence, I got nervous. Though other wives and players were cordial, I knew they all thought I was a slut. What would folks say if I were with child? Nervously scratching my hair at that thought of isolation and embarrassment, the flakes underneath my fingernails made me sick again. I headed straight to the bathroom in the back of the plane and threw up.

When we got home hours later, the first place I went was to the toilet. Dillon's footsteps grew louder and louder. I didn't even have to rise up from the toilet, I knew he was towering over me.

"You are pregnant, Shari. You always get sick at first. Oh my, gosh, what have you done to us? Why did you even let me make love to you that night, you knew you had just come back from getting busy with some pretty boy? I was trying to let all this blow over, just get past it. I was trying to own up to what I'd done to you to get you to fall in the first place. But now you're pregnant. You know when you're ovulating. Why didn't you tell me that night?"

He flung a fake plant across the bathroom. I could see where he was going with his tacky accusation. But he was concluding the wrong thing.

"You didn't tell me because you wanted to make sure we had sex to cover yourself. You never even knew I'd find out you were with someone else. I never thought you'd do this to me."

Grabbing the toilet tissue off the cold holder, I wiped my mouth from left to right, flushed the toilet, stood, and looked straight at my husband.

"I did not set out to trap you or try to cover up anything. I was never intending on being intimate with you. Think back. You came on to me. You know how I dream. I didn't even think the first few moments were real, we had such discord. Did I seduce you? No. Did I come on to you first? No. If I'm pregnant, and you know I might not even be, I pray it's yours."

"So you didn't even use protection. Do I need to get an AIDS test?"

Though he had another good point, I walked around him and sank to our tub. This was hard. I was losing it. The more I tried to make sense of all that was happening the more consequences began to show themselves, reeking havoc on my life.

He turned to me and said, "Come on, let's prove you are."

Washing my hands with soft soap, drying them quickly on a white T-shirt, I leaned over the sink.

"I'm goin' and getting a pregnancy test," he said.

"Drug stores are closed," I said in a frustrated

voice, wishing he'd let me handle this with a doctor's visit.

Not phased he said, "That's fine, I'll drive a few extra miles to Wal-Mart. They are open twenty-four hours. We need to solve this tonight. You need to get out a calendar. Calculate out the timing and show me the probability of something. What's the likelihood that I'm the Dad. Forget what you say you want, what are the facts."

He should have been gone only an hour or so, but my husband was gone for three. I tried to figure out the whole timetable thing, but all the dates were so cloudy in my mind. Being on tour I hadn't tracked my period, my cycle was so irregular I was everywhere. I was on such personal highs and lows that I didn't remember any of that stuff. I didn't even realize that I hadn't had my cycle.

Ever since Starr was born, that time of the month for me had been irregular. Dillon was right, some months I did know when my egg released from my ovary because it was sheer pain. But I didn't remember feeling it this time.

What I did know was that in my heart, my husband wanted me so that our moment together was much more passion filled and perfect than my time with Bryce. Hopefully, that counted for something. Thinking of Bryce as my child's dad was a farce.

On edge, I called Dillon's cell phone a few times. Only his answering machine picked up. He was dodging me. That fact alone burned my core, but what could I do about it. I knew he was somewhere driving, furious that I had put him in this situation.

Issues always seemed to plague Dillon and me. We could never be truly happy for long. There was always something job related, sex related, task related, or just stuff always between us and now it was baby related.

When he finally came through the door, I was so happy he hadn't had an accident. Before, I'd held off going to the bathroom because I knew I'd be required to give a sample for the test. However, I was about to explode. So I quickly grabbed the box, tore open the wrapper, and peed so hard on the stick that I didn't care what color it was. I felt relieved that the test was finally done.

We both sat in the bathroom not saying a word to each other. The five minutes we had to wait seemed like the whole three hours that he was gone. When I looked at the stick there were two lines and on this particular test that meant yes, yes, yes, I was pregnant. I showed it to him not even thinking that he didn't know what the two lines meant.

After he shrugged his shoulders, I uttered the words, "I'm pregnant."

He smiled quickly. Then that sweet look faded. His squinted eyes and mean frown scared me.

He said, "You said, *I'm* pregnant. I really wished you had said *we*."

"Baby, I didn't mean anything by that," I said to him as I kneeled down on the floor, unable to figure out how I felt about it anyway.

This would be my third child. Maybe this was the boy I always wanted and that just might be my luck for doing the wrong thing. Would it be my son with Bryce? After all he did have two of them already. I was really messed up because I had to come face-to-face with the reality that if it wasn't Dillon's, it was a no brainer for what I wanted to do. For sure I'd keep the child, but could Dillon live with me.

Seeing my strong guy's weary eyes made me know he was wrestling with some of those same tough thoughts. Neither of us shared what was going on in our minds. I stood to my feet and started running my hot shower water. I saw my husband leave out of our bedroom door. I wanted to flee behind him and say it was going to be okay. But I couldn't tell him that with such certainty.

Being that my hair was dirty, I just put my head under the hot steamy water and let my mind go to a better place. One where my husband was in the shower with me, rubbing my back telling me how excited he was of the thought of being a dad for the third time. Letting me know how special I was to him. When I opened my eyes and saw Dillon standing with me in the water, he didn't have to say anything, just him coming back into our space, sharing that with me, let me know he was going to be with me. We held each other. He was loving me and it felt right. I felt God watching over us, telling us the ride might be bumpy, based on our past sins, but He'd be there to help us through the consequences.

"I love you, Dillon. I'm sorry."

He kissed my brow. We weren't free from drama. However, even with our problems, we held each other until the steamy water turned warm.

It seemed so surreal as I printed out the last page of the first draft of my manuscript that had taken forever to complete. When all of the pages were out of the printer, I smelled the bundle and kissed the top sheet. Then I prayed over the whole stack. It was such a blessing to get to this point.

Life had been so upside down that most times things had gone wrong. But the symbolic part of the completed first draft showed me that I was getting things in my life together. Finally, I was walking where He wanted me to walk. I was finally going where He wanted me to go. I was finally feeling good, even though physically, after going to the doctor and being confirmed that I was nine-weeks pregnant, I felt sick all the time. Nothing stayed down and nothing tasted right. I had an appetite for nothing. I was truly tired of the saltine crackers and ginger ale, but I could only hope that I would continue to keep them down because I certainly didn't want to go to the hospital and receive fluids.

With Dillon constantly either at the football facility or on the road, it was easy to complete my manuscript. My husband had agreed that this was his child by faith. I accepted that there wouldn't be any more discussion about it. We were trying to find the right time to tell our family, and when my grandfather requested his children and grands to come to Thanksgiving dinner, Dillon and I agreed that that would be a good time to share our news.

Stuff was coming together, things were working out, but even if my baby was a girl, I truly didn't care anymore; that longing for a son itch had been scratched away. All I truly needed was to have this baby be Dillon's biologically. Whatever sex God had for us was cool with me. The Lord knew best.

Dillon and I didn't talk about how we were going to tell the girls. So when Stori walked in and saw my head in the toilet, I quickly stood, not wanting to explain. However, turning around I didn't realize that my bulge was growing. It was very noticeable to her. She made no bones about asking what was going on.

"Mommy," Stori said inquisitively, as she came up and touched my stomach. "Is there another Stori in there?"

I knelt down beside her and giving her a big hug, I confessed, "Yes, mommy is having a baby."

I didn't know how my little three and a half year old was going to take this. She and her sister were inseparable, but on that same note they often times got on each others nerves. So I held her and prayed she'd be excited about this. My heart was overjoyed when I gave it to God, because there He let me hear sweet words from my oldest baby.

"Wow, Mommy," she screamed, and left my arms as she screamed out looking for her little sister. "Starrie, a baby's coming."

Squeals came from them both. They came running full speed. Starr was so cute, not only did she have her walk down, but she was flying. This was good.

The next day I was flipping through the channels when I saw Bryce doing an interview on BET. I'd gotten him out of my system or so I thought, because I was frozen when my brown eyes spotted him. He was talking about his latest transition from Christian to R&B. The brotha' was looking good. He'd recently been in more tabloids discussing his nasty divorce. The ballads that he had on his albums talked about true love.

The interviewer asked, "Are you acting these emotions, or do you know something about it?"

"What are you asking me?" he said seriously to the female commentator.

"Well, I've got to ask . . . that lady that wrote that book . . . are you and she an item?"

Thank goodness she didn't know my name. I moved to the front of my bed, picked up one of the towels that had been before me, desperately needing to be folded, and threw it at the tube.

No part of me wondered why I cared so much about his reaction to that question. I didn't want him back, even though the brotha' was fly, he was a dog. I didn't want him to tell any falsehoods about where we stood. I had a marriage and a family to protect. This wasn't just some cheesy tabloid that could twist the facts. This was Bryce talking. Whatever he said would be consumed by black America. He had to get it right.

He said, "A brotha' never kisses and tells. Of course she and I were aversely affected by a lot of things. I can say the pictures were made to look one way and totally distorted the truth. The paparazzi seem to have it out for me. I hated that the lady you mentioned was dragged through such a scandal."

Right away the interviewer said, "Those sleazy magazines are always misrepresenting mé too."

"Alright then," Bryce said, "she and I are just friends. She helped me through a difficult part of my life and I only wish her the best now."

I exhaled. He didn't do me right a few months back, but he didn't do me wrong then. Wow!

"And your ex-wife, Pamela?"

"You said it all. She's my ex. And the pictures surfing the Web with her and my brother aren't fake."

"Oooh," she said as she covered her mouth, "that's why I like this album. It's really true to a lot of folks' lives. Marriage isn't easy, love isn't easy, and somewhere in all that, if you let yourself go just a little bit, you will feel something good."

"Exactly," he said. "Hopefully my music will help you and yours get to that good place. Check out the album, it's in stores."

I thought I had put to bed the whole issue of this baby being Bryce's, but seeing him on TV protecting me and being honest about what's going on in his family made me want to reach out to him. So without thinking and without praying, I just called.

"Hello," I heard him say as I immediately wanted to hang up. "Shari?"

"Yeah, it's me, I hear tons of noise in the background. I can catch you another time," I said, hating I called on impulse.

"No, I'm not busy. What are you up to?"

"I just saw you on BET. I'm sure you're swamped with folks in the green room and stuff."

"No, I taped that last week. I've got some folks at the crib, but I just watched it too. You saw what I said about you, huh? The writing good? How have you been? You still married?"

With his questions bombarding me, I didn't know what to answer first. I skipped all his questions. Some were so personal I needed to keep our conversation at a distance. It needed to be cordial, not intimate.

I said, "I just wanted to let you know that I appreciate what you said on the air."

"That benefited both of us. Just sorry things got

so out of hand. That tabloid has been banned from publishing our picture."

He asked me a few questions as I heard the voices in the background fade. I guess he walked away to another room. It didn't matter what he was saying, I shut him up with my next words.

"I'm pregnant," I said. Immediately I wanted to take back my words. Shucks, I didn't even know who the father was. Why did I say that?

Bryce abruptly yelled back, "It can't be my baby. I didn't get excited until I was on my way out the door, you know what I'm saying. I came out."

"It would have only taken a drop to get me pregnant, Bryce," I said, before slamming down the phone when I happened to look up at my bedroom door and saw my husband glaring at me with disappointment.

I couldn't even finish the call. I was so into the chat that I didn't even hear Dillon get in from work. Based on the steam I could see shooting from my husband's ears, I knew I was in trouble. I knew he knew who I was talking to and what I was talking about.

He yelled, "I want a paternity test done, Shari."

Those horrific words sent chills up my spine. This was a nightmare. Regrettably, the moment I was living was not even close to a blissful dream.

Chapter 14

Constellation

With anger in my gut, heavier than Santa Claus's stomach, I got to my feet and went to my husband. "A paternity test? What in the heck are you talking about? You told me it didn't matter whose child this was, that you were ready to love and accept this baby as yours."

Quickly, putting his hand on his face and walking around me, I knew I needed to give him a little space. The brotha' was trying to calm down. He huffed for a few seconds.

Then Dillon said, "That was before you decided to tell the other man you were pregnant. I can't believe you were on the phone with that Negro who gave me doubts in the first place. Why would you be talking to him and how often have you done it? Does he have our number? Shari, I thought we had built something again. I thought we had trust. What in the world would you have to say to him? Why are you telling him about the baby? I'm not being a fool no more. I want a test."

I couldn't cry. I was too annoyed to cry. I couldn't hit him, as mad as he was, I knew he was capable of hitting me back. And then we'd have even crazier drama. Tapping my foot and placing my hands firmly on my hips, I tried to calm myself down. Like in the airplane, you have to put your mask on yourself before you can help someone else. Since I had a baby in my stomach, I didn't need to get myself all worked up. I was already weak from not being able to eat. I had to get this under control, but it wasn't working. I was tapping my foot faster and faster.

Dillon wasn't even looking my way. He was staring out the window. I don't know what he was getting from all those stars up in the sky. They didn't even really look beautiful or spell out any meaning. They were just haphazardly up in the sky.

Then he turned and faced me. His eyes held a distant cold stare. It made me grab my chest with one hand and prop up my back with the other to pay attention.

"I thought I was okay with not knowing for sure," he said to me, "but now I want a test. How soon can you get one?"

I walked over to him and turned his face toward mine and began pleading my case. "Listen, Dillon, you don't understand. Please."

"You're right, I don't understand why my wife told me she was through with any communication with the dude she had an affair with. But then, stupid me giving too much trust, comes home to catch her on the phone rapping with the guy. How can you explain it?"

"For the record we never discussed Bryce. But to set things straight, this was the first time I called him. I saw him on TV and he put the whole affair thing to bed on national television."

Moving to the other side of the room, he said, "Well, this is just great. My players are going to flip out about this when I go to practice tomorrow. I can't believe he was confessing his love for you on TV."

"No," I said, "it was just the opposite. He said the tabloids changed some images and made some stuff look like something that it wasn't."

"Oh, so he lied on TV and you were grateful."

Dumbfounded that he didn't think this was good, I said, "Well, I mean, I know he was doing it to save his own neck too. But this is a good thing, yeah. So I thought I owed him a bit of thanks."

"You owed him, I thought you owed me, your daggone husband. You forgot about that. Have you forgotten about me? Or forgotten about our family? Seems like you have to me. I just came upstairs to tell my wife I'm here and give her a big hug. Trying to do what she says I don't do."

I was so sick of him referring to me in the third person. I was right before him. Why not shoot direct?

"I was going to change all that and try to be a better man. I come upstairs and find my wife on the phone with the man she scr . . . know what? I can't even go there. When can you get the test, Shari? The rest of this is bull."

"Okay, I'll have the test," I said to him. "And if the test proves that you're not?"

Dillon didn't respond. He just gathered his toothbrush and night clothes. He basically sent my heart into a rigid freeze as his answer to my question was to walk out the door. He didn't have to tell me that was his way of saying, if the kid wasn't his we'd have severe trouble. His actions said more than his words ever could.

I fell to my knees and prayed. I so wanted to operate in God's will and not my own. If I wasn't here for the Lord, I needed to surrender more so that I could. After praying, I got off my knees and went over to the window where my husband stood moments before. I too looked out and saw that the stars were still all over the place. Usually that was a beautiful sight, but maybe tonight, because of my mind set, the sky looked crazy. I wanted to bring order to it. Maybe the test was my key.

The next day I made an appointment with my doctor. God was so good I didn't have time to stay down long, after the appointment was confirmed my phone rang again. It was Tina.

She said, "I'm loving this manuscript, there are a few changes we need to make here and there, the chapters are way too long for instance but that's easy to fix when you do it in three sections. We can just break it all apart, and instead of fifteen chapters we can have say forty-five. Oh, this is going to be a great story, so much about your life. No, you don't even have to say it, I know its not about your life. But the way you made it read even more dramatic is fabulous. Oh, this is just great, this is your best work yet. I really think you hit the jackpot. I'm going to find a mainstream publisher that's going to eat this thing up, it's hot. Oh, the only other thing I think you need to change is the ending."

Tina was good at taking my work to the next level. I was waiting for her to say you need to fix this and that. *You just need to have a little bit more yumph, a little more zazz.* After the affair she makes up with her husband, yup; it ends a little to quickly for me. You need just one more hard bump, how about I make it so that's she's pregnant? And, of course, Tina chimes in and said, *We don't know who the father is.* Then what we find out in the end is that it's her husband's. No, we find out in the end that it's the guy she had the affair with but, because of love, her husband expects that and they all lived happily ever after. Oh my, gosh, perfect; *make the changes send it to me.* I can shop it from the first three chapters and the synopsis. And you know I've been making notes as I've been writing this thing; it's hot. *Uh, this is great, but wait,* she said before getting off the phone. I knew she had picked up on so much of this book it really could almost be a parallel to my life. I thought I'd get away with her not asking me questions when I mentioned that about the ending, just on the—

"You're not pregnant are you?"

"Let me just get the changes back to you," I said.

"Oh my, goodness gracious, I'm praying for you, sweetie. Our actions do have consequences that's the one thing I do like about this book."

The next day as I sat in the doctors office waiting for her to come in and administer the test, I knew Tina's words rang true.

Bad actions did have nasty consequences, but I could only pray for grace. I knew I had to turn this whole thing back over to God. If my husband needed to know, he'd have proof. This was the last thing I had to do for us to move on the right way. Even though God didn't get me into this mess, I had faith He'd show me the way out. My out might not be a golden fairy tale but as long as the Lord wouldn't leave me it felt good. I felt peace before having to get the long needle stuck through my belly, I knew I'd be okay. God wouldn't have come with me this far and leave me. He'd give me strength to make the few days until the results came in.

As if I hadn't gone through punishment enough for my sins, I had to sit at Thanksgiving dinner nauseated. My aunts, uncles, cousins, and parents were digging into the food. Even my little girls and especially Dillon, everybody but me. Oh, I tried to play the role, but I didn't want to put too much on my plate and not be able to eat it all. Dillon and I had planned to tell my family that we were expecting, but because of the whole testing thing, we decided to just hold off a bit.

However, the candied yams were a little too creamy for my stomach, and the green beans just didn't mix. Before I knew it, I was headed to the bathroom, and unfortunately I didn't make it before green and orange gook hit the bathroom floor.

My mom had cooked the bread we were eating. My dad was so proud to show off their place in Columbia. In Greenville, they lived a modest life, not wanting anyone in his school district that worked for him to see. When he got a raise, the folks in the town were mad. He was mad too, because somehow the newspaper got a hold of his salary and posted it. It wasn't like he was the highest paid superintendent in the country, but a hundred and seventy-five thousand dollars compared to the bus drivers salary of only fifteen grand, well, I could see why folks would be a little angry here and there. However, when he came home to Columbia no expense was spared.

My time would have been comfortable had he left his coarse joking in Greenville and not rushed into the bathroom, touched my stomach I was trying to hide with larger clothes. "What's going on with you, baby girl, you pregnant?"

The next thing I knew, I had about ten family members around me. The ones not around me were around my husband congratulating him and hitting him on the back. When Dillon didn't smile the room grew silent, and as I came out of the bathroom while my mom got a mop and tidied up my mess, I got all kinds of crazy looks from my relatives. They didn't have to say it, I knew what they were thinking. *Whose baby was this?*

My dad was such a sarcastic man, but I knew he loved his little girl. Every time I got backed into a corner, someway, somehow, he'd pull me out. That's kind of what he did then. When he got back to his seat, he asked for the greens to be passed. As he piled more and more on his plate than we all knew he could eat, he diverted attention to himself.

He said, "I was just so thankful when that singer dude got on TV and said those pictures weren't real. Taking back all that they said about my baby."

My aunt, Velda, who was still here visiting, said, "I can't believe people can do some amazing things to pictures, putting folks heads on other people's bodies that's crazy."

I'd already confessed to a few of them that the affair was legitimate. However, they wanted to protect me. Or at least they wanted my husband to be comfortable enough to believe that they thought beyond a shadow of a doubt that it was his. I winked at my dad and smiled at my aunt.

I was thankful for a lot of things. I was thankful for the Thanksgivings that I'd spent with my grandma. I looked at my grandfather at the other side of the table and felt sad that he looked lonely and out of place. I knew that I had to soak up every bit of life, the good and the bad, because it was short. I needed to make it sweet. I was thankful for my family who cared enough to turn my crazy situation into one that made a little sense. I was thankful that the writer's block had gone.

But when my husband got up and came over to my side, placing one hand on my tummy the other hand around my waist, he pulled me closer to him and said, "Yep, we're having a baby." I was overjoyed and cried worse than I had the week of the funeral.

"I love you." I didn't have to wonder what turned his heart or what changed his mind. I knew God did it, just like He said He would in the word. In the Bible, He says in the book of Matthew, *"Come into Me all ye who labor and who are heavy laiden and I will give you rest."*

I could have collapsed in my husband's arms at that moment, just hearing him say what he said was comfort, was peace, was joy, was serenity, and it was rest. God did it, but as we drove back to our house my husband confessed.

"I saw the last chapter of your new book lying on your desk when I went to get some paper, and I couldn't find any, the desk was a mess."

"You saw the chapter?" I said.

"I more than saw the chapter, babe, I read it, and I don't know. I was shocked to kinda see our life story sitting on pages of your next book. But the character, the ending, the husband, the forgiveness, and his actions were Christ-like. He'd responded naturally, he responded supernaturally, and they're going to raise that baby. It honestly brought tears to my eyes. I repented because I knew I was operating out of God's will. No different from you and your own faith in me. God led me to read that, to show me how I needed to change. Your book spoke to me."

"But you seemed so angry earlier in the evening, you hardly said anything."

"I know, I wasn't just wrestling with myself, but actually the spirit and the flesh. When a lot of your family basically looked at me insinuating this might not be my kid, I knew it was time for me to stand up and let them know this is my kid."

I was more excited than a tennis player winning Wimbledon. I leaned over and hugged him so hard the car swirled to the other side of the road. Thankfully no one was there. I guess the roads were empty because people were still eating their Thanksgiving turkey.

When I got home, I went to use the telephone to let mom know that we were back at our place. Before I dialed her number, I scrolled through the caller ID box. My mouth formed a grin when I saw that my agent, Tina, had phoned me on a holiday. She had to have good news from a publisher. This day was going great.

When I went upstairs, my husband was already pushing play on the answering machine. Tina's voice said, "Hey, Shari, the three editors I pitched it to turned it down. I just wanted to let you know as soon as I got word. Don't be upset. Don't feel dejected. I still love this story. I know it will get placed. It might take us a little longer, but we'll find it a home. I'll be in touch next week. Oh, and happy holidays to you and your family. Dillon congrats on the baby, oops, am I not supposed to know?"

"Tina is crazy, huh," I said to my husband as he turned around seeing me standing there.

The sweet look in his eye let me know he hated the news I'd just received. With his arms stretched out wide I fell into them and wept.

"It's okay," he said. "She still is going to fight to get you a deal. You believe in the work. You love the story. I just told you it changed me. It's going to get placed, you'll see."

"No, no I'm not crying about that, and I know we need the cash and all. I'm crying because I love you and I'm so sorry for everything I took you through. For you to say you love me, our family, and this baby . . . who needs the Lord to give 'em a book deal. Writing Christian fiction, I've always felt that if my writing touches a life, then I've been used to better the Kingdom."

He wiped my face and said, "That's good."

"Well, you just told me that my book blessed you. So I know my writing wasn't in vain. You've already given me the best prize of all, where my writing is concerned. The tears I'm shedding are of joy."

After being comforted in a intimate way by my husband, I laid beside him stroking his chest. "You awake?" I asked.

"Yep," he said, kissing my forehead. "You hungry? You want me to fix you a sandwich or something?"

It was like a honeymoon for the two of us. The girls were still at my parents house with all the relatives. No one wanted us to take our own babies home. It was fine though. I wanted to connect with my husband. Spending time with him without interruption was moving. We could have laid in that bed for the rest of the night for all I cared. But I knew the Thanksgiving meal had probably dissolved.

"Naw, but I need to get up and fix you something."

"You need to eat. I'm concerned about you throwing up everything."

"I'm not hungry though. Plus, I'm just so full on our love."

He shook his head, as if to say I was crazy. My lips found their way to his. We enjoyed the moment.

Then he said, "Before that message from Tina came on, I got a call from Parker Rex. You remember him, right?"

"Your old teammate that has been in the news about the top football job for Maryland," I said, trying to find something nice to say about the jerk I remembered to be a male chauvinist.

Proudly he said, "The Terrapins hired him. He is heading to Maryland. He wants me to come up there and talk to him about a defensive coordinator position."

Shocked I said, "You don't need to talk to him about that, we're not moving."

"I'm not saying I plan to take it, but when we

were estranged, Parker and I talked about which-
ever one of us got a head-coaching job first would
look out for the other one. That's my boy, and he
is going to need a black face up there dealing with
all them knuckleheads. I'm tired of being a position coach," he said, pleading his case.

"Don't you think you'll get promoted here?" I
asked, pleading back.

"I don't even know if my head coach is going to
keep his job."

"You know he will, y'all been winning like crazy.
You might get other offers and they might at least
be closer than Maryland."

Stroking my hair, he said, "Baby, I just want to
make double my salary as a coordinator. You'd not
have to sweat about this book thing. You're going
to have another baby and you need to be home.
You can still write anywhere. Yeah, your parents
won't be there, but they don't even live in Columbia right now anyway. If you're not going to support me, then I need to call Parker back right now
and tell him I'm no longer interested."

As Dillon got up from being close to me, I knew
he was angry. Taking my bare body out from
under the covers, I went over to the closet and
threw on a robe. I was amazed at how my stomach
was growing. No wonder my family knew for sure I
was pregnant without it having to be verbally confirmed.

As my husband sighed, I knew I had to let him
know I was onboard to fully support him. After all,
my family was changing. We were always struggling
with finances, even with my man bringing in six figures we still barely made it. At the end of paying
bills, we didn't usually have a lot of money to save

or do hardly anything with. Dillon getting a promotion, moving him into what he always wanted, and that being a head coach in the NCAA, I knew being a coordinator was pretty much a prerequisite. And I had to face the music, how often did black men get an opportunity like that? I certainly didn't want to be out of God's will anymore by not following my man or supporting him. He had turned toward the window and wasn't looking my way anymore.

I went over to him, sat on the side of the bed, and said, "You know what, I'm sorry for thinking so selfishly. Go for it. You deserve to be running a defense."

As he hugged me, I had confirmation knowing that this was right. Later that evening, my husband was in the basement studying film when the doorbell rang. I had no idea who it could be. I hoped it wasn't any of the relatives, I certainly needed to pick up a few things around the house before having company. I just hadn't felt up to it. I couldn't be happy when I opened the door and saw the face of my girlfriend Josie because her beautiful mocca skin looked weary and her big eyes red. Being that we were on the opposite ends of the city, I knew that something was dramatically wrong.

"What's going on? Why aren't you with your family on Thanksgiving? You okay?" I asked as I let her in.

"I want a divorce, girl. I'm just sick of him and his mama. When she comes to town he loses his mind. I thought I was first, but he went off on me in front of her because she said I erased her messages."

Knowing that Dillon would be occupied for a

long time on the bottom level, I took Josie up to our guest room. No need for him to hear us doing any husband bashing. I was very upset that my girl's husband had disrespected her. Josie was such a strong woman. I very rarely saw her shaken, but as she followed me through my hall she was rambling so incoherently. I knew she was serious about this possible divorce thing.

"Calm down, Josie, maybe you can get him to see he can't dog you," I said, rationally thinking about her boys without a dad.

"His mom is so dependent on him, Shari. It's so sickening. She told him, in front of my face mind you, that he was crazy to put down family to please his wife. And when I looked at her like I could strangle the heifer, she rolled her eyes at me and left the room. Then my husband got so mad at me," Josie said with frustration. "It all started the night she got here. She went on and on about how much she missed her grandchildren. But yet she won't even let me and my husband go out on a date. She just wants him to sit up and be in her face all the time.

"How'd you handle that?" I asked.

"You know I give them their little time to run around and do their thing. However, I thought she was going to offer to take the kids somewhere, but she didn't. Just trifling. Then after being influenced by her, he comes trotting to me and tells me we need to give his sister money. The same wench that we had to kick out of our house for being disrespectful and for neglecting my children. That ungrateful chick caused so much drama between me and him, I wouldn't give her a dime."

"I agree," I told her.

"And check this out. She wants him to give her money, but she hasn't even called her brother since she left. I ain't giving her jack and I told my husband. I guess he told his mama 'cause that's when she made that snide little comment, like I was going to be shaking in my boots. I guess his mom wants to fight me. He took her side. I just don't even need the headache you know. I got a good job. I bring in more money than he does. I'm leaving."

I'd always support my girl. I loved her so much and I really agreed with what she was saying, but I couldn't go with the whole thing of her walking out. They needed counseling. Neither one of them were in church. And though it had been a while since I'd been, I daily talked to God.

I just held her hand and said, "You know what, lets pray."

I had no clue what I was going to ask the Lord. It felt like I needed to say something to her to give her hope. Thankfully, I just lifted up the name of the Lord and the rest poured out of my mouth.

I prayed, *"Lord, I love this girl. Josie's always been here for me . . . always been my rock. And sometimes, Lord, I know the advice she gives me might not really be aligned with Your word. I know it would be so easy for me to say yup leave that man, let him have a taste of what it would be like to live without her, but that's not what Your word says. However, this is hard. Husbands are supposed to leave their fathers and mothers and cling to their wife. He's not doing that. So I just pray for both of their hearts, that they will make You first and then find their way to each other. Help Josie know how much her husband does care for his family. Right now both she and I think he is crazy. But then again, what family ain't. I certainly got some issues with my mother-in-law too. So, Lord, I just pray that maybe she and her husband can start praying together and going to church together more. Start having a heart that wants to please You above all, because if they put You first they'd be fine. I don't want her to walk down that crazy road that I did looking for another to satisfy her. Give her hope in her marriage again, Lord. Show her the way home. In Your precious Son, Jesus' name I do pray."*

"Amen," she said as she hugged me tight. "You think God can help me."

"I know He can," I said as I looked her straight in the face, gripping her hand so tight she knew I was serious.

Two days later I got a phone call from Josie. She and her man were working things out. The mother-in-law had gone home. Her husband had stepped up to the plate and told his mom that she had to respect his house or she couldn't come back. Josie bent and decided to give the sister money, so everybody was happy all the way around.

I was happy for her, but I was a little nervous. It was time for me to go to the doctor's office and get the results. Dillon knew where I was going. Since he didn't say a word to me, I figured he wasn't going. When I grabbed my purse and keys, he stood up, grabbed his coat, and followed me.

"Going to work," I said to him.

"Naw, babe, I want to be there with you. You don't have to worry, whatever the results are, its our baby. I know you are nervous, you didn't sleep a wink last night. Plus, I'm concerned about you not eating. I want to go with you to this doctor's visit. I claimed it. We are okay."

Sitting in Dr. Rhymer-Anderson's office, he

held my hand as we waited for her to come in. All of a sudden I became very agitated. I couldn't sit down in the chair. I started biting my lip. I went over to the doc's window and just looked out it. This whole mess was crazy. I didn't deserve for it to work out, therefore, my mind was playing tricks on me. I believed it wouldn't.

"I hate this," I blurted out loud.

Dillon got up and came over to me. He placed his hand around my waist and allowed me to rest my weak body on him. Leaning my head on his chest was comforting.

He said, "Last night, all the tossing and turning you were doing made me get up, go to the window, and close the blinds. I thought maybe all the light was keeping my wife up. But then I got caught in the gorgeous sky. It wasn't like the night before when all the stars made no sense. I looked up at the ones twinkling. The stars clearly spelled out, *all good now*."

"What do you think that meant," I asked.

"To me, it meant our life was all good," he said as he touched my stomach. "It's all good. So don't you fret, baby."

We heard the door open and female footsteps come in. I squeezed his muscles so hard. She was going to say it was Bryce's baby. Lord, I thought, I'm so sorry.

He whispered in my ear, "It doesn't matter what the doctor tells us. I believe in that constellation."

Chapter 15

Star

"Well, based on the embrace I see before me I'd say the two of you don't need my results for a happy ending," Dr. Rhymer-Anderson said to us.

I couldn't tell what she was going to say next. There was no emphasis in her voice. But she wasn't overly happy either. She was a straightforward person. She motioned for my husband and I to take seats in front of her desk. We did so and continued to hold hands as we awaited the outcome. She opened up a folder and turned it toward us. Showing us some data that neither of us really understood. We weren't scientific people. All we saw was ninety-nine point five percent conclusive, that meant whoever she would say was the father was certainly the father.

Dillon scooted up in his seat. "Doc, I'm an old college football coach, I don't understand that technical stuff. Please spell it out for us."

"Certainly," she said, before going off on a tangent. "I went to South Carolina, so first let me say congratulations to the Gamecocks for having such a great season. My husband, who also went to South Carolina, says word's out that we might lose you because you have an offer to become a defensive coordinator. I certainly hope those rumors are not true."

Dr. Rhymer-Anderson was very good at her job. Though she wasn't a psychologist, she knew what to do to calm my husband down a bit. Yes, he would be supportive, and yes if the baby wasn't his, I truly believed he would keep his word and we'd be a family. But Doc knew he needed to take some deep breaths, probably because the news wasn't in his favor. The best way to do that was to speak his language, not medical science, but football. Her tactic worked as he smiled ear-to-ear and became a little bit more relaxed.

She said, "I'm a big football fan, but I know that's not why you guys are here today. And having delivered both of your girls, I remember there was a little bit of disappointment in the sex. And now you are here for a paternity test. This visit makes my job even harder."

I squeezed his hand really tight at that moment. I was bracing myself for the bad news to come. She looked at me with a sad expression.

She said, "I have to deal with ladies who can't have children. I see patients with babies that aren't healthy in the womb."

And as soon as she said that it was like God released my fears. It didn't matter about the sex or the paternity, I just needed the baby to be healthy. I looked at Dillon with a serious glance, he mouthed, *It's okay.*

"Oh, maybe I'm not making myself clear," Doc said, guessing that we were reading her wrong.

"That's not the kind of news I have today. It's all good."

"You mean my baby is healthy?" I said to her, thinking of absolutely nothing else.

"Yes, Shari. Your baby is healthy."

I embraced my husband so hard I saw veins pop out of his neck.

She said, "But that's not all the good news I have for you guys today." I looked back at her with watering eyes, as if I was perspiring or something. My face was so moist. She pointed to the chart, and said, "Dillon McCray, it says right here that you're ninety-nine point five percent the father of this baby boy."

We both just stood up in the doctor's office and screamed. I ran around to her side of the table and hugged her. The Lord had given us a miracle. The angels up in heaven were looking out for us, and when they gave my husband a sign the night before, saying it was all good, they were more than correct.

She went on to talk about her concerns about my eating habits. She told me that if I didn't start taking in more in a week's time, she would have to admit me into the hospital for fluids. With all the stress of the situation, she also was a little concerned about my blood pressure and the baby's heart rate. Thankfully, after a thorough exam, all was better than expected.

Dillon and I were so relieved. However, we wanted our marriage to work more than anything. So we entered couples counseling with Mrs. Kindle's husband.

During a session, Dillon admitted, "I'm so excited, pastor. I just don't want this to happen again in our marriage. The whole infidelity thing almost wiped out our love. And my anger sent her to a place of needing to find comfort in the arms of another. I do wonder if we can really trust each other again to not let the other down."

"That's normal, son," Pastor Kindle said as he stood erect in his chair, looking at us both with such eyes of wisdom. "Naturally, there is a side of you that can't trust until you guy's talk about all of this. Though the details may be more than you want to know, honest communication will aid in building back the trust. So, Dillon, I ask you, why do you think your wife needed comfort from another man?"

Scratching his head, he leaned forward and said, "I was hard on her. I wasn't affectionate. Football is my job, which is understandable since it pays the bills, but I kinda made it my world. The mean, nasty mentality that a defensive player needs to have to be ruthless and stop an offense, I displayed in my house. And when my wife made me angry, I was a little too abusive verbally and one time I threw things and punched the wall."

A tear welled up in his eye. Then it rippled like a peaceful creek being blown by a cool breeze. I slid my body close to him. I knew then that he regretted hurting me.

Dillon continued, "I pushed my wife away. I regret that."

"That's good, son. Let it out," pastor said, nodding in approval. "And Shari, why did you feel that your husband couldn't give you all that you needed? What did you do to prevent him from being the husband you longed for?"

Reaching for my husband's hand, I kissed it. "My husband was a tyrant. After my last pregnancy, I felt things going downhill for us. We pulled away from each other. I now know we didn't pray enough and give our early issues over to God. I was so down myself that he couldn't lift me up. Instead of turning to God for my strength and help, I waited for my husband to give me what I now know only God could. When he didn't fill me, I sought refuge with another. The grass looked greener, only to find out it was burned up."

We looked at one another with sorrow. Our marriage was scarred. Though God's grace had saved us, we knew the mark was there.

"I'm sorry," I confessed with truth that would pass a lie detector test. "I will never do that again."

With seriousness, Dillon said, "Can you be sure of that? If I do get the job in Maryland, I don't even know if I should take it. In the early stages, I'd be away from you a lot. How do you know you won't cheat on me again?"

I said, "Honestly, no one knows what the future holds. But I do know I plan to walk with God. I'm trusting Him to help me keep my halo on. I fear Him more than I fear you. And that's how you can believe in me again; trust God to hold me accountable to the vows of our marriage. You know I don't want to move now that we are having a baby. My parents are so close, I've got a good network system here, but baby, I'll go whereever you need me to go. I don't want to be resistant to you anymore. I really want to be the helpmate the Lord called me to be for you. I love you."

"Hearing you say that, baby, is like a dream come true. I'm sorry for taking my own insecurities out on you, being mad that I didn't get the promotion the year before, bringing all that stuff home. God hadn't left us. I believe we are going to be okay. Pastor, will you do the honors?" Dillon asked.

Reverend Kindle renewed our vows. It wasn't a real ceremony, but for the two of us, it was so symbolic. We were recommitting ourselves to each other again. We were starting fresh. We were blessed to be children of the King and we were blessed to have love that forgave.

Though I was the one that committed the act, I was thankful that my husband saw that he was just as guilty as me. Now with that being washed away, as far as the east is from the west, we were able to focus on what was to come.

"Heavenly Father," Reverend Kindle prayed, before we left his office, *"continue to bless this union. May this bride and groom now stay before You to keep their marriage strong. May they keep You as a guide, until their footsteps and a light upon their path show them daily that You're all they need to survive. Give them a clear understanding of Your direction. Show them the joy that comes with being a person that wears the crown of righteousness on straight. Crowns shift, but they are to be worn. We praise You for making the broken, whole again, in Your precious Son, Jesus Christ's name we do pray, amen."*

Dillon and I said amen also. When the pastor instructed Dillon to kiss his bride, it was declared that the kiss sealed our renewed commitment.

The next day was a good day. I was pumped. My husband was back at work and I had time to love on my girls. Also, I was so thankful to God for everything. After we watched *Barney* tapes, did hair, and played dolls, I was able to put them down for a nap.

As soon as I got back downstairs, my cell phone rang. I rushed to it hoping it wouldn't wake my babies. When I saw the number, I froze like an item that had been in the freezer for weeks. It was Bryce.

Though I knew Dillon wouldn't walk in and hear me talking to him, I knew I needed to cut this whole thing off. Our relationship was like a falling star shooting down from the sky, I needed to get out of the way before it burned me.

"Hello," I said, after deciding to answer the phone.

"So tell me, am I going to be a dad or what."

"Quit playing, like you told me, you knew you pulled out before the small explosion. The baby is my husband's."

It was weird, but he didn't seem relieved that he wasn't tied to me anymore. I, on the other hand was excited that my family was intact. What was up with him, though?

I asked, "Why did you call? You know if it had been your kid I would have told you."

"Yeah, yeah I believe that. You don't have to be so cold with a brotha'. I thought we were friends. I straightened everything out with the media."

"And," I said, almost rushing him to the point to say what he had to say and be done with it.

"*And* . . . I need to talk. I miss you."

Okay, I was going to handle this conversation. The truth of the matter was, I didn't miss talking to Bryce at all. I had everything I'd ever wanted. I certainly didn't want Bryce to be misled. He had been my friend when I needed one. Though he took advantage, I wanted him then. However, this was now. I had to cut this off. He didn't think twice about my feelings when he got up the next day and said it was over to me. So I didn't have to feel bad needing to do the same. Truth be told, I should have listened to Lacy. She tried to tell me he was no good, but like a fool I had to find out the hard way. Well, I would not be sucked in again.

"Look, dude, we had a good friend time. But when I was with you I left my religion. It was like the halo God gave me when I accepted His Son, was cracked and on the ground. I'm not into that anymore. I may not be perfect, but I at least want to wear my halo," I said, not caring what he thought about my declaration.

He was quieter than the girls sleeping. They snored. Bryce uttered not a peep.

I continued, "I wish you the best. I'll even be praying for you, but Bryce you can't lean on me. You need to work it out with your wife."

He ranted, "Yeah, right please. I told you she got with my brother. No, that's over. I'll see my boys, but we are through."

"Well, take some time to work it out with God then. You used to be one of the best gospel artists out there, now it's all this R&B stuff."

"And it's not doing that well," he revealed.

"Well, maybe that's a sign that you need to only sing for Him. I don't know. I've already said more than I should. This is your life and you've got to get it right with God. I can't talk to you anymore."

"I understand, but I do want to keep in touch with the lady who's now showing me life isn't all about me. Maybe it is God I need. Maybe He's the only one that's right in my life."

Though I didn't want to talk longer, I knew witnessing about God was permissible. "I thought you could make me happy. But I know God is the only one who can set things right. Life ain't supposed to be easy. God's got a great place for us in the next world. But we got to give ourselves back to

Him so we can get there and partake in what He's prepared. We'll have the ups and downs of life until we get home. Take care of yourself,"

"Wow," he said. "You really don't need me anymore. You sound so confident. I need what you got. Good for you, girl. Good-bye then."

That closure call felt good. I was no longer hanging onto something I needed from the superstar. I was letting go of all of that. I was living in the truth. Truth that God loved me so that He sent His only Son to get me back on the right path. And along the way He would give me a few extra good nuggets. My life after this crazy storm was more serene then swinging from an old maple tree, feeling the kisses of angels blowing on my face.

Winning the last two football games of the season put us in a BCS bowl. That meant more dollars for the school, a higher ranking, and the possibility to be able to get the national championship.

It was six o'clock in the morning when our phone rang. As I listened to Dillon say a few words, it sounded like he had panic in his voice. The next thing I knew, he was frantically putting on his clothes. He was bumping and stumbling in the darkness until he made his way over to turn on the light.

I said, "What's going."

"It's coach. He said he urgently needs to talk to me. I don't know if he's got wind of the fact that I'm going up to Maryland for an interview or what. I don't know, this isn't good. I certainly don't want to get fired."

"No worries, if so, your buddy practically told you it's your job there."

"Yeah, but I shouldn't have set up the interview before I talked to coach. I was planning on telling him before I went out there, but this might blow up in my face now."

I grabbed his hand and calmed him down. I was so thankful God was truly leading our family. Somehow I knew God would take care of us. I couldn't sleep for the next two hours. Though the girls were quiet, I just felt concern for my man.

Worried, I prayed, *"Lord, let Dillon and me have peace. Help us to get the right formula here. Help us trust You and not get so frazzled. I calm him down then, but as soon as he leaves, I get knots in my belly. Or is that my baby boy. You demonstrated that You have us in the palms of Your hands. I want that to be enough. Minute-by-minute, day-by-day, step-by-step help."*

The phone rang. My husband was ecstatic. The news was that our defensive coordinator was just offered the head job at the University of Central Florida. So now there was an opening at USC.

He said, "Yeah, coach wanted to tell me he had heard about me wanting to go someplace else. He said no one wants me to leave and since I have been pretty much running the defense he wanted me to take the job. Shari, he told me whatever the salary I was looking for I could name my price. You were right . . . look to God."

I just squealed. Put down the phone. Did a little dance, and felt hungry all of a sudden. I knew building my intake would keep me from having to go to the hospital for fluids. It was real good news that I was starving.

Picking up the cordless, I said, "Dillon, I'm hungry. I've got an appetite."

"Baby, yeah, you feel like eating? Well, that's right on time, I'll be right there to take you out," he said with enthusiasm. "Coach told me to go home and celebrate with my wife. He wanted me to tell you in person, but I couldn't wait. He said congrats on our little boy too. He hopes he's still coaching and can get him on the field one day. I'm coming home and taking my girls out for breakfast."

As I got up to get a shower, my phone rang. This time it was Tina. I felt like this day was too much when she told me that three companies were bidding for my book. They were three of the best in my opinion. I was just ecstatic at what a great lesson it was for me to learn. When I turn things back over to God, He gives me everything I longed for.

I just needed to be content with what He was doing. Not try to do His job anymore. He wasn't just the star of this team, He was the whole team. He didn't need me to play. As I understood my role, I realized how good He was.

When I told Dillon at breakfast my news with three book companies, he said, "When you do things God's way, it can't fail."

"So are you happy?" my mom asked as she helped me fold clothes in Starr's room.

"Yeah, I'm so happy, Mom. Not just for what I have, but for what I know. And how I plan to live the rest of my life," I said, so filled on God's love. "And I don't know what kind of bid I'll get for my book, but three companies wanting it . . . wow. For the last book, I got an advance of ten thousand dollars. If I double that, I'm excited. My agent seems to think because of this whole national scandal and that all these companies aren't Christian publishers, so they like the drama, it may come back in my favor. She keeps saying we're now looking at a sizable advance. I don't know what that means, but with Dillon getting a promotion we're already good."

"I'm just happy you don't have to move. And your dad is thrilled about the grandson," she said, rubbing my belly, which was uncharacteristic of her.

"Sorry I haven't always been the daughter that really understood you. I know I gave you many sleepless nights."

She nodded. "But I'm so proud of you. I've got to do a better job of wanting to be close to you myself. Not just keeping your kids, but being there for you as only a mom can. I could open up myself more. I didn't have that closeness with my mom, since I was the oldest and she was so young herself she barely knew how to be a mom. Then when I lost my dad at such a young age, a part of my lovey-doveyness faded, but holding your babies, my grands, in my arms . . . seeing you struggle . . . let God show me that I needed to step up and be a better mom to you. And not just criticize you all the time."

I reached over and hugged her. She didn't have to apologize anymore. I didn't have to say anymore. The embrace meant, hopefully, from this point on we wouldn't have any more regrets. I could come to her as me and she would except that, and I could take in what she wanted to say without feeling like I was letting her down. It was a beginning.

My mom was kind enough to watch the kids while I went to lunch with Josie. I hadn't talked to her in a while. I was so glad to hear that her marriage was still intact as well. Her husband had been sticking to his decision that she was right. His wife came before his mom. He couldn't walk the fence nor could he choose his mom, if he valued his marriage.

She said, "Girl, I've been thinking about your prayer for a bit. There was a void in my life. A hole that no husband could fill. Feeling desperate to be better in every area, I turned to God and asked Him to complete me Himself. When I talk to Him now, I sense Him relating to my every word. The satisfaction I feel is like I was royalty or something."

I wasn't expecting it when Josie told the waitress she didn't want a midday cocktail. Which for her was a little strange. She was different. My carefree fun-loving best friend that thought she had so much time to get her life right with God, now was filled with the Holy Spirit.

"I got your e-mail. All is well in babyland, huh? And it's a boy. Well, you know I've got the two and can give you advice. Hopefully, I'm having a girl and you can give me advice on raising them. Guess it looks like we're pregnant together again."

"Oh my, gosh," I screamed so loud that folks in the restaurant looked at me like I was crazy. "My girlfriend is pregnant."

We both just smiled as we rubbed our bellies with one hand and held each others hand with the other. Then I just naturally closed my eyes and prayed for the Lord to bless us both, as we go through our pregnancies, bless our families and continue to guide and direct us.

Later that night I knew that I hadn't talked to Mrs. Kindle to tell her the results of my paternity test. I felt bad that I'm sure her husband had to tell her. But when I said, "Hello," she wasn't mad at all. She just started shouting, "I knew it! I knew every-thing was going to be great. Oh, and girl, it gets better. My son needs to talk to you tomorrow. Some Los Angeles production company wants to put the song you wrote for your grandmother on an album."

Clutching my chest to avoid a heart attack, I said, "Are you serious?"

"Oh honey, yes. My son said he's working on a movie soundtrack. Supposedly in the film a grandmother passes. When he played your song for the director and producer they loved it as is. Congrats," she went on to tell me before we finished the call.

I walked outside after placing my jacket on and looked up at all the glowing lights in the sky twinkling toward me. The whole fact that opportunity was possible was just a God thing. I'd learned many lessons and gotten something meaningful out of the detour from my walk with Christ. I came away from this past six months learning that if you don't stand on God's path in the end, your end might not be with Him. Many folks say they believe, but a life that has truly opened their heart to God lives differently. A believer doesn't have to have a miserable life on earth.

Hearing the phone chime again, I went back inside. It was Tina. I didn't allow my heart to race, but I couldn't help it beating a little faster.

"You're not going to believe this," she said with excitement before I could get a word out. "Wait this is Shari, right?"

"Yes, it's me," I said, biting my lip hoping at least one publisher didn't bail out on still wanting the book.

"Landon Home Publishers bid one hundred fifty thousand dollars for your book."

"What?" I uttered, knowing I'd heard her wrong.

"Yeah, I got you a one-book deal for a hundred and fifty grand. That's like what . . . fifteen times what you got on your first book. Looks like getting dropped from your other contract was a huge blessing. God has a way of making a masterpiece from dirty, nasty mud."

Crying at the Lord's mercy, I said, "You are the best agent in the whole wide world."

"No, you humbled me a little bit. I wanted to be your agent, your mom, and your publisher. Sometimes I was a little too condescending, a little too hard on you. Wanting to help you before you made bad choices. Looking back on stuff, it looks like I might have pushed you into more mess than I meant you to get into. Most ungrateful authors talk about me behind my back. You got me straight though. Before you cut me loose, you gave me another chance to do my job. And thanks to the Almighty, I was able to come through."

"Thanks for not giving up on me either when I was being ridiculed in the press. Your loyalty is priceless."

"Shari, I'm so happy for you. Because the book is already written, when you sign, you'll be getting a very nice check too, girlfriend."

"Oh, Tina, this is just so amazing. Thanks again," I said before we agreed to talk the next day to go over other deal points.

When I hung up the phone, I saw lights coming toward me from the dark street. I knew it was Dillon. I so hoped his day was great because I couldn't wait to tell him about mine.

Unfortunately, he entered the house and threw down his coat and keys. The frown on his face explained he was bummed about something. Before I could talk to him, to share my news and cheer him up, he went in the bathroom.

When he came out, he bitterly said, "Though coach told me to name my price, the athletic director is only offering one hundred and fifty grand. My buddy in Maryland has it cleared to pay me fifty thousand more. To keep you home with the kids, we're going to have to move after all. I'm sorry. I really wanted to be here too, but financially we just need more."

I blurted out, "Well, hold up, let's not get ahead of God. Don't you think three hundred thousand will be enough?" He looked at me like I didn't hear him. I explained, "You are looking at the newest Land Home author whose book just got picked up for a hundred and fifty grand advance."

"What, that book you were writing and I read is getting a hundred and fifty grand upfront. God is really honoring our staying together." Dillon swung me around, and my stomach kicked hard.

I teased, "Wait now, your son doesn't like that. He's getting jealous."

"Well, he's going to have to stand in line, big daddy's here now."

We kissed under the moonlight. My life was perfect when I followed God. He gave me way more than I ever deserved. It was as if the lights and stars winked at me. I thought of them as angels saying, "See, all you got to do, girl, is stick with the Man and life will be more than okay." Letting them know I fully understood and would not be wavering anymore from God's plan. From now on I'd keep my halo on, take my burdens to God, and always follow His star.

Enjoyed
Stephanie Perry Moore's
WEARING MY HALO TILTED?
Check out
CHASING FAITH,
available now wherever books are sold!

Chapter 1

Venture

I'm young, attractive, and intelligent, so why am I lying here with this guy when I don't even love him? It's an early November morning and C-SPAN is blasting from the other room. I'm annoyed. I was getting real tired of the casualness of our relationship. I tried to cover my naked body with the silk sheet thrown across the bed. I moved carefully so Mr. Three Times in One Night wouldn't wake up and want to go another round.

Troy Evans and I had been seeing each other intimately, with no strings attached, for seven months. Neither of us wanted any commitment other than our jobs. We were coworkers and a darn good team, both on the job and under the covers. He was hitting thirty-three and I was almost twenty-eight. However, I now wanted more than a fling. I didn't know what it was I was chasing, but I did know Troy wasn't the answer.

As an FBI agent, I considered myself to be tough. Upholding justice was my life's work. Ever since my alcoholic dad left my mother, little sister, and me when I was ten years old, I felt I had to protect the three of us. I was the oldest, so I had to take care of my family.

My mother raised us in church, so the only father I knew was a Heavenly Father, and most times I wondered if He was even there. You know, when Mama couldn't pay the rent, when we had no food, or when I wore shoes to school that were way too small because we had no money for new ones. Where was God when my mother couldn't get folks in our small church to help her? Out of desperation she turned to a local drug dealer for a job. It destroyed her life, and not having her there for me sent me searching for love in all the wrong places. So here I am with Troy.

Troy and I found our way into each other's arms after work one day. It was early April, and I'd been on Troy's team for eighteen months. It was my tenth assignment since coming out of training—I had been an agent for almost five years. We were working a money-laundering case. We'd tracked our suspect, Rudy Roberts, from our hometown and headquarters in D.C. to New York City. Troy, another agent, and I were in a surveillance van, following Roberts in a cab. Suddenly the yellow taxi pulled over and Roberts got out, smiled at our van, and started walking briskly down the sidewalk.

Very annoyed that the guy had somehow found us out, Troy ordered, "You guys stay in the vehicle and follow me—I'm tailing Roberts."

He hurled out so fast that he didn't take a radio. When Roberts ducked down a dark alley, Troy followed him. We couldn't see either of them.

After waiting a few minutes, panic began to set in. I opened the van door.

The other agent yelled, "We need to stay put."

"We can't even see him now," I rationalized. "What if he's in trouble?"

I ducked down that same blind alley and heard a scuffle. With my gun drawn, I crept up the sidewall behind a green, industrial Dumpster. Suddenly the struggle ended.

Roberts laughed. "You've nothing on me. Get ready to die."

Taking a deep breath for courage, I walked a few paces more and saw Roberts on top of my case leader, his gun in Troy's face.

I identified myself by saying, "Freeze—FBI!" When he cocked his gun, I shot mine on impulse.

After the smoke cleared, I realized I had shot a man for the very first time in my life. I suddenly felt this awful guilt. Although I'd spent countless hours at the firing range, I was not prepared for the emotional reaction that I would have when I was actually in that situation.

"What have I done?" I mumbled.

Then Troy was in front of me, taking the warm weapon from my hands. "If you hadn't shot him, he would have killed me. I'm forever grateful— and glad you disobeyed my order and got out of that van." He smiled.

After Internal Affairs investigated for days, they concluded I did the only thing I could have. Still, I was mentally drained and shaken. After the shooting I couldn't handle my emotions in the field, so my boss, Agent Thomas Hunter, decided to keep me chained to my desk, reviewing cases and talking to confidential sources, gathering evidence until he thought I was ready to get back out there.

Troy understood my disappointment. Not too long after I was benched, he asked to buy me a late meal. Since the shooting, I didn't like being alone at night, so I accepted his offer. We went to a local steak house and ate and drank for several hours. Later, Troy saw me to my door. I was slightly inebriated and he wanted to make sure that I got in safely. He opened the door for me with my keys but didn't say good night.

Troy looked deep into my eyes that hazy April night and told me I was beautiful and sexy. I hadn't heard that from a man in too long.

I pulled him close to me and kissed him deeply. I wanted to be found attractive again by a man. It had been years since I'd felt the warm hands of a strong man all over my body. No part of me hesitated as I slipped into his arms.

Though Troy made it clear he didn't want anything serious, that was the first of many wonderful, sensual nights that we would spend together. Law enforcement wasn't the kind of career that lent itself to settling down. The women Troy had dated before me didn't understand that. The long hours and spur of the moment out of town trips for weeks at a time without a decent night off weren't the kind of thing most women could deal with. He was one of the FBI's best agents, so he handled some of the biggest cases in the world. Romance came second to adventure for Troy.

At first, that wasn't high on my priority list, either, so we made a good match. We'd get together whenever we felt like keeping each other's bed warm. Other than that, neither of us had any expectations. Months ago that was okay, but now, lying next to him, I was suddenly sick of the arrangement.

As I gazed at his muscular body, toffee-colored skin, and handsome face, I thought maybe, just maybe, I was ready for more than just casual sex with no commitment. Something inside made me see this as wrong. Was it the Holy Spirit at work?

Stepping out of bed, I hurried to the bathroom. It was almost two A.M. Spending the night this time was not an option. I had too much going on inside me. Not only was I starting to hate our no-strings-attached relationship, I was also starting to despise my profession. I was honestly burnt-out personally and professionally. Our unit worked closely with the Drug Enforcement Agency, following seedy characters from state to state until we finally got enough evidence for an arrest. But each time I saw a major drug dealer get off on a technicality, it made me want another job. And watching others work on cases in the field while I was still tied to a desk didn't help matters any.

Standing at the sink, I stared at my dim reflection in the mirror. Troy often complimented me on my smooth brown complexion and warm, hazel eyes. I was just glad my eyelashes were long and thick so I didn't have to use mascara. I never wore much makeup, preferring to rely on my own natural, God-given attributes. Glamour and guns only mixed in the movies.

I really needed to redo my highlights, though. I ran my fingers through my short hair and thought about the fine man in the next room. Suddenly my insides started churning.

One part of me wondered why I was tripping.

Maybe I just needed to crawl back into bed with him and get some more loving. Or maybe I needed some space. It seems like just yesterday that my first and only love, Max Cross, broke my heart. Max and I dated all four years at Baylor. I majored in Criminal Justice and he was a Business major. We met at a freshman party and were inseparable from then on. He was an exceptionally sexy man with creamy clay skin and hazel-brown eyes that made me melt. I thought we'd get married, and I was devastated when we broke up. I shouldn't have told him I was pregnant. The abortion broke my heart—and our relationship.

To get over that pain, I took on more shifts at my job at a local restaurant, Texan Grill, where I'd been working to earn money to send back to my mother and sister. It hadn't been more than three months before the married manager, Damien, and I began having an affair. I knew it wasn't right. But Damien just treated me so well—like a queen, and I hadn't been treated like that before. He bought me things and took me on trips. I didn't know what he told his wife and didn't care until the day she caught us in the act.

Over the next six months, I applied and got accepted into a training program for the Federal Bureau of Investigation. It's been less than six years. After doing well on other assignments and saving Agent Evans's life, I now enjoyed the respect of my colleagues. They started calling me "the woman with everything going on." It was true. I was good-looking, well put-together. Whatever I wore always suited me. And I'd never had a problem attracting a man. But what difference did all that really make? I wasn't happy. There had to be more to this life than survival. I felt empty and needed to be filled by something everlasting, but how could I get that. The only thing I knew was that I had to change the crazy way I was living.

I sighed and reached to turn on the faucet. That's when I saw the condom Troy and I had used just hours before. The shriveled-up thing wasn't balled up in the wastebasket, but curled up on the sink, positioned as if it had been inspected.

"What the . . . ?" I screeched out, completely lost in anger as I realized what must have happened.

Troy's voice came suddenly from the other room. "You got a problem?"

"Yes," I snapped. "What is this?"

He made his way to the bathroom, and eyed the condom beside me. "Would you calm down, baby. I'm sure it's no big deal."

"Troy, don't play. Did this burst?"

"I . . . I don't know. I'm not sure."

"What do you mean, you're not sure. You're a grown man, Troy."

Troy scanned my naked body with hungry eyes and tried to pull me close, but I held back. Didn't he get that I was pissed?

"I can open another one," he whispered. "It'll only take a second for me to put it on."

"You knew the condom broke, didn't you?" I said, scanning his guilty face and ignoring his new erection. "I can't have a baby and work in the FBI!"

"Don't even sweat that. You're cool. I'm over thirty. I've been sexually active since my teens. I've been with lots of women and never had any children. Trust me, it'll be okay. I know what I'm doing."

He tried to lead me back to bed, but I shoved him out of the bathroom and closed the door in his face.

See? I chastised myself. *That's why I shouldn't be doing this.*

Troy's frustrated voice filtered through the door. "Shut me out, then. I'm gonna fix me something to eat. I'm telling you, don't worry. I know you're fine." His confidence made my skin crawl.

When I heard him storm away, I took the only clean washcloth in the place from under the sink and began to freshen up. Emotions started to bubble up. I needed help. I needed something different. I needed not to be in this casual sex relationship.

Deep down, I felt there was only One that could fix this, so I looked up at the ceiling and said, "God, You gotta know this is not a good time for me." I shook my head. What was I doin'? He wouldn't listen to me. I'm sure He gave up on me a while ago.

But something—sheer desperation—spurred me to get down on my knees and continue. "Well, if You're still in the forgiving business, I need help. There's got to be more to this life than living and dying. There has to be more than just trying to get by. If there's a better plan, God, help me see it."

My mom used to make us pray every night, trying to lift our spirits. But ever since I had the abortion after the breakup with Max, I'd strayed away from God. Somehow I just felt unworthy of His love. But at that moment in Troy's bathroom, I needed to feel close to Him.

I emerged from Troy's bedroom fully dressed and headed to gather my stuff. Troy heard my steps and caught my arm before I picked up my bag. He pulled me to the television in the living room.

"Can you believe this?" he raged.

A news conference was being held on C-SPAN. A U.S. senator, the Reverend Steven Stokes, was addressing the nation from Atlanta, Georgia. For a brief second, I forgot that I had planned to head to my own apartment.

"Did he say he's running for president?" I asked.

"Yeah," Troy confirmed.

I shrugged. "Maybe he can win. He's a popular senator," I said, recovering from shock.

"Please! I don't care who he is. Jackson's, Chisholm's, and Sharpton's poor showings at the polls over the years should be enough to prove this nation ain't ready for a black president."

"I don't know," I said, lowering myself onto the couch. "That was years ago. Colin Powell and Condoleezza Rice have since held cabinet posts—they've changed America's outlook about having a black person in politics. Maybe the nation is ready."

"Yeah, right," Troy dismissed.

The reverend's wife, a beige-skinned, petite lady, strode up to her husband with a bright, confident smile. She wore a navy suit, tea-length with a rounded white collar pressed to perfection. Pearl accessories added a touch of elegance. I admired her style.

Their three children followed, all seemingly in their twenties or early thirties. The eldest, Steven Jr., had a young family of his own with him. But the bad-boy look in his eye told me this guy was probably a bit of a troublemaker.

The daughter, Savannah, was a younger version of her mom. She looked to be in her early twenties. She walked up to her dad, took his arm, and gave him an adoring smile.

The middle child, Sebastian, had a muscular build that made me do a double take. He wore dark-rimmed glasses and a charcoal-colored suit and tie that made him look like an overpriced lawyer.

I didn't know them personally, but the Stokeses had been in the spotlight lately. The press loved talking about how much the family was putting Georgia on the map. I had seen headlines touting the way their community involvement had helped decrease the number of homeless people, increase the number of corporate headquarters in Georgia, and raise the state's literacy rate. I'd always felt that though we hadn't had a black president yet, we needed more politicians to keep reaching for it. And what better candidate than a family man who had been a politician and the leader of a church. Plus, I could get behind someone who wanted to work for America as president and not just push his own agenda. Reverend Stokes seemed like that type of person.

"They seem like the real deal," I said.

"Whatever," Troy grumbled, heading into the kitchen. "Wait 'til the press starts eating them up. All their dirty laundry will be out there." Troy poured himself a shot of gin. "White folks don't want a brother in the White House. They're afraid we'll get in there and make our own rules." Troy laughed to himself.

"White people aren't the only ones who vote. You'll vote for him, won't you?"

Troy chugged his drink. "I don't know anything about the man."

"He's black and he's a Democrat. Plus, he has a good track record," I said, angry at his stubbornness. "What else do you need to know?"

"Chris, if you ever meet them you'll probably see they aren't that impressive. I bet those smiles are only on the surface. Most politicians I come across are phony."

"All of them can't be bad," I said, gathering my stuff. "I imagine their life is pretty wonderful."

"Then I suggest you apply for the Secret Service temp job, guard them for a while, and find out all their dirty little secrets. Then you'll see that the rosy picture you're talking about isn't so perfect."

I spotted my toothbrush and makeup case and stuffed them into my Gucci overnight bag. Walking back to the living room, I said, "Temp job? What are you talking about?"

"It was posted through the inner office e-mail system. Something about because it's election time, the Secret Service needs bodies to help them cover the presidential candidates," Troy said before kissing me on the cheek and opening his apartment door.

Once on the other side of his door, I raised my eyebrow, nodded my head, and thought, *Good riddance, Mr. Evans. And maybe I should look into that temp job.* It was time for a new venture.

Don't miss Rhonda Bowen's

Get You Good

On sale now!

Chapter 1

Sydney was never big on sports.

It wasn't that she was athletically challenged. It was just that chasing a ball around a court, or watching other people do it, had never really been high on her list of favorite things.

However, as she stood at the center of the Carlu Round Room, surveying the best of the NBA that Toronto had to offer, she had to admit that professional sports definitely had a few attractive features.

"Thank you, Sydney."

Sydney grinned and folded her arms as she considered her younger sister.

"For what?"

"For Christmas in October." Lissandra bit her lip. "Look at all those presents."

Sydney turned in the direction where Lissandra was staring, just in time to catch the burst of testosterone-laced eye candy that walked through the main doors. Tall, muscular, and irresistible, in every shade of chocolate a girl could dream of sampling. She was starting to have a new appreciation for basketball.

Sydney's eyebrows shot up. "Is that . . . ?"

"Yes, girl. And I would give anything to find him under our Christmas tree," Lissandra said, as her eyes devoured the newest group of NBA stars to steal the spotlight. "I love this game."

Sydney laughed. "I don't think it's the game you love."

"You laugh now," Lissandra said, pulling her compact out of her purse. "But when that hot little dress I had to force you to wear gets you a date for next weekend, you'll thank me."

Sydney folded her arms across the bodice of the dangerously short boat-necked silver dress that fit her five-foot-nine frame almost perfectly. It was a bit more risqué than what Sydney would normally wear but seemed almost prudish compared to what the other women in the room were sporting. At least it wasn't too tight. And the cut of the dress exposed her long, elegant neck, which she had been told was one of her best features.

"I'm here to work, not to pick up men," Sydney reminded her sister.

"No, we're here to deliver a spectacular cake." Lissandra checked her lipstick in the tiny mirror discreetly. "And since that cake is sitting over there, our work is done. It's playtime."

"Focus, Lissa." Sydney tried to get her sister back on task with a hand on her upper arm. "Don't forget this is an amazing opportunity to make the kinds of contacts that will put us on the A-list. Once we do that, more events like this might be in our future."

"OK, fine," Lissandra huffed, dropping her compact back into her purse. "I'll talk to some people and give out a few business cards. But if a player tries to buy me a drink, you best believe I'm gonna take it."

Sydney smirked. "I wouldn't expect otherwise."

"Good." Lissandra's mouth turned up into a naughty grin. " 'Cause I see some potential business over there that has my name etched across his broad chest."

Sydney sighed. Why did she even bother? "Be good," she said, adding a serious big-sister tone to her voice.

"I will," Lissandra threw behind her. But since she didn't even bother to look back, Sydney didn't hope for much. She knew her sister, and she'd just lost her to a six-foot-six brother with dimples across the room.

Sydney eventually lost sight of her sister as the crowd thickened. She turned her attention back to their ticket into the exclusive Toronto Raptors NBA Season Opener event.

The cake.

Sydney stood back and admired her work again, loving the way the chandelier from above and the tiny lights around the edges of the table and underneath it lit up her creation. The marzipan gave the cream-colored square base of the cake a smooth, flawless finish, and the gold trim caught the light beautifully. The golden replica of an NBA championship trophy, which sat atop the base, was, however, the highlight.

She had to admit it was a sculpted work of art, and one of the best jobs she had done in years. It was also one of the most difficult. It had taken two days just to bake and decorate the thing. That didn't include the several concept meetings, the special-ordered baking molds, and multiple samples made to ensure that the cake tasted just as good as it looked. For the past month and a half, this cake job had consumed her life. But it was well worth it. Not only for the weight it put in her pocket, but also the weight it was likely to add to her client list. Once everyone at the event saw her creation, she was sure she would finally make it onto the city's pastry-chef A-list, and Decadent would be the go-to spot for wedding and special-event cakes.

She stood near the cake for a while, sucking up the oohs and aahs of passersby, before heading to the bathroom to check that she hadn't sweated out her curls carrying up the cake from down-stairs. She took in her long, dark hair, which had been curled and pinned up for the night; her slightly rounded face; and plump, pinked lips; and was satisfied. She turned to the side to get a better view of her size six frame and smiled. Even though she had protested when Lissandra presented the dress, she knew she looked good. Normally she hated any kind of shimmer, but the slight sparkle from the dress was just enough to put Sydney in the party mood it inspired. OK, so Lissandra may have been right—she was there for business—but that didn't mean she couldn't have some fun, too.

By the time she reapplied her lipstick and headed back, the room was full.

She tried to mingle and did end up chatting with a few guests, but her maternal instincts were in full gear and it wasn't long before she found her way back to the cake. She was about to check for anything amiss when she felt gentle fingers on the back of her bare neck. She swung around on reflex.

"What do you think you're doing?" she said, slapping away the hand that had violated her personal space.

"Figuring out if I'm awake or dreaming."

Sydney's eyes slid all the way up the immaculately toned body of the six-foot-three man standing in front of her, to his strong jaw, full smirking lips, and coffee brown eyes. Her jaw dropped. And not just because of how ridiculously handsome he was.

"Dub?"

"Nini."

She cringed. "Wow. That's a name I never thought I would hear again."

"And that's a half tattoo I never thought I'd see again."

Sydney slapped her hand to the back of her neck self consciously. She had almost forgotten the thing was there. It would take the one person who had witnessed her chicken out on getting it finished to remind her about it.

Hayden Windsor. Now wasn't this a blast from the past, sure to get her into some present trouble.

She tossed a hand onto her hip and pursed her lips. "I thought Toronto was too small for you."

"It is."

"Then what are you doing here?"

"Right now?" His eyes flitted across her frame in answer.

"Stop that," Sydney said, her cheeks heating up as she caught his perusal.

"Stop what?" he asked with a laugh.

"You know what," she said. She shook her head. "You are still the same."

He shrugged in an attempt at innocence that only served to draw Sydney's eyes to the muscles shifting under his slim-fitting jacket.

"I can't help it. I haven't seen you in almost ten years. What, you gonna beat me up like you did when you were seven?"

"Maybe."

"Bully."

"Jerk."

"How about we continue this argument over dinner?" he asked.

"They just served appetizers."

The corners of his lips drew up in a scandalous grin. "Come on, you know you're still hungry."

He was right. That finger food hadn't done anything for her—especially since working on the cake had kept her from eating all day. But she wasn't about to tell him that.

Sydney smirked. "Even if I was, I don't date guys who make over one hundred thousand dollars a year."

He raised a thick eyebrow. "That's a new one."

"Yes, well," she said, "it really is for your own good. This way you won't have to wonder if I was with you for your money."

"So how about we pretend like I don't have all that money," he said, a dangerous glint in his eyes. "We could pretend some other things, too—like we weren't just friends all those years ago."

"I'm not dating you, Hayden," Sydney said, despite the shiver that ran up her spine at his words.

"So you can ask me to marry you, but you won't date me?"

"I was seven years old!"

"And at nine years old, I took that very seriously," Hayden said, his brow furrowing.

Sydney laughed. "That would explain why you went wailing to your daddy right after."

He rested a hand on his rock-solid chest. "I'm an emotional kind of guy."

"Hayden! There you are. I've been looking all over for you!"

Sydney turned to where the voice was coming from and fought her gag reflex. A busty woman with too much blond hair sidled up to Hayden, slipping her arm around his.

"This place is so packed that I can barely find anyone." The woman suddenly seemed to notice Sydney.

"Sydney!"

"Samantha."

Samantha gave Sydney a constipated smile. "So good to see you."

Sydney didn't smile back. "Wish I could say the same."

Hayden snorted. Samantha dropped the smile, but not his arm.

Sydney glared at the woman in the red-feathered dress and wondered how many peacocks had to die to cover her Dolly Parton goods.

"So I guess you two know each other?" Hayden asked, breaking the silence that he seemed to find more amusing than awkward.

"Yes," Samantha volunteered. "Sydney's little bakery, Decadent, beat out Something Sweet for the cake job for this event. She was my main competition."

"I wouldn't call it a competition," Sydney said, thinking it was more like a slaughtering.

"How do *you* know each other?" Samantha probed.

Hayden grinned. "Sydney and I go way back. Right, Syd?"

Samantha raised an eyebrow questioningly and Sydney glared at her, daring her to ask another question. Samantha opted to keep her mouth shut.

"So this is where the party is," Lissandra said, joining the small circle. Sydney caught the flash of recognition in Lissandra's eyes when she saw who exactly made up their impromptu gathering.

"Hayden? Is that you?"

"The very same," Hayden said, pulling Lissandra into a half hug. "Good to see you, Lissandra."

"Back at you," Lissandra said. "Wow, it's been ages. I probably wouldn't recognize you except Sydney used to watch your games all the—oww!"

Lissandra groaned as Sydney's elbow connected with her side.

"Did she?" Hayden turned to Sydney again, a smug look in his eyes.

"Well, it was nice to see you all again," Samantha said, trying to navigate Hayden away from the group.

"Samantha, I can't believe you're here." Lissandra's barely concealed laughter was not lost on Sydney or Samantha. "I thought you would be busy cleaning up that business at Something Sweet."

Sydney bit back a smirk as a blush crept up Samantha's neck to her cheeks. Samantha went silent again.

"What business?" Hayden looked around at the three women, who obviously knew something he didn't.

"Nothing," Samantha said quickly.

"Just that business with the health inspector," Lissandra said, enjoying Samantha's discomfort. "Nothing major. I'm sure the week that you were closed was enough to get that sorted out."

Hayden raised an eyebrow. "The health inspector shut you down?"

"We were closed temporarily," Samantha corrected. "Just so that we could take care of a little issue. It wasn't that serious."

"Is that what the exterminator said?" Lissandra asked.

Sydney coughed loudly and Samantha's face went from red to purple.

"You know," Samantha said, anger in her eyes. "It's interesting. We have never had a problem at that location before now. It's funny how all of a sudden we needed to call an exterminator around the same time they were deciding who would get the job for tonight's event."

"Yes, life is full of coincidences," Sydney said dryly. "Like that little mix-up we had with the Art Gallery of Ontario event last month. But what can you do? The clients go where they feel confident."

"Guess that worked out for you this time around," Samantha said, glaring at Sydney and Lissandra.

"Guess so," Lissandra said smugly.

Sydney could feel Hayden eyeing her suspiciously, but she didn't dare look at him.

"Well, this was fun," Sydney said in a tone that said the exact opposite. "But I see some people I need to speak with."

Sydney excused herself from the group and made her way to the opposite side of the room toward the mayor's wife. She had only met the woman once, but Sydney had heard they had an anniversary coming up soon. It was time to get reacquainted, and get away from the one man who could make her forget what she really came here for.

By the time the hands on her watch were both sitting at eleven, Sydney was exhausted and completely out of business cards.

"Leaving already?" She was only steps from the door, and he was only steps in front of her.

"This was business, not pleasure."

Hayden's eyes sparkled with mischief. "All work and no play makes Sydney a dull girl."

This time her mouth turned up in a smile. "I think you know me better than that."

His grin widened in a way that assured her that he did. "Remind me."

She shook her head and pointed her tiny purse at him.

"I'm not doing this here with you, Dub."

He stepped closer and she felt the heat from his body surround her. "We can always go somewhere else. Like the Banjara a couple blocks away."

Sydney scowled. Him and his inside knowledge.

"If we leave now we can get there before it closes."

She folded her arms over her midsection. "I haven't changed my mind, Dub."

He grinned. "That's not what your stomach says."

Sydney glanced behind him, and he turned around to see that Samantha was only a few feet away and headed in his direction. Sydney wasn't sure what string of events had put Samantha and Hayden together that night. The woman was definitely not his type. Or at least she didn't think Samantha was.

"I think your date is coming to get you," Sydney said, her voice dripping with amusement. "Maybe *she* wants to go for Indian food."

"How about I walk you to your car?"

Without waiting for a response, he put a hand on the small of her back and eased her out the large doors into the lobby and toward the elevator.

"What's the rush?" she teased.

"Still got that smart mouth, don't you."

"I thought that was what you liked about me," she said innocently, as he led her into the waiting elevator.

"See, that's what you always got wrong, Nini." He leaned toward her ear to whisper and she caught a whiff of his cologne. "It was never just one thing."

Sydney tried to play it off, but she couldn't help the way her breathing went shallow as her heart sped up. And she couldn't keep him from noticing it, either.

His eyes fell to her lips. "So what's it going to be, Syd? You, me, and something spicy?"

He was only inches away from her. So close that if she leaned in, she could . . .

"Hayden!"

A familiar voice in the distance triggered her good sense. Sydney stepped forward and placed her hands on his chest.

"I think you're a bit busy tonight."

She pushed him out of the elevator and hit the DOOR CLOSE button.

He grinned and shook his head as she waved at him through the gap between the closing doors.

"I'll see you soon, Nini."

For reasons she refused to think about, she hoped he kept that promise.

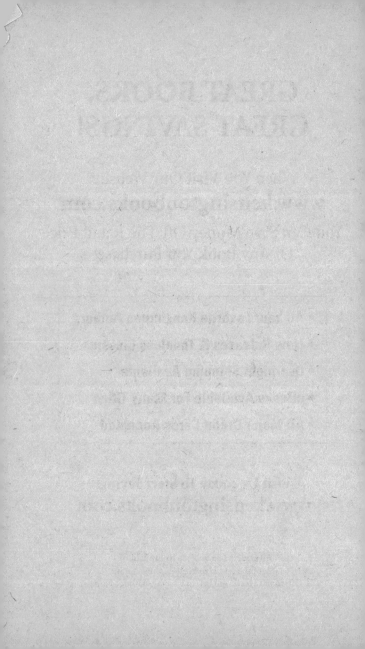